Crimes of Summer

Robin Timmerman

Order this book online at www.trafford.com
or email orders@trafford.com

Most Trafford titles are also available at major online book retailers.

Printed in the United States of America.

ISBN: 978-1-4907-4794-1 (sc)
ISBN: 978-1-4907-4793-4 (hc)
ISBN: 978-1-4907-4795-8 (e)

Library of Congress Control Number: 2014917742

Trafford rev. 10/06/2014

 www.trafford.com
North America & international
toll-free: 1 888 232 4444 (USA & Canada)
fax: 812 355 4082

For Keith

PROLOGUE

*C*ormorant, (corvus marinus, the sea raven).
   A prehistoric-looking large black bird, expert at diving to catch small fish.
   Origin dates back to the very earliest modern bird, perhaps seventy million years ago.

Dawn on a morning in late June, a humid mist hovering over the lake.

The sun is rising like an immense pink pearl from the luminescent half shell of the water. A group of cormorants are headed out for their breakfast ground, forty birds in a crooked black line, flying low. In the reeds by the shore, other birds, swans and geese, are noisily feeding.

The cormorants continue silently on through the wreath of mist that is slowly rising like steam in the warming day. The birds pass the old lighthouse tower on the Point, where the sun glints like a piece of gold ice on a broken window pane. The only light that has flickered there for decades, a mere faint, winking eye above the shore rocks.

But the cormorants pay it no attention. Light or no light, it makes no difference to them. Decades make no difference to them, nor centuries either. The waves are their home and they have fishing to do.

A lone vulture is interested though. He's spotted some movement down in the water by the shore. He dips his featherless raw-red head to consider, then stops and turns in his flight.

1

To northern peoples, summer is an annual miracle. Yet the three summer months last only a quarter section of the long year.

So much to do, so little time!

Most Canadians head as often as possible to the nearest body of water. Some to merely contemplate the serene blue waves where so recently there was rigid ice. Others to roar frantically over the surface in whatever loud, exhaust-spewing, water-roiling vehicle they can afford.

The bay that Middle Island shared with the neighbouring city of Bonville, was visited by both types. Unfortunately, farmers and jet-skiiers don't mix. So when the telephone rang, Jane Carell, office manager and nerve centre of the Middle Island police station, smallest independent police force in the province, resigned herself to listening to yet another complaint.

Would it be about a speedboat coming too close to a dock? Or a couple of jet skiiers having a race? Or maybe some raucus partying folk who had camped uninvited in a farmer's field. And the summer had just begun! Personally, Jane was already dreaming about quiet autumn when the holidayers would go home. She sighed now and called past the room partition to her boss, Chief Bud Halstead, "Do I have to answer?"

Halstead grinned and waved. "Be nice."

But the phone had blessedly stopped ringing. *Thank you, lord, for small mercies.*

When it started up again, she grabbed without looking, her mind on the schedule of the day ahead. "Middle Island police station," she said warily. "How can I help you?" Then she stopped and began listening.

"Is he dead?" she asked after a moment.

"Who's dead?" asked Officer Pete Jakes, coming out of the small room that served as a coffee and common room for the three police officers on staff. He carried a half eaten muffin in his hand.

The chief rose from his chair, echoing his own "Who!"

In a community as small as Middle Island (pop. 4500), the question was all-important. Jane whose wide network of her own family, plus siblings, nephews, nieces and grandchild were all local residents, waved the two men to silence, while she listened some more. Then turned, her expression serious.

"Some American tourists in a boat near Lighthouse Point, they say they've seen a body floating by the shore."

* * *

Lighthouse Point, one of four notable promontories on Middle Island, was about a fifteen minute drive from town. The southernmost and easternmost point on the Island, it jutted out into the main lake, where shipping traffic (from west to east and vice versa) had travelled for three hundred years. In this time, the vessels had undergone some changes, from sail to steam to oil powered. But the shipping routes had remained the same. Wind and water patterns don't change much in a century or two.

The Norris Lighthouse, that had served for over a century as a warning beacon to hundreds of ships, had seen better days. Far better days. The wood frame tower still stood straight and true but the roof boards leaked and the windows of the light cupola had long ago been broken and blasted out by winter gales. Wooden shutters now closed them up and the mud nests of swallows clustered under the eaves.

On a summer day though, with the swallows diving and soaring about, the place was an attractive picture-postcard ruin. In fact, there was a postcard of the lighthouse sold in the village drug store and it was a favourite subject for local painters.

This morning though, Jakes rocked the cruiser along the dirt road that led past the lane to the Lighthouse, barely sparing the structure a glance. Halstead braced himself as a particularly large rut loomed. The cruiser was fairly new and it had been hard enough to get the car included in last fall's budget. But Jakes, with the confidence of youth's good reflexes, easily navigated the bump. A half mile further on, he pulled the vehicle to a shuddering halt. The two men got out and stood briefly atop the metre-high slope that led down to the water.

"There's the folks who called in," Pete pointed to a nice-looking yacht, tethered about twenty feet out from the shore. A woman looked back at them, waving wildly. She wore sunglasses and brandished a huge pair of binoculars.

Halstead grimaced, looking at the other boat, a battered aluminum outboard bobbing forlornly against the narrow strip of rocky beach. "I was afraid it might be Mel Todd, and that sure looks like his boat."

He sighed. "Better get down there."

There was a bright yellow dinghy pulled up on shore as well. A grey-haired man came towards them. "He's over here, officers."

"I saw right away that I couldn't help," he explained. "So I didn't touch him."

Now Pete could see what looked like a bundle of sodden rags, bobbing between the old outboard and the rocks. Halstead stepped forward and uncaring of wet shoes and trouser cuffs, stepped into the water. He tugged at the body's jacket shoulder, just enough to turn the face partly up, and nodded.

"It's him. It's Mel Todd." Luckily he hadn't been in the water all that long. Possibly just overnight.

"You know him?" asked the grey-haired man.

"He's a local fisherman," Halstead said. "Or he used to be, anyway."

"Like I said I'm sorry we couldn't help. My wife there, she was just looking for birds, or ducks or something and she gives out this little shriek and tells me she's looking at a body. I didn't believe her at first but when I saw that she was right, I lowered the dinghy and came right over. But the guy was long past help," he finished. "Just as you see."

The three of them looked down again. A sombre sight.

"Help me move him to shore," Halstead said to Jakes.

"Harry!" came a strident call from the boat. "Are you telling the policemen the story? You don't know beans about telling a story. Come and get me! I'm the one who found the body."

Harry looked apologetically at the two officers. "Do you need to talk to her, should I get her?"

Jakes heaved at the body's legs and Halstead placed Mel Todd's head as gently as he could on the stones.

"Sure," Halstead said. "go get her."

It would be better than listening to the woman hollering from the boat.

Halstead made the necessary calls, one to Chris Pelly, the doctor from Bonville Hospital, who doubled as Island coroner when needed. The other to the ambulance service to pick the body up. They would probably be awhile but unfortunately, there was no rush.

Meanwhile Pete took down the statements from the couple on the yacht. Their involvement was slight, though the woman tried to make the most of it. To be fair, Pete amended, she had suffered a shock. Still, she was obviously thrilled by the excitement and already planning the story she would tell her friends.

"I was looking through the binoculars when I saw the boat. I gasped, didn't I Harry, when I saw the foot tangled in the mooring rope. Then I saw the body bobbing beside the boat."

She glanced quickly at the sodden heap of clothes that had once been a living man and shuddered theatrically.

"We saw a vulture circling. They haven't haven't been at him, I hope? The poor man!"

Basically though, they had little to tell. They'd spotted the body about an hour ago, and had seen no person or other boat anywhere near the site. They were from a town in New York State, were on vacation and had never met the deceased. The woman hadn't been quite so thrilled about having to view Mel Todd's dead face but she did her duty, alongside her husband.

"Poor fellow must have slipped on the rocks," said the husband.

Pete thanked them for their help and they set off in their yellow dinghy across the twenty feet of water to their boat, Mrs. Harry looking reluctantly back. She had wanted to take a picture but much to her disappointment, Halstead wouldn't let her.

Now he looked up the slope. "Mel would have a camp somewhere nearby. He liked to get away sometimes and do his drinking."

The spot was only a few yards away. Just a rough camp, comprised of a pup tent pegged down in the long, rank grass. Inside there were some empty whiskey bottles and a damp, foetid sleeping bag. Pete couldn't guess the original colour. At the entrance to the tent there was a smell of whiskey and some shards of broken glass.

Halstead stooped to pick up a piece of glass. "Looks as if Mel was pretty looped," he said. "Or he wouldn't have been spilling good whiskey. He must have wanted to get something from his boat, gone back down there and fallen in the water."

"Came here a lot, did he?" Pete asked.

"He practically lived on the lake, grew up on the fishing boats. His father and grandfather were fishermen, and Mel carried on the family business. Then the government took away the commercial fishermen licenses. Mel was only in his sixties, he didn't know what to do with himself. So he started to drink."

A familiar story.

Halstead shrugged. "He liked to come here. He used to say he could find his way blind drunk along the Island shores and if he couldn't, his boat would manage by itself, like an old horse. He was never any trouble, we left him alone."

He looked down at the body on the beach, and shook his head.

"And now he's drowned himself. Even if was lying there needing help, no one would know."

It was a quarter mile walk in from the road, the nearest house a mile away. A solitary spot. Obviously why Todd, had liked to come there.

"Maybe he had a heart attack," Pete said. "That happens to a lot of older guys."

Halstead felt a resonant twinge in his own chest – the twinge he got whenever he read an obit of a middle-aged man who succombed to cardiac arrest.

"Here's Chris," he said brusquely, turning at the sound of the coroner's car.

A half hour later, Chris Pelly rinsed his hands off in the lake water. A slight man, with cowlicked brown hair, Pelly greeted them with his usual boyishly cheerful grin. His at times grim work never seemed to get the man down.

"Looks as if the man drowned," he said without irony. "He must have stumbled getting in or out of the boat."

The three men looked out over the picture postcard scene. Blue sky, cotton puff clouds, the lake stretching to forever.

Halstead sighed. "I hope Melvin went looped and happy. At least he died out here, not in the Bonville drunk tank. The lake was pretty good to him and from the stories he used to tell of being caught out there in some bad storms with his dad, he had a few lucky escapes already."

Pelly grunted, gathering up his heavy case. "Yeah well I guess his luck ran out this time."

2

Ali Jakes poured coffee into three mugs and sighed. She'd rather not go back into the living room and keep on being polite to her husband's army buddy. But if Lieutenant Tyler Cotes made one more put-down comment about the Jakes' Middle Island friends and neighbours, he might just get a cup of steaming coffee in his lap!

Ah well, into the breach.

Cotes was a good-looking fellow, at thirty-four only a few years older than Pete. Dark where Pete was blond, a bit taller, but to her mind there was no contest. She'd fallen for hunky Pete three years ago in war-torn Afghanistan – she was teaching on a United Nations project and Pete's unit was assigned to safeguard the teachers – and she still considered their meeting the luckiest event in her life.

It seemed there was a contest between the two men though, at least in Cotes' mind, His voice was loud as if he was always striving for attention, like a toddler she thought. Like her own toddler Nevra, upstairs in her crib and recently bathed, read to and lullabied to sleep.

And kissed goodnight by her handsome Daddy, who never looked more attractive, Ali thought, than when he was gently holding their precious little daughter. That was a kind of maleness that Mr. Macho Tyler Cotes with his endless stories of guns and battle, obviously knew nothing about. And what was he going on about now?

She plopped the tray unceremoniously down on the coffee table and forced a smile,   "Sugar, Tyler?"

Neither man was wearing army fatigues – Pete because he had thankfully left the forces when they married, and Cotes because he had suffered a combat injury three months ago and was now recuperating, very unthankfully in a rented cottage on the south shore of Middle Island. At times Ali regretted that the Jakes had ever made the suggestion.

But she could hardly have argued against the idea either. Although she had never met Cotes, she knew that he and Pete had served together for two combat tours. On the bookcase by the window, there was a framed photo of six young soldiers, in camouflage gear, smiling and looking ready to take on whatever the Afghani insurgents, or indeed the world, could throw at them. And sadly, they did get thrown at.

The bodies of two of the young smilers had been brought home in flagged coffins to Canada. Two others had been diagnosed with post traumatic stress syndrome. After the combat tours, Pete had signed up for the U.N. project where he'd met Ali. Ironically it was while escorting a visiting dignitary from Canada back to the airfield in Kabul, that Pete and the rest of the convoy had been blindsided by a roadside bomb. An experience that led to his own tough recovery.

And now here was the last of the six, Tyler Cotes sprawled across the Jakes' living room couch, his foot cast propped up on cushions. Not that she begrudged the man a dinner, for heaven's sake, nor comfort for his foot, wounded in the service of his country. It was a bad injury that required orthopedic surgery, and several months recovery involving intensive rehabilitation therapy.

She could even endure the seemingly endless tales of danger-filled days on patrol in the desert, on one of which he had been shot. But she did dearly wish that the man could be a little more sensitive in his comments about Middle Island life and its inhabitants. He had already complained of the country silence and worse, no highspeed internet service. He had also mocked the village Main Street for its lack of bars and restaurants.

"Maybe I should look into opening up a fast-food franchise," he was saying now. "You could use one of the big chain burger-pizza places here. Even that guy with the chip truck does O.K. I was talking to him the other day and he says he takes his wife back to Portugal every winter for a holiday."

Ali winced. 'Oh but you wouldn't want to take away Benny Sorda's living. They've still got a couple of kids in high school. Pete coaches his son in hockey."

Tyler shrugged. 'Business is business. Besides if the Island becomes a more happening place, there could be lots of money for everybody.'

Pete caught the look on his wife's face – it had been a long evening -- and quickly jumped in.

"So Ty, do you want to get out on the water tomorrow, catch some fish?"

Tyler grinned. "I don't know buddy, think you can tear yourself away from your important Island cop stuff? Maybe some old lady will jaywalk while we're out on the lake. Or somebody will park illegally on Main Street and deputy Jakes won't be there to write up the ticket."

Pete didn't mind the ribbing but Ali bristled.

"Pete and the Chief had to retrieve a body from the lake today," she said tartly. "That wasn't a lot of fun."

"Somebody offed the guy?" Tyler asked, just as irreverently.

"No," Pete shoook his head. "An unfortunate old drunk who passed out in the lake. Sad, though."

"That's too bad," Tyler said, quelled at last.

And thank goodness, Ali thought. A tragic accident was hardly something to joke about. Although dreadfully, for just a moment, she had found herself almost wishing that Pete could say he was involved in a homicide. Just to shut Tyler up.

That's how much the man irritated her. What shabby thoughts he drove her to.

Because of course she was grateful that Island life was rarely plagued by violence, that was one of the reasons they had stayed. She and Pete had experienced more than enough violence in troubled Afghanistan.

Now Pete yawned and stood up. "We should get going early tomorrow morning Ty. That's the best time to catch those walleyes."

"You know it, buddy," Tyler swung his leg out over the couch pillows.

When he had arrived on the Island a couple of months ago, Tyler was on crutches, now he wore only the foot cast and used a cane. Ali noticed though that he still winced as he stood up, and once again felt contrite. She wrapped up some of the dessert pie for him to take home.

Nevra Jakes, curled up so sweetly in her crib, was a beautiful child. But Ali supposed all parents felt like that. A darker blond than Pete and with Ali's Turkish heritage reflected in her olive skin and long dark eyelashes, the little girl was an exotic blend of her parents' genes. *Nevra* for new. They had chosen the name to symbolize optimism and peace in a troubled world. Ali looked happily around the room, the pretty flowered wallpaper, the shelves of books and teddy bears. A suitable setting for their tiny princess.

She tiptoed back across the hall, kicked off her sandals and stretched her elegant honey-coloured legs right down to her toes. It seemed she had been tense all evening.

"That's too bad about the fisherman," she said to Pete. "Did he have any family?"

"A married son who lives out West. The chief didn't think he was likely to come back for the funeral, though. Some bad argument, years ago."

Fathers and sons, so often the case. Pete's own father hadn't come to their wedding and in fact Ali had yet to meet the man. But it wasn't the time to bring that up.

She sighed. "I hope that Tyler isn't serious about opening a fast food place on the Island. We don't need it, there's enough of those ugly places in Bonville."

Pete shook his head and pulled back the bed covers. "Tyler just needs to be optimistic about some sort of plan, honey. He's worried that he won't pass the physical to get back into the army, though I'm sure he'll be fine."

He laughed. "Besides, you don't have to worry that he'd ever seriously consider moving to the Island. You've heard what he thinks of the place."

Ali rolled her eyes. "Exhaustively!"

Then she scolded herself. Pete was right, cut the man some slack, he'd been through a traumatic experience. Emotional healing could take a lot more time than physical healing. As had happened in Pete's case. Even now, he occasionally had that recurring nightmare about his own encounter with an Afghani road explosive.

"Where do you think he would settle then – if ever?" Crossing her fingers behind her back, hopefully far from Middle Island.

"Do you think he'll ever get married again?" she added.

Apparently Tyler had been married young, in his early twenties. The couple had no children and the marriage didn't last. Pete had given up this information only reluctantly. When she asked if there had been anyone serious since, Pete had given an embarrassed shrug.

"I haven't asked him, honey - guys don't ask each other things like that."

She rolled her eyes. "And men wonder why their wives' number one complaint is 'lack of communication!'

Pete hopped into bed and patted the pillow next to him. "Come on over here gorgeous, and we can communicate all you want."

She smiled and turned off the light.

"Don't worry," he said sleepily, later. "It's all talk, with Tyler. He's just restless and tired of being laid up. Once he gets the O.K. from the doctors, he'll be off to the action again. Wherever the army sends him, he'll be raring to go. Ty's a good soldier, the kind of guy you're glad to have at your back when the artillery starts going off. I should know. We saved each other's necks, more than once over there."

He nuzzled her cheek. "So you can thank him for that."

And she did. But lying there, looking out at the country moon, Ali wondered if sometimes Pete too, missed the action. She could tell he had enjoyed the evening, talking with his old buddy of exciting times from the past. There was danger yes, and plenty of it, but camaraderie too and the thrill of the adrenalin rush.

Had Pete found the evening's stories and memories a welcome change from changing diapers or reading bedtime stories to Nevra? She was so happy herself, and delighted that they'd bought the house, which she saw as a commitment that they were planning to set down roots in Canada. But was Pete getting restless, was he bored with life on Middle Island? That was a disturbing thought.

* * *

In the frame house across the road, identical to the Jakes' but painted celery green instead of white, seventy-five year old Miranda Paris poured a glass of wine and patted the head of Emily Dickinson, her dog. Of border collie heritage, black and white with a long feathery tail, Emily was a good companion and a good listener, which was an asset for those humans who live alone. Now Miranda looked approvingly towards the Jakes' home. It was good to have lights there, to have neighbours there in the country dark.

The Island needed newcomers, if only to keep the population up. The old ones were dying off, that's for sure. Not that Mel Todd had been all that old. His father, Walter, had only died a couple of years ago, at ninety-two. But then Walter Todd hadn't been a drinker like the son. If Mel hadn't drowned like that in the lake, he would likely have perished of cirrhosis. It was only a matter of time.

So, she would attend another funeral. The lake had provided the Todds and others with a living for decades, now it had exacted a price. Another link with the past gone. A century of Island commercial fishing days had ended two years ago, cancelled by a government decision. Poor Mel, she remembered him as a little fellow, playing around his father's boat. He'd taken over the business eventually and fished all his adult life. When the Ministry decision came down, Mel hadn't been able to adjust to changing times.

She too, knew how tough that was. She still missed her teaching years in the Canadian Arctic, the pleasure of being around young folk who were just starting out in life, rather than finishing up. She had taught reading, both English stories and translations of Inuit legends and often felt she'd learned as much as she'd taught. It was a good thing she still had a brain – she could hardly bear to look in a mirror now, at the stringy old crone she'd become.

Sometimes she felt as old as the cormorants that nested on North Island. She'd read that the creatures' history reached back millions of years, to the very origins of birds. Millenia of living, of being part of the natural rhythms of earth. While the much more recent and probably short-lived, garbage-strewing human history bumbled on below, of no interest to the cormorants, or indeed to the universe.

"And you know," she said to Emily. "The birds might just be right."

3

It was a five minute walk from the church to the Island Grill. Having paid their formal respects to Mel Todd, Chief Halstead and his marine patrol officer Art Storms, had decided to skip the post-funeral coffee and lemon squares in the church basement and opt for a farewell brew to speed the late fisherman on his journey.

There wasn't much of a crowd in the dim, cool diner. Several of Todd's drinking buddies had died off too, in the past few years. Hence Todd's solitary camp-outs. Storms got the first round, bringing a couple of glasses to the table. An easy-going bulk of a man, face and neck tanned and weathered from years on the water, he had worked with Halstead off and on for fifteen years.

Halstead raised his beaded glass. "Here's to Mel. May his nets always be full in the great beyond."

The coroner's report hadn't yet arrived (a busy week in the provincial office) but they expected it to be pretty well a rubber stamp of Chris Pelly's examination. Death by falling drunkenly into the lake, and imbibing a lot of water, in simpler terms, drowning.

Art snorted, "Well the Fisheries Ministry won't be sad to see him go, that's for sure. Mel could be a real pain in the butt to them."

"That's for sure," Halstead agreed. "Todd never did get over his grudge against them, for stopping his commercial fishing license."

The Ministry's action had roused emotion and support in the rest of the community too. The Island fishing families had been working the waters of the lake for two hundred years. But in recent decades the catch of perch and walleyes had dwindled and the fishermen ran into conflict with sportsmen who demanded their share of the lake's fishing as well.

Halstead chuckled, "Remember how Mel drove his boat around for months with that crazy sign." A crudely painted copy of the Ministry logo, and below that a hand with finger upraised, in the universal signal of rude disrespect.

They drank again, in salute to the passing of an Island character, a true original.

Storms popped a piece of nicotine gum into his mouth and grimaced.

"I've been on this stuff for six months trying to kick the habit – now I think I'm addicted to the damn gum. Still coughing too, so sometimes I wonder what's the point."

Halstead had gone cold turkey twenty years ago, but he was sympathetic.

"Stick with it," he said. "Think of all the money you'll save. So how's the summer shaping up?"

Storms had spent a decade with the Great Lakes Coast Guard before coming to the Middle Island force. Now in his early fifties, he was spending the summer as he had for the past couple of years, working with the auxiliary coast guard to train student recruits in search and rescue work.

He was also Middle Island co-ordinator of a province-wide initiative to reduce alcohol and drug related impaired boating. The task was to get the message out that impaired boaters faced the same penalties as those for drinking and driving -- suspension of license, a fine, and impoundment of the boat. And that no alcohol could be consumed while the boat was underway, not even by the passengers.

"That one is a an unpleasant surprise to a lot of folks," Art said. "The boat has to be at anchor or tied up to a dock."

"The program is a good idea," Halstead approved. "What's your crew like this summer?"

"A bunch of good kids. Greg is pleased." Greg Jackman was head of the local auxiliary coast guard.

"And what's new in the smuggling world this week?" Halstead asked.

Art always had some good stories he'd heard from his regular coast guard pals. Some exciting, some funny. The distance across the lake to the American shore was never more than twenty kilometers away, and from some of the lake islands, half that. Hence a constant temptation to smugglers and there were some mighty dumb crooks out there.

Such as the young Canadian scuba diver who thought he'd just swim over to the U.S. side, a plastic cylinder packed with a couple of kilos of marijuana, strapped to his back. No doubt he thought this was the first of many lucrative trips. However, the long swim through rough waters was pretty tiring and the police had no trouble picking up the exhausted diver on the other side.

Or the Niagara cheese smuggling ring members, who had been driving across the border with U.S. cheese, sold at at one-third the price of Canadian brands, to sell to Ontario pizzerias.

"A driver could make a couple of thousand a trip," Art said.

Halstead frowned. "I read about that gang. Not so funny, there were some police officers running that fiddle. Then one of the cops had to pay a $50,000 fine. He lost his job and his wife left him. I hope he thought it was worth it."

Art picked up a cheese-topped nacho and looked at it assessingly.

Halstead laughed. "Don't worry, that's good Canadian cheddar. Gus gets his cheese like the rest of us, from the dairy north of Bonville, always has."

But serious smuggling, run by gangs, was a mighty serious problem, costing Canada an estimated $2 billion in lost tax revenue annually. And the cost of surveillance of the watery border between Canada and the U.S. wasn't cheap either.

"Basically cigs going north and marijuana going south," Art said. Further east on the St. Lawrence River, smugglers were known to simply drive their trucks across the winter ice. 'Couriers" could make $6000 a week. Occasionally there were some other smuggled goods, when prices were temporarily markedly cheaper in either country. Halstead remembered there was once even a brisk trade in disposable diapers from the U.S.

It was a constant, unwinnable battle, a cat and mouse game between the RCMP and the smugglers. At least nowadays, the Canadian and U.S. police worked together so smugglers coudn t escape simply by scooting over to the other country s water zone.

"Luckily we're a bit far down the lake for the big smuggling operations," Halstead said.

Storms nodded. "The most excitement I get is ticketing speedboats."

Halstead pushed back his chair and his empty glass. Wouldn't do for the Island Chief of Police to have a blood alcohol level over the limit.

When he tried to pay, Gus Jones the proprietor of the Grill insisted the brews were on the house. "Mel Todd stayed at the motel here all last winter. We'll miss him."

Jones an aging hippy, who in the summer served behind the bar in shorts and blue singlet, also owned and operated the one motel on the Island. Once the tourist season was over, he was happy enough to rent rooms out at a cheaper monthly rate for the winter.

Halstead nodded his thanks.

"Gotta go, Steph is expecting me for lunch."

* * *

YourSpace Retreat the sign read against a backdrop of painted peonies. The real peonies were long past but tall delphiniums nodded along the driveway. Though it had been nearly a year since their wedding, Halstead still hadn't got over the thrill of arriving home and seeing Steph there. Ever-graceful even in old gardening jeans and a tied off shirt, she greeted him with a breezy smooch. Slim and smart, he bet she could still slip into the cheerleader outfit she'd worn at highschool football practice thirty years ago. Back then, he'd never thought of her as any more than the pesky kid sister of his best buddy. But years later, post-widower (him) and post-divorce (her) they had become re-acquainted.

She brought out cool looking things from the fridge. A bowl of what she called nicoise salad -tuna and egg as far as he could see- and a pitcher of iced tea.

When there were no guests at the Retreat, and on occasions when Steph's daughter Livy was home from university, they ate in their own kitchen. On Retreat occasions, guests could make their own breakfasts and lunches in their cabins, then meet in the common room for a communal meal at night. Preparing the meal was part of the 'experience' for Retreat participants, Steph had explained to him. Personally he couldn't see wanting to pay good money to go somewhere where you had to make your own dinner, but it seemed to work for Steph's guests and that was fine with him.

"So, how did it go?" she asked, as she arranged pretty napkins and plates. A reflex with her, to create beauty. That was part of the appeal of her successful mid-life business venture -- providing an elegant getaway Retreat for other successful businesswomen who wanted to repower their psyches and energies. Or so Steph's brochure described the Retreat experience.

"Not much of a crowd," he said. "Most of those fishermen were Mel's father's age and they're all gone."

She poured the amber-coloured tea into tall glasses, adding a fresh lemon slice on the rim of each.

"Well, it's a sad thing, watching the old ways go. In the future, kids will think fish only comes in cans for lunchtime sandwiches."

He scooped out some salad. It looked tasty whatever she called it. "Gotta roll with the punches Steph, that's what folks have always done."

She sipped at the tea, thinking. "The stories of Mel Todd and the other fishermen may not have the romance and excitement of the earlier days of sailing ships but their stories are part of the lake history as well."

"Then maybe you can include something about them in the Save the Lighthouse project your group is working on. I'm sure that Mel would be tickled pink."

"That's a good idea," Steph said. "I'll talk to the others about it." She and Ali Jakes were members of a group who were working to preserve the old structure at Lighthouse Point. In a cost-cutting move, the Canadian government was looking to divest itself of hundreds of disused lighthouses across the country. On the Island, the move had aroused a howl of protest.

He took another helping of salad. "So who have you got lined up for the Retreat this month?"

She pushed a brochure across the table. "Have a look at this," she said excitedly.

He handled it dubiously. The cover was a montage of swirling mauve butterflies. *A New You!* The copy read. *New Perspectives for Women in Mid-Life.*

"This woman's sessions are very popular," Steph said. "I've managed to book her for a retreat in August. It's a real coup."

"That's great," he said, already making plans for his own type of retreat. Preferably something that would involve fishing and beer. But he was admiring of Steph. For a woman who moved easily in the realms of meditation and spirituality, she had a smart and savvy business sense.

Now she tinkled the ice in her cup and looked thoughtfully down towards the lake that sparkled beyond her artistically designed flower paths.

"That woman who found Mel sounds awful," she said. "The worst kind of tourist. We don't need that."

Halstead shrugged. "It seems the village businesses are glad to get any kind of tourist."

Steph sighed. "I hope things don't change too much. The quiet pace here is what I love and that's what attracts my clients as well."

Halstead stretched out his long legs and yawned in a Saturday afternoon, post- beer way. "I wouldn't worry. Middle Island is pretty quiet. I reckon we've had our quota of excitement on the water for this week."

4

A bright, sunny day on the lake. The breeze was clear and snapping, the police launch bouncing playfully over the waves. A sailboat tacked across the Bay, tangerine coloured sail billowing like a freed balloon. Pete looked back towards Middle Island, enjoying the view. There were no big beaches on the Island, just rare bits of smaller, sandy shoreline, fronting on the farmland. He could see the rocky outpost of Lighthouse Point and further down the shore, Cedar Grove cabins where Tyler was staying. An inlander, born and raised in a city, Pete had really taken to the water since moving to the Island.

So when the chief had told him to grab his hat and head for the docks, he was eager to go.

"What's up?" he asked as they drove the few short blocks to the marina behind the Island Grill.

Halstead shrugged. "Not sure. There was a call from the Ministry of National Defense. Their guy working on South Island apparently needs some police assistance."

The Middle Island jurisdiction was made up of three areas. Middle Island, only technically an Island as it was joined to the mainland by a causeway, was by far the largest chunk of the domain. A pretty, rural landscape with winding tree-lined roads and pleasant views of farmland fronting on bay and lake waters.

South Island, a tenth the size, was a limestone almost soil-less outpost, populated only by clumps of spindly cedar trees and scratchy juniper. North Island, the smallest of the three, and the hangout of the local cormorants, was barely more than a rock with a handful of trees sitting on top, like candles in a birthday cake.

Halstead squinted his eyes at the approaching island. "The guy at the Ministry office didn't say much."

Pete frowned, with a policeman's instinctive wariness. It was generally helpful to have some idea of what you were walking into.

"Probably just another boatload of sightseers," Halstead said dismissively. "Their man likely needs help shooing them away."

"Maybe he's actually found a bomb," Pete said. "Or sorry, a UXO." The acronym was government shorthand for Unexploded Explosive Ordnance. Or simply a bomb, as Pete had put it.

"There are no bombs on South Island," Halstead said wearily. "Never have been."

Personally, he thought the Ministry expedition to scan the island for old ordnance was a lot of blow over nothing, and potentially a big pain in the neck for his police force.

It was true that sixty-odd years ago, during World War II, some other spots along the lake had served as practice bombing ranges for Commonwealth air crews. These areas had been posted and closed off to the public years ago. But South Island had never been posted and never would have been, save for the recent discovery of a sheaf of dusty maps in some dusty drawer in Ottawa. One of the maps supposedly indicated that some ordnance might once have been dropped on South Island.

Now the Ministry had sent a bomb expert to scout out the area. The news heralded a flurry of activity. Except for courting teenagers, no one usually bothered much with rocky, scrub-covered South Island. But then the Ministry posted a notice in the Bonville Record, warning people not to land on the Island while Ministry staff investigated the situation. Not surprisingly, that worked like a magnet to attract thrill-seekers. During the first week of posting, they flocked in their boats to the site, hoping to witness an explosion. Art Storms and the auxiliary coast guard had to be out there every day to control the situation and Halstead cursed the Ministry for creating an unnecessary sideshow.

The notice also touched off a flurry of creative and wild speculation as to the true reason the Island had been closed to the public.

It's some kind of government cover-up.

They're going to test a missile.

They're going to bury some toxic stuff.

And the ever-reliable old chestnut, *They've found a martian spaceship.*

By now though, the novelty had worn off a bit and as the launch approached the Island, Halstead could spot only a couple of boats moored at the dock. One was the white Ministry boat, with the big green government logo on the side. The other boat was bigger, a fine-looking yacht.

A fluorescent-yellow sign posted at the end of the dock, read:.

National Defence Advisory - Explosive Hazard Warning
KEEP OUT. DOCKING HERE IS PROHIBITED
Be advised that there is a risk of serious injury or death to persons entering the South Island area. Unexploded explosive ordnance (UXO) could be buried in the area.

If you find something that could be UXO:

Do not touch it.

Remember the location and leave the area.

Contact 911 or your local police as soon as possible to report what you have found.

Pete coasted the launch in, past a few of the water snakes that inhabited the island shore. The police seemed to have arrived in the nick of time, as the two men on the dock looked about to come to blows. The shorter one, who must be the government fellow, was a trim, compact man wearing the green cap and khaki shirt of the Ministry. He was easily outmatched by his opponent, a burly man with a red, angry face. Both men were yelling, but the Ministry man was standing his ground.

"Get back on that boat!," he commanded, brandishing a fist, about six inches upward into the other man's beard.

The big man appeared about to pick up his adversary and shove him into the water.

Pete leapt off the launch, made a scrambling landing and straightened to interject himself between them.

"Hey!" he said. "Police. Back off."

The men, breathing heavily, looked at him in surprise. The Ministry man settled down first, taking a step back. When the other man tried to push forward, Pete gave him a shove.

"Hold it buddy. Fun's over."

By this time, Halstead was also out of the launch. The big man acknowledged a setback, laying his muscular arms across his chest with a snort of angry disgust.

"I just want to know what right he thinks he's got, to keep me off this island," he muttered trucently. "It's not government property."

The Ministry man stepped forward. "Wesley Sedore here," he said to Pete, extending a hand. "Thanks for coming. Maybe you guys can get this bozo to leave."

He turned and said with exaggerated diction, "Can't you read that sign there, Mac? It says KEEP AWAY, DON'T LAND HERE. That means you and anybody else."

Bozo was obviously not the best choice of words for the situation. Pete saw the big man tense and quickly brought out his notebook. The mere sight of the book and a request for identification often helped to defuse a tense situation.

"What's your name please, sir?"

"Gerald Tice," he said belligerently, "and that's my boat there. I'm a legitimate businessman and I want to know why I can't work along the shores of this island."

Halstead glanced towards the boat, an expensively rigged out craft, with the nameplate *Finders Keepers*. That figured.

"What are you looking for?" he asked. "There's no wrecks here. They're all further out in the lake."

"Just lookin'," Tice said evasively. "We've got a right to be here," he repeated.   Halstead belatedly noticed two young people staring over the side of the boat. They looked chagrined, embarrassed by the fracas.

Sedore snorted loudly. "I know what you're 'just looking' for. You're one of those crazy Arrowheads, diving for those old airplanes in the lake." His face screwed up in disgust. "It's been fifty years man, don't you nuts ever give up?"

Halstead sighed. Another wild goose chase, in his opinion. UXO hunters *and* Arrowheads, all in the same morning, all unfortunately in his Middle Island jurisdiction.

Some self-described 'Arrowheads' arrived every summer to search the local waters. Fifty years ago the Canadian government had invested hugely in the production of the Avro Arrow, an airplane ahead of its time in aerospace technology. The factory producing the plane employed thousands of people and several five hundred pound models were tested over the lake.

Despite great hopes of putting Canadian airplane production on the world stage, the then government inexplicably cancelled the project, destroying all the specification records and ditching the models in the lake. It was the Arrowheads' passionate quest to recover these artifacts, a process that involved increasingly expensive diving projects. Thirty metres down and seemingly unretreivable, the plane models remained stubbornly undiscovered and for some the quest had taken on obsessive, even mythical proportions.

Tice snarled, "Yeah, well if I'm so crazy, why is the government trying to keep us away from here? You don't want us to find those plane models. It'd be too embarrassing for you guys."

"*You* should be embarrassed," Sedore retorted. "You're a looney, man. Nuts."

Hastily averting a return of hostilities, Halstead moved forward. "The sign says it all, sir. For the time being, at least until Mr. Sedore has finished his job here, South Island and its shores are off limits to the public."

As Tice seemed about to sputter some more, he added tellingly. "*And* if you don't leave immediately, we'll be booking you for harrassment."

Tice left, still trucelent but at least moving in the right direction, towards the *Finders Keepers*. Halstead tipped his cap to the young couple who watched warily as Tice came aboard. They were a good-looking pair, early twenties he guessed, athletic and tanned from long days on the water. And they'd been in the water, too he saw, noting the stack of neatly piled diving equipment on the boat deck. The dark-haired young man scowled at Tice's back, and the girl, a pony-tailed blonde just looked wearily resigned. He wondered if they were employees and whether they were beginning to regret their choice of a summer job.

Sedore exhaled deeply, as the boat moved away. "Thanks fellows. Some of those Arrowheads can get real upset after years of throwing away their time and money looking for those things."

Pete looked down into the water, cleaned crystal clear to the bottom by invasive zebra mussels that ate every speck of algae in the lake.

"Doesn't seem as if anything much could stay hidden in this water," he said. "Let alone a five hundred pound model of an airplane."

"Yeah, but tell that to Tice and his type, they won't believe you. Anyway, from the look of that boat, he's got lots of money to waste on the search."

"You're right about that," Halstead said. He looked enviously after the *Finders Keepers* departing wake. "A nice boat like that could cost a half a million bucks. We don't see that too often in these waters."

"Even if the guy did actually find the plane model," Pete asked Sedore. "How would he plan to retrieve it?".

"Oh he'll have a plan all worked out," Sedore said. "If he doesn't have a winch on the boat, he can get one that does. Not that he's ever going to find anything. I feel sorry for his daughter."

"His daughter?"

"Yes she's the girl you saw on the boat. She and her boyfriend have to work all summer with her bozo father. They're Tice's divers," he added. "Tice introduced them to me at the beginning when we were still being civil. The boy at least is a professional diver."

He gestured to the shore. "How about a cup of coffee? Least I can do for you."

The campsite was neatly kept. A state of the art tent, stacked boxes of supplies and equipment and a portable cookstove in the firepit. Poles apart from Mel Todd's derelict haven, Pete thought.

While Sedore boiled water on his stove, he chatted happily about his work. "It was quite exciting to see the map, the first new information we've had in decades."

"So there's really something here?" Halstead asked sceptically, accepting the cup of instant. "Just what are we talking about, some kind of bomb, a landmine, what exactly?"

Sedore offered sugar and powdered cream from plastic tubs. He grinned enthusiastically. "Could be that, or grenades, artillery shells, even unused bullets. You wouldn't credit the stuff our crews have dug up across the province."

"Dangerous work," Pete said, thinking of his own experience. It was depressing too, to think that in many parts of the world, new ordance was even now being dumped to endanger future generations. Small powerful landmines, strewn like a toxic crop in fields and along roadsides.

Sedore nodded, "Yessir. Over the years, the department has incurred several fatalities and many more injuries. And then of course there are the public fatalities. These testing ranges were set up in areas that were once considered remote, but now they're populated. One injury happened when a farm employee ran over a buried pyrotechnic device. Another shell killed two curious boy scouts, and three workmen died when they were loading topsoil into a truck."

Halstead winced. "I can see how maybe the kids might be careless, but what about the grown men?"

Sedore nodded. "Over time, the ordnance can lose its original shape, or the paint and markings wear off. By now, it may look more like a piece of old pipe, or maybe a car muffler or any other bit of rusty metal. The government has spent millions of dollars trying to find the stuff but we'll never get it all."

Halstead scoffed, "And you really think there might be one of those things here on South Island? That's what your maps say?"

"The maps aren't always that clear," Sedore said glibly. "Usually we have some corroborating evidence."

"But you don't have any corroborating evidence in this case?" Halstead guessed.

"It's a lot of work," Sedore said defensively. "There's not always the time or the money. People have to read through stacks of archives and military records. Sometimes they even go out and chat with old timers in small towns who remember the war years."

"My dad was overseas then," Halstead said. "But I never heard my mother talk about any bombing near here. And she and her friends would have known, believe me. There's no keeping secrets on Middle Island, especially among the ladies."

"They would just have been practise drops," Sedore said impatiently. "Sometimes night time runs. The bombs weren't actually going off."

"Not till now, anyway," Halstead said wrily.

"That's why I'm here," Sedore said, his good-humour restored. "The Ministry doesn't want anyone to get hurt."

He proudly showed them some of his bomb detecting equipment, which included sophisticated metal detectors and magnetic pulsing sensors.

"Good thing that guy Tice didn't see my maps," he laughed. "He'd have taken them as proof that we're looking for his precious airplane models."

"Never mind UXO's," Halstead said. "Half the folks over there on Middle Island think you've found a UFO here, a spaceship." He snorted, "Bombs, model planes, spaceships." He waved a hand, "Have you looked around you at the terrain? It's all rock, I doubt you could plant a carrot seed here, let alone conceal what you're talking about."

Sedore took no offense. "There's some pockets of dirt here, piled up over the years. Lots of nooks and crannies too."

"Well good luck to you then," Halstead said. "And watch where you step."

Sedore saw them back to the dock, where a pair of cormorants perched on the struts, drying their blue black feathers in the sun. The birds didn't move as the people approached.

"They're used to me," Sedore said. "I like to watch them fish. They're quite remarkably skilled."

"Remarkable shitters too," Halstead said. "They're not popular with a lot of folks around here. Luckily there's nothing much to ruin on North Island."

"We're a pretty messy species too," Sedore said mildly. "You only have to take a boat trip around Lake Ontario to see how ten million people can really mess up a shoreline."

Jakes, a birding enthusiast, who had often had this discussion with the chief, managed not to laugh.

They sped away in the boat, leaving Sedore alone on the island.

"You think he's O.K. there?" Pete asked.

"He's got his phone, he's got our number," Halstead said testily. "He's got the cormorants for company. And the snakes."

5

Ali jiggled her wriggling daughter on a hip and searched her backpack for another fruit bar. "Shush darling," she cautioned. "Mommy wants to hear Auntie Miranda talk."

Despite the distractions of a gorgeous July afternoon and gulls wheeling lazily in the warm air currents above the lighthouse tower, Miranda was doing well. The talk was an informal run-through of the presentation she planned to give to the Ontario Heritage Foundation next week. She wore slacks, blouse and sandals and wisps of her silver hair poked out from under an an olive-green Tilly hat. Ali thought she looked far younger than her years, though at times maybe a little too lean for comfort.

In a concise fifteen minutes, Miranda had managed to encapsulate the history of the old lighthouse that had once been part of a network of beacons that protected shipping traffic on the lake. Even so, there had still been many shipwrecks in the days of sailing, as captains would risk the violent autumn storms to get their valuable loads of barley over to the States. Miranda's great-grandfather had been a lighthouse keeper, in the days when the light was still provided by oil lamps that had to be tended through the night.

The Norris Lighthouse was a white frame construction, with a shed at the back which had once been the house for the keeper and his family. At the top of the tower was the windowed cupola that had enclosed various lighting systems through the decades. By the beginning of the twentieth century, the early oil lamps had been replaced by electric light but the keeper's duties still included radio and weather communication, tending fog alarms and providing rescue services.

In the 1980s the keepers themselves were replaced by the new, fully automated systems that were installed all along the lake. Shipping had changed too, boats were bigger and faster and steered by modern GPS systems. Many of the old beacons such as the Norris Light, that had helped protect so many lives, fell into disuse and neglect.

"We must act to preserve this important piece of our heritage," Miranda finished in ringing tones. "We will light the light again. I urge the Foundation to save the Middle Island Norris Lighthouse from delisting and destruction and to grant the structure official heritage status and protection."

There was a ragged round of applause from the small group assembled on the grass. Even little Nevra caught on and delightedly added her bit.

"That was wonderful, Miranda," said Stephanie Bind, events co-ordinator for the Save the Lighthouse group. "If you make that speech on our picnic day, we should get lots of donations."

Ali looked up at the old lighthouse tower. For a few moments, Miranda had brought those earlier days alive.

Then a cruder voice broke into her thoughts.

"Wow you ladies have bitten off a lot here," Tyler Cotes said. "Looks to me if you want to save this place, you'd better hurry up. That roof looks as if it will blow clear off in the next thunderstorm."

Ali hadn't been thrilled that Pete had told Tyler about the meeting. She had even rather meanly hoped that he wouldn't come. He must be really bored at the cabin.

Now he seemed to read her face and said defensively,

"It's good of you folks to try, though. I just meant it was going to be a challenge to save the place. You're going to need big bucks."

Stephanie Bind nodded. "We do have some options, the picture isn't all bleak. Obtaining heritage status for the lighthouse is an important first step. Then there are various government grants we can apply for."

Her glance swept the site. "There's nearly two acres here. In the past, the lighthouse keeper would have grazed a milk cow to provide milk for the family. They likely also kept a few chickens, most everybody did. Fisheries and Oceans would actually sell us the entire property for a dollar but then we would have to raise money constantly to maintain it."

"So, not much of a deal, " Tyler said.

He looked over at the lighthouse. "Can people go inside the tower? Climb up to the top and see the light?"

Stephanie sighed. "We wish! It would be a great draw for tourists, but we couldn't allow it in its present state. Ali and I have been up there but the staircase is too rickety for public use. We're getting an estimate on repairing it right now but it's going to be a big extra expense."

"Too bad. Of course I couldn't get up those stairs anyway, not on this shaky leg of mine. I'd really like to see that view."

He explained, "I've been looking at some books about the old shipping days on the lake. There's nothing else to read, they're the only books at the cabin. But some of it's pretty interesting. There was one whole book about smuggling booze during Prohibition in the States."

Miranda nodded enthusiastically, "Yes, that was an interesting time. But there's always been some smuggling happening on the lake. Escaping slaves from the States, liquor, criminals. And a lot of jettisoned cargo."

She looked out at the shimmering waves. "Lots of bones," she intoned stagily "and lots of tales about what's down there under the water."

Her words seemed to cast a shadow over the view but it was just a cloud obscuring the sun for a moment. Tyler spun on his cast and looked around the site.

"Say, that dead guy last week. Didn't they find him somewhere around here?"

Trust Tyler to bring *that* up, Ali thought angrily.

It was true that the discovery of Mel Todd's body only a short distance up the shore, had put of bit of a damper on their planned lighthouse picnic fundraiser. But the executive committee intended to go ahead with the event.

"We've already booked the tent and picnic tables," Stephanie pointed out.

"And it won't be for another few weeks," Beth Harrison said. "So it won't seem too disrespectful."

Beth, sixty but with well cut frosted hair and a body kept buff at the Bonville recreation centre, had eyed Tyler's t-shirted biceps with interest. The Save the Lighthouse executive committee was all female and Ali the youngest member by decades. There were husbands and sons available for heavy work when required but most of them, like Pete were busy during the day.

Now Beth,who had grown sons of her own, showed a not so motherly interest in Tyler. She actually giggled, "There's lots of work to do. It will be good to have a big strong fellow like yourself to help."

Tyler sketched a corny bow. Ali doubted he would be much help, more likely he would see his role as critic.

Plans for the event included an informational tour of the lighthouse exterior and a chance to have a photo taken in the eighteen foot old lifeboat, which the grade ten high school class had taken on as a project to clean up and paint. There was also a summer-long raffle of a local artist's painting of the lighthouse, and Ali was designing a treasure hunt for the kids. A project for another summer and hopefully more funds, would be to fix up the lighthouse keeper's shed as a small museum to house a ship's anchor and other sailing artifacts.

"How about a smuggling exhibit?" Tyler asked. "I read there were once actual pirates on the lakes."

"Oh I don't think that would be appropriate." Beth sounded shocked. "Pirates and thievery are hardly the sort of picture that we're trying to present."

"Barley shipping or rum running, it's all history," Miranda pointed out. "We don't get to pick and choose, that would be censoring the truth. Besides," she added gleefully, "it's more than likely that your great-grandaddy as well as many of my relatives, were smugglers with the best of them."

"Maybe your folks were criminals," Beth huffed. "Not mine."

"Tush," Miranda said, rolling her eyes.

Tyler grinned and said his goodbyes. He had rented a car for his stay on the Island and trips to his Bonville physiotherapy appointments. Beth looked long and longingly after him, while the others sat about on the grass or in collapsible fold-up chairs. Ali followed Nevra around the perimeter while her daughter pushed a toy schoolbus through the grass. The business of the meeting over, there was time for chitchat about the busy waterways and the boaters and tourists who returned in summer like the swallows.

"And don't forget that fellow looking for bombs on South Island," Steph laughed. "That sure has everybody stirred up."

"Do you remember any bomb testing then, Miranda?" Ali asked, thinking that Miranda would have been ten years old at the end of the war.

Miranda shook her head. "My cousin said there was some down Lake Erie way, but never here."

Ali rolled the toy school bus back to Nevra. "So there's no danger of an explosion?"

Miranda patted the younger woman's shoulder. "No danger at all, my dear. But we must let the government men have their fun."

This was followed by a group laugh.

Eventually, the women trailed lazily back to their vehicles. They had chores to do and supper to make. Miranda, travelling with Ali in the Jakes' SUV, looked back at the old lighthouse, its neglected lines mellowed in the late afternoon sunshine. If she squinched up her eyes, she could imagine it renewed and looking spruce again, though she wouldn't want to displace the swallows. Some of those nests must be decades old.

But to relight the light, even symbolically, now that would be something. She could picture the lighted beacon visible from far out on on the darkened lake, a light that hadn't shone there for many long years. Or as the Bard would put it, leading the way through *'unpathed waters, undreamed shores.'*

She hadn't taught English Literature for forty years without collecting some handy quotations.

6

Eight p.m. and the day was just beginning to wane over the water. Long evenings, one of the joys of summertime. Pete tossed the styrofoam chicken wing containers into the recycling box, with mental apologies to the planet and Miranda, a kindly, if unrelenting fount of environmental no-no's. He'd been over at the Bonville courthouse that afternoon and thought he might take a fast food fix out to Tyler at the cottage.

"Thanks buddy," Tyler raised his beer, "for a reminder of civilization."

Pete tipped his own drink. "You're welcome. Just doing my bit to keep up the spirit of the troops."

"So, what's the scoop over at that island?" Tyler asked curiously. "Is there anything to that old buried bombs story?"

Pete shook his head. "The chief says it's a load of hooey. I have to admit though, I was still a bit edgy walking around there yesterday. And it turns out we did run into some fireworks."

He explained about breaking up the the argument between Sedore and Gerald Tice.

"I see that fancy boat out on the water most days," Tyler said. "And the divers. What's their game?"

Pete explained about the Arrowheads.

Tyler whistled. "I remember hearing something about those planes. What would it be worth to find one of those models?"

"No idea," Pete said. "But the government would probably demand to have them back."

"After ditching them in the first place!" Tyler marvelled. "It might be interesting to talk to this Tice guy though."

"I doubt it, he's not exactly friendly."

Tyler flexed his arms. "I can take care of myself buddy – even on one foot. And I'd like to find out more about the airplane story."

"Ali said that you came to the Save the Lighthouse meeting. That's good of you – you weren't bored?"

"Nah, your friend Miranda knows a lot of neat stuff about the place. She gave me a book on the old booze smuggling days."

He indicated the small pile of books and pamphlets on the coffee table.

"I've been taking the boat out in the afternoons, figure I might as well check out some of the locations mentioned in the books."

Tyler had rented a speedboat from a Bonville dealer soon after he arrived at Cedar Grove. When Pete, who was content to fish from an outboard from Peterson's Marina, asked why Tyler needed so much horsepower, Tyler had shrugged and looked at his foot cast.

"I can't do much on land these days, might as well have some fun on the water."

He wasn't much impressed with Bay fishing anyway.

"It's way too quiet here for me. Not like that summer I worked in Florida on a marlin fishing boat. I don't get how your boss can sit out there for a whole day waiting for a bite on the line and even then, the fish is likely so small that you have to throw it back. Now, racing some of those rum-running boats, that sounds like fun."

Pete looked out past the small lawn, where the fading sun threw a glittering cutlass-like blade across the water. "They say several of the local fortunes are based on that rum money." He grinned. "Of course the folks are all right and proper now."

"So, what did you think of the old lighthouse tower?," he asked. "Kind of a neat place."

Tyler snorted. "I wish Ali and the others luck. Last I heard the government isn't throwing away much money these days."

"At least they've stirred up some local interest," Pete said. "I think it would be cool if some of that old smuggling money ended up helping to save the the lighthouse that guided their grandfathers to port."

Tyler stirred restlessly. "I think I'll go out a bit farther in the boat tomorrow. Take that book of treasure maps and have a looksee."

"Those maps are just a come-on for tourists," Pete warned. "If there was any treasure out there, someone would have found it long ago."

Tyler waved a hand. "Ah, it's something to do."

"Wear your lifejacket," said Pete the policeman.

"So, what else you been up to lately, supercop? Some kids been stealing apples?"

"Peas," Pete said dryly. "The apples aren't ready yet. How's the leg coming along – still doing the physio?"

"Coupla hours a day. It's slow going though."

"Ah you'll be jogging around the Island any day now."

Tyler smiled sourly. "Yeah but what am I going to do then? What if the army won't take me back -- I've never done anything else."

He looked frustratedly at the cast. "And it's not as if the army will care what happens to me, not judging by the stories you hear. You take a bullet, risk losing the use of your leg for your fellow citizens and all you get is a crappy disability cheque."

"Maybe you could think about changing careers *in* the army," Pete said. "In ten years maybe you've done enough combat tours."

He knew that Tyler had been on patrol in some of the toughest battles in the moutainous Afghani terrain. Ty was proud of himself as a man of action, a risk taker, the guy who was always out in front of the unit. In the battle where his foot had been nearly shattered, ten other soldiers had been wounded and two killed.

"You could work in emergency relief for instance," he encouraged.

"Lugging sandbags, or handing out bottles of water after a hurricane?" Tyler scoffed. "I don't think so. It's different for you,

you wanted to leave. But that isn't me. They might as well shoot me now and get it over with."

"There are lots of different jobs," Pete objected. "All that rescue work has to be organized. you're a smart guy, you could do that."

"A desk job, no way! I'm off to fight in Darfur. If they'll take me, that is," he scowled again at his foot.

"You'll be O.K." Pete assured. "It just takes time."

He looked around the cottage. "You're good here for awhile anyway, so just relax and enjoy taking it easy. It'll work out."

"Yeah, sure buddy. And maybe one of these treasure maps is for real."

Pete stood up, "Well I gotta go and stake out some pea snatchers."

"Stay for a beer man, it's early."

"Sorry, I haven't been home yet and I promised Ali I'd help her move some furniture around."

Tyler scowled. "Yeah I know, the old ball and chain is calling. I lose more buddies that way than to Afghani road bombs."

"I'll tell Ali that, she'll love the ball and chain part."

"Ah, you know what I mean, bud. Ali is a knockout of a woman in every way. I envy you. You look good. The whole package looks good, beautiful wife, the baby, the house."

"Thanks," Pete said. "I know I'm a lucky guy, other men died in that road attack. You're lucky too. That bullet only hit your foot."

Tyler slumped back on the couch. "Yeah, but you survived that attack for a reason. I don't know what my reason is – it's not clear yet anyway, that's for damn sure."

He kicked out angrily with his good foot, against the cottage siding.

"Careful there," Pete warned. "You don't want to spend another few months in physio. It will work out, buddy. You'll be back over there by September. I guarantee it."

But Tyler didn't look much comforted.

* * *

Ali stood with hands on hips, admiring her work. She'd found the little dresser in the Island thrift shop and knew it would be perfect for the nursery. She'd worked for a week on it in the back porch, stripping off the old surface and re-painting the wood a rich, creamy white. Then she'd found some neat old-fashioned china knobs for the drawers.

"What do you think?" she asked Pete now. "Isn't it sweet?"

She had to repeat the question.

"Sure honey," he said absently. "It looks terrific."

"Did you have a nice time with Tyler?" she asked teasingly. "Swapping the old war stories?"

He smiled. "Sure, it was fun."

"What does the specialist say about his leg?" She knew he'd had an appointment that week.

"It's coming along. Not fast enough for Tyler though. He's pretty restless."

"But he's going to get better, isn't he?"

"Sure. But maybe Tyler should think about his future, he can't stay in the army forever."

"What else could he do? What's he interested in, other than renovating our village Main Street?"

He smiled ruefully. "I don't know. I don't think that Ty has thought much about it before this. He always seemed to be fine with what he was doing."

She fetched wine and they sat on the back porch watching the bats swoop in the dark. Crickets hummed from a neighbouring field and fireflies were beginning to glimmer in the grass. She thought she would never tire of the natural peace of the Island. Of the rhythms of the year, that she had only learned to appreciate since they had moved here.

But now she felt again that vague disquiet, wondering if Pete felt the same about their new home as she did. He was very quiet tonight. He was a quiet man altogether though usually she was fairly privy to his thoughts, as he was to hers.

But he and Tyler shared a past that she couldn't enter. Pete's mother had died when he was fourteen, his older brother had joined the army and been killed in Bosnia. His relationship with his father was non-existent. Tyler was like the family Pete had never really had.

Was she just a teeny bit jealous? Because she'd never seen Pete close to anyone else?

Ali was horrified at the thought. What was wrong with her? Tyler was Pete's best friend, for that matter the only friend or link with his past who she had yet met. No, she assured herself. She was glad for the insight, for the chance to glean anything more about Pete who was reticent about so much.

"Ty said that he came to your lighthouse meeting," Pete said. "Thanks, it was good for him to get out and see some people."

More guilt for Ali. She would try harder to get along with the man.

"How is the heritage grant application going?" Pete asked.

"Miranda and Beth are doing most of it," Ali said. "I gather there there are all sorts of hoops to jump through. It took months just to get our charitable status so that we can give tax receipts for donations."

"It would be nice if you could save the old lighthouse," he said. "Really nice. It's a piece of history."

She felt the same. They had seen so much destruction in Afghanistan.

"Miranda has been trying to figure out the best way to light up the tower on the evening of the picnic. Beth said she could find us a generator for the night, and then we'd have electricity. But that would be noisy and spoil the mood, so Miranda would rather have a lamp, like they used back in the day. We're going to see if we can get something from the museum. If not, we'll just take a couple of hurricane lamps up there to make our symbolic gesture."

"Sounds neat," he said. "I could help."

She smiled and reached across the chair arms to hold his hand in the dusk. "That would be nice. It's a fun project to be working on."

Their house was on an inland road but Ali always felt that she could smell the lake. In winter it roared in on wet, snow-soaked gales. But on a summer night like this, the tantalizing, watery, reedy scent wafted in deliciously on the gentle breeze. A charmed night, a charmed moment, one of those rare occasions when you could almost believe that everywhere was peace and that nothing would ever go awry again.

7

Wes Sedore thought he liked this time of evening best. In the natural world, the daytime shift was giving way to the night time shift. Some critters were getting ready to bed down, many others were just awakening for the nightly food hunt. Now there was this soft, magically blurred in-between time.

He had camped often with his kids in the provincial parks and wished impractically that they could be with him now. He chuckled to himself. Wouldn't his twelve year old son love this particular camping trip. Hunting bombs with Dad -- now there would be a tale for the annual How I Spent My Summer Vacation essay.

Despite his enjoyment of the job (this is work? he asked himself often) he had to admit the day had been unproductive. He'd spent most of it checking out what looked to be an intriguing anomaly on the map. But though he'd scoured the area with the modern day equivalent of a fine tooth comb, he'd found no clue to buried ordnance. It was time to pack it in for the day, the fireflies and bats were coming out. He would have to try again in the morning.

Back at camp, he heated milk for cocoa. But when he'd kicked out the fire, some light remained in the dark down by the shore. A boat? Some tardy boaters coming in to the Marina., or a late-night fisherman? He couldn't hear a motor though. It was almost ghostly. He thought of the creepy stories he'd told his kids, their wide eyes *as they grabbed their blankets tight and huddled by the comforting firelight.*

He called out towards the light, but no one answered and the light went out.

8

Mid-morning and it was already hot and humid. So humid that South Island appeared only as a shimmering mirage bobbing somewhere ahead of the launch. Pete was sweating in his blue short sleeved shirt and sometimes he felt that the peaked policeman's cap held in more heat than it warded off.

The call from the Ministry Regional Office hadn't been very specific. Just that Wesley Sedore hadn't made his regular call into the office the day before. And he wasn't answering his cell phone either.

Pete cut the motor as they neared the Island and they coasted in. The Ministry boat was still moored at the dock, looking just as it had a few days ago. Was it his imagination or did the small island seem almost eerily quiet? It was odd that Sedore hadn't come out to greet them. He should have heard the launch arrival.

"Hit the airhorn," Halstead said. "Let him know we're coming."

But there was no answering shout.

On shore, they headed for the campsite, moving urgently but cautiously as well. By now, it was pretty certain that something must have happened to Sedore and they were on high alert.

"Maybe he's actually found a UXO," Pete said, "and accidentally set it off. He could be hurt."

"There are no UXO's here," Halstead said tiredly. "And if the fool actually did blow one up, we'd have heard the damn thing over on Middle Island."

"If not a bomb, then what?" Pete asked. He found his own nerves jumping at the prospect.

They had reached the campsite. The firepit was long cold, Pete thought it hadn't been used recently. Everything was tidy and ship-shape. The frying pan wiped clean, no dirty coffee-cup from a camp breakfast.

Halstead looked in the tent flap. The sleeping bag was laid out neatly and undisturbed on the camp fold-up cot. "It doesn't look as if Sedore even slept here last night."

They circled the site. There were scuffed bootprints in the dirt, but lots of them. Sedore had obviously taken different routes in his scanning of the island.

"Here's a graph," Pete said. "Looks as if he's divided the island into sections and is marking them 'clean' when he's finished there. The way the shaded areas are filled in, it looks as if he was over this way last."

Halstead nodded grimly. "Let's go see."

Pete looked doubtfully past the cleared area, to the spreading mats of scratchy juniper bushes and dry clumps of burdock that made up the bulk of the island's vegetation.

"I sure hope that map of Sedore's is wrong," he said. "I've already had one bad encounter with a bomb in my life."

Halstead grinned sympathetically. "There's no bombs buried here Jakes. I guarantee it."

"Stake your life on it?" Pete asked only half sarcastically. "That's what it comes down to sometimes."

Halstead shrugged. "Like I told Sedore, lots of the local old timers were kids then. If there was a chance of the air guys dropping a bomb anywhere in the vicinity, they would have walked on water to find the thing. And they never did."

"O.K. then, away we go." Pete led the way, crunching into a patch of five foot high burdock. An hour later he stopped in the scant shade of a lonely pine and looked back at the chief, face dripping sweat and arms plentifully scratched, like his own.

"Maybe we need Sedore's fancy equipment to detect *him*."

Halstead shook his head, said seriously. "We'll have to call for some back-up for a more intensive search. But personally, I'd swear that the man is not here."

Pete looked towards the dock, where the green and white Ministry boat was tethered. "So what did he do, swim away? But why, and where the heck would he go?"

"Maybe somebody picked him up to go fishing."

"For two days? And his cellphone doesn't work, he doesn't answer his boss?"

"Maybe it was a mermaid who picked him up. Remember that movie with Tom Hanks."

Mermaid or not, Halstead radioed for assistance. Within an hour, Greg Jackman and some volunteers from the auxilliary coast guard had arrived. Art Storms came too, with his young crew from the search and rescue training course. Both boats carried emergency medical equipment as well. With Halstead and Jakes, that made a team of a dozen to fan out and thoroughly work their way over the small island.

"Watch out for martians, " one of the kids warned and the others laughed.

The searchers were done by five o'clock but had turned up no sign of Sedore.

"I can tell you one thing," Halstead said, when they reconvened hot and tired at the dock. "The man is not on this island, not even his ghost."

Art's crew, four boys and two girls, had already stripped down to their bathing suits and plunged thankfully into the lake. The adults in their various uniforms looked on enviously.

"What next?" Jackman asked. In his forties, he was a quiet, capable man who had seen a few water tragedies in his time.

"You can go, thanks, " Halstead said. "Jakes and I are going to stay here overnight. On the off chance that we've missed something or that Sedore comes back."

Jackman shook his head. "Yeah, well good luck. "But if the guy drowned somehow, his body won't show up here. The current will carry him over your way, towards Middle Island."

The search and rescue trainees had their swim, shouting and splashing with the cheerful oblivion of youth. Halstead was doubly glad they hadn't found an actual casualty this time. After everyone had cooled off, he thanked the searchers for their diligence and waved them on their way.

"What exactly are you expecting?" Pete asked, watching the old tub used for training the kids, move off in ungainly fashion from the dock. "That Sedore will just calmly arrive, step out of some friend's boat, say he's been fishing and what's the fuss?"

Halstead shrugged. "At least we'd have fresh perch for supper." He moved towards the fire pit. "So let's see what he's got here for us to eat."

After making cell phone calls to their wives and Jane at the station, they found some cans of chili in Sedore's food case. There was also a powerful battery-operated lantern to bring out once it got dark. Pete heated the chili on Sedore's little gas stove, then made coffee and stirred in the powdered cream substitute.

"Sedore is an organized camper," he approved. "Everything neat and handy."

Halstead nodded, taking a sip of the coffee. "Let's hope the guy is alright."

They sat companionably in the dusk, thinking of the cheerful, innocuous man they'd visited only a few days earlier. As the sky darkened, a faint glow appeared from the city on the American side of the lake. Nearer by, there were the pinpoint lights of some farmhouses on Middle Island.

Ali and Nevra are there, Pete thought. I'm not looking at the stars from some desert plain in Afghanistan. I'm looking at the lights of home.

"So, what do we know about Sedore?" Halstead asked. While they'd been searching the island, Jane had been busy gathering and forwarding information from the man's employers to Pete's laptop.

"Wesley Sedore is forty-three," Pete said. "He's been at his job with the Ministry for fifteen years. Divorced, two kids, a fourteen-year old daughter and a twelve year old son."

Young teenagers who needed food, clothes and college for another five years at least, Halstead noted. Seemingly never-ending responsibilities. Some men were overwhelmed at the task.

"The dangerous age," he said. "The time when men buy red sports cars and take off."

"Only what this guy needed was a boat," Pete pointed out.

Halstead tipped out the dregs of his cup. "He could have arranged something, could have been organizing his escape for some time."

"I saw a movie once about a guy who did that," Pete said. "He just disappeared one day, never even said good-bye to his family." He stirred the fire embers. "You've been forty-three, chief. I can't see you doing something like that."

"You know what they say, son, about walking in another man's shoes. We don't know yet what troubles Sedore might have had. Or maybe he was just bored."

Pete grinned. "I can't ever imagine being bored with Ali. Not if I live to be a hundred and three!"

Halstead patted his shoulder. "Nor can I Jakes"

He got up gingerly, stretching his back. He'd probably feel a whole lot worse in the morning – it had been awhile since he'd camped out.

"By the way," he asked, "how did that movie turn out?"

"The guy had a heart attack. He'd fallen into a ditch behind his own house and the town tractors covered him up. No one found him for ten years."

"That's a cheery bed-time story."

Halstead yawned and looked askance at his blow-up mattress. He could feel his back rebelling already. Bats gathering insects, swooped outside their lantern's small circle of light

"Guess if Sedore hasn't turned up by morning, we'd better go talk to some of the people in the man's life. See if we can find what he might have been intending to escape."

9

"Yes?" said the slight blond woman who opened the door of the tidy-looking bungalow in a Bonville suburb. She wore the uniform of a popular donut chain and a name tag that said *Assistant Manager*. She looked tired. And apprehensive. It was a common reaction, Pete knew, to the sight of a uniformed policeman.

"Cathy Sedore?" he asked.

"Yes?" she said, panic beginning. "Oh my god, my kids. Are my kids O.K!"

"I'm sure they're fine," he said reassuringly. "I'm here about your husband, actually your ex-husband, Wesley. Can I come in for a moment?"

"Wes?" she drew back, opening the door and ushering him in. "We just saw him last weekend, he took the kids to the movies. Is Wes alright?"

She hovered in the small hallway, then flustered, led him to the living room.

"Is Wes alright?," she repeated. "What's happened?"

"Hopefully nothing," he said. "But he hasn't reported in to the office for a couple of days. We thought maybe you could help us, tell us something about him."

She sat finally, on the sofa, looking at a loss for words. "Wes is pretty ordinary I guess," she said. "He's a good father, he takes the kids camping and swimming. Is that the sort of thing you want to know? He's certainly never done anything even near criminal, I can tell you that."

"You're divorced," Pete said.

She shrugged and actually managed a smile. For a moment, he could see the pretty young woman she had been before she got so tired.

"I didn't say Wes is a saint. But then neither am I. We gave it our best and it wasn't good enough."

"What are his interests? What does he like to do?"

"He plays in a jazz band on the weekends. The Barista, a little place downtown."

"Do you know if he's seeing anyone currently. Is he dating?" Nearly three years on this job and he still squirmed inwardly when prying into people's personal lives. But it had to be done.

Cathy Sedore nodded. "He has a girlfriend, Fran Reilly. She runs the Barista. That's where they met last year. You can find her there, or maybe she's gone away too." She looked worried again. "Though I can't imagine Wes doing that without saying anything to me or the kids. It doesn't sound like him at all."

She chewed at an already bitten nail.

Pete stood. "Thank you for your help, Mrs. Sedore. I'll check out that club."

She looked as if she was about to catch at his arm. "I hope he's O.K.," she said. "I'm going to leave him a message right now on his cellphone."

She was entering the number as he left. Obviously not a vindictive ex-spouse.

* * *

The Barista occupied a narrow slot between a dry cleaners and a sporting goods shop. A few lunch-time patrons were scattered around the wooden tables but most of the Bonville lunchtime trade would be filling the parking lots of the fast food strip up by the mall. The place was self-consciously retro, with a chalkboard menu over the counter that advertised grilled cheese sandwiches and sodas.

The woman at the counter was younger than Cathy Sedore but not by much. She was taller too, red hair caught back loosely in a clip. Had Sedore met both his women in restaurants? He'd heard that waitresses did well in the romance department, also stewardesses. That combination of warmth, friendliness and of course food. He could certainly feel this lady's charm, as she turned to smile at him. Was this woman the mermaid who had possibly enticed Wes Sedore away?

But then where did she take him, and why was she still here, pouring coffee in this little hole in the wall club.

"What can I get you officer?" she asked. "I make a mean bowl of chili."

"Thanks, I might take a raincheck. I believe you're Fran Reilly?"

"That's me," she said brightly.

"I'd like to ask you a few questions about Wes Sedore." He looked around the cafe. "Is there somewhere more private?"

Her smile lost a bit of its lustre. "Sure, I guess we can go in back to the storeroom. I better warn you though, it doesn't have the elegance of the rest of the place."

When she got there, she turned around, arms crossed hostilely across her chest, all bright chatter gone.

"So, officer, just what have you got to tell me about Wes?"

"When did you last hear from him?"

"I saw him on Canada Day, last Friday. The band he plays with had a gig in the park in the afternoon."

"That's five days ago – is that usual?"

She shrugged, "Wes and I don't live together, though we're thinking of it. And he wanted to get back to the island where he's working for the summer."

Her expression changed and she asked warily, "Why the questions, officer. What's all this about?"

"He s supposed to report into the office daily but they haven't heard from him for a couple of days. And he seems to have disappeared from the island."

"He's gone off somewhere on the boat, you mean?"

"His boat is still there."

Before she could fully take this in, he asked about the jazz band.

She laughed warmly, "The Loco Locals, they call themselves. They're just a bunch of guys who get together and play for beer. A couple of times a year they maybe get a charity gig, stuff like that."

Her expression sobered. She seemed utterly bewildered at the news, at the mystery of what had happened to Wes Sedore.

"Wes wouldn't go anywhere without telling me," she insisted "He wouldn't just *leave*. We were planning a trip to Spain in the fall."

"Can you give me the names of the band members," Pete asked. "A way to get in touch with them?"

She looked confused. "You could try Harry Silso, the sax player. He teaches at the high school and he would know how to get in touch with the others." She tore a sheet off her menu pad to write down a telephone number.

"What does Wes play?" Pete asked.

"The trumpet, " she said flatly. And watched unsmilingly as he went out the door.

* * *

"So, what do you think?" Halstead asked Jakes. "Is one of those women hiding something?"

Pete shook his head. "As far as I could tell, both of them seemed genuinely shocked at his disappearance."

Halstead rocked thoughtfully in his chair. "The wife isn't acting like a woman scorned? The girlfriend doesn't begrudge the child support Sedore has to pay?"

"Nothing like that. Cathy Sedore says he's a responsible ex, the lady friend likes the kids."

"His workmates at the Ministry?"

"They've known him for years."

"The band members – the Locos or whatever they call themselves – I don't suppose they're all coke addicts?"

"I checked. The saxaphonist guy has taught music at the high school for forty years, is about to retire. Clarinet guy is on the board of the Children's Aid Society. Another is a local lawyer. All husbands, one of them is a grandfather. Wes is the kid in the group, they all like him."

"There must be *something*."

"Not a bad word from anywhere." Pete shrugged. "By all accounts, Sedore is about as ordinary a guy as you could expect to find."

Halstead gave the chair a final tight spin. "Yeah well his life isn't ordinary any more. Now it's different and once it comes to our attention, that's rarely good news."

He tossed the file on his desk. "Keep working on the usual routines, checking whether he's using his credit cards for accommodation, gas, meals, whatever. Or whether anybody else is."

10

MYSTERY ISLAND -- GOVERNMENT BOMB EXPERT
DISAPPEARS
Local Residents talk of 'strange doings' over there.
'Like that X-files TV program.'

The Bonville Record was having a field day with the story.
With an angry grunt, Halstead tossed the newspaper into his
wastebasket and dialled the editor's number.

Bob Denys, also the captain of the local old-timers' curling
club to which Halstead belonged, answered cheerfully.

"Hi Bud, fine fishing weather we're having. The walleye
running out your way?"

"Fishing, smishing," Halstead growled, "I've just been reading
that trashy rag you call a newspaper. What's with this *Mystery
Island,* crap? Is that really worthy of you Bob?"

"I thought you'd be pleased," Denys said innocently. "You
folks are always complaining that we don't give the Island enough
coverage." He lowered his voice, speaking in mock conspiratorial
tones,

"So what is really going on over there chief? A UFO sighting,
or has a flying saucer landed? You can tell me."

"Why – so you can start some kind of aliens invasion panic? There's nothing going on over there – a guy went fishing and hasn't reported home for a couple days. But I guess there's no headline for you vultures in that."

"Who are you kidding, Bud? That was a serious, all-out search that you guys carried out over there. Do you suspect foul play? Can I quote you on that?"

"Quote this." And Halstead slammed down the receiver.

Bob would make something up anyway. He was good at that. Though he'd been born and raised on Middle Island himself, and his sister and her husband still lived there, he delighted in writing about the place as if it was some kind of rural dogpatch, populated by benighted rustics.

"I'm a businessman – it sells papers," he insisted and was unrepentant.

The next caller was even less welcome. And worse, he came in person. Vern Byers, County Clerk, whose office was a stone's throw up the block in the Middle Island Municipal Office. At times, Halstead had seriously considered testing the hypothesis.

Vern gave a great Eeyore sigh that seemed to come from the depths of his skinny frame and not waiting for an invitation, sank into the chair across the desk from Halstead.

"Mornin' Vern," Halstead said, feigning cheerfulness, "how's it going?" With Vern you had to be over-hearty, just to achieve a balance. In concession to the hot summer day, Vern was wearing a yellow striped short-sleeved shirt above his customary baggy grey trousers. He looked almost festive but Halstead knew better.

The clerk looked as if he was sorting through grievances, loath to concentrate on merely one. Finally, he chose.

"Had quite the session over to Bonville yesterday afternoon. They're a bossy bunch. 'Specially that jumped-up, full of himself Stuckey."

This was familiar territory, the clerk harboured a long-standing resentment of the city across the causeway, particularly of Mayor Stuckey. The rant was predictable and Halstead could produce a grunt at appropriate intervals. He spun his chair a half turn and set himself to contemplation of the photo of his boat, the *Lazy Loon*.

"It's bad enough they take over the whole darn Bay every August first," Vern began, "Now they want our police force too."

The issue of the moment was the August holiday celebrations, still nearly a month away or in Vern's anxious view *only* a month away. The event involved entertainment from local bands, dragonboat races, a food court and in the evening a fireworks display. Fun for all, or for most anyway.

Vern rolled on scathingly, his long horsey face animated for once.

"*His Worship* doesn't seem to realize or care that I am not about to leave the Island open to god knows what criminals for an entire day and evening just to help him supervise his darned firecracker show."

Now it was Halstead's turn to sigh. Reluctantly he swivelled away from his view.

"Now Vern, calm down. You know we go through this every year and things generally work out just fine. We just send over a couple of officers, like good neighbours. Our Island folks enjoy the show too, you know."

"Yes but this year, you're short a man again, " Vern said in grim triumph. "Have been ever since that last recruit left in February. So, who's going to mind the store?"

Halstead forebore pointing out that the store or Island in this case, didn't need much minding. The main work would be out on the Bay itself, where Art Storms and Pete would be patrolling in the launch to ensure that unruly boaters didn't get to drinking and disrupting the event. However, it was true that he wasn't likely to get a new recruit till at least the end of the summer now. It wasn't easy to attract young ambitious police cadets to the Island.

"I'll be here," he said. "I'm sure I can handle things. I've got one of these neat new gadgets called a cell phone, if I need any help." He held the phone up, to illustrate.

Vern grimaced. "Har de har har." He spotted the *Record* on Halstead's desk.

"And now we've got aliens or martians or whatever running over South Island. The Bonville committee people had a great laugh over that."

"Ah, they're probably just jealous," Halstead said. "What summer attraction have they got to rival martians?"

"It's O.K. for you, Bud," Vern said. "You don't get the hassle that I get. Every time I turn around, somebody else wants to complain."

He sounded genuinely tired, "Want a new job?" he asked.

Halstead looked up in surprise.

Vern nodded. "I mean it. I'm sick of being acting Mayor. I want to go back to accounting – I'd rather work with numbers than people. You've been talking about retirement."

"I was thinking that way a couple of years ago," Halstead protested. "When I was trying to save our Island police department. You and council were about to turn the job over to the provincial police, if you recall."

"Yeah but you saved it," Vern said. "Now you could retire and run for Mayor. You'd likely be acclaimed, and then you could just take it easy, spend the days out on your boat."

Halstead laughed. "You've just spent the last while grouching and telling me how miserable the job is."

Vern leaned across the desk. "Miserable for me, maybe. But you've got more of a way with people. You could stick up for yourself and the Island. Come on, won't you think about it?" He straightened up, said gloomily. "Or else I'm stuck to finish out the term."

"You'd make a terrible salesman, Vern."

* * *

"So, no sign of Mr. Sedore yet?" Steph asked, holding out a spoonful of sauce for Halstead to taste. Always a hearty eater, he never seemed to add an ounce to his lanky frame, much to the envy of some of Steph's clients.

"No sign, " he said now said through a mouthful of sauce. "Wes Sedore has to all intents and purposes, simply disappeared."

He smacked his lips and made the thumbs up sign for the sauce. "Those folks who think Sedore ran into some aliens over there on South Island, might just be right. Gus says they're laying bets at the Grill."

He sighed and reached for his beer. "And who am I to judge? The way this investigation is going, that's as good an answer as any."

"Maybe he bumped his head and has amnesia," Steph said. "And he'll wake up soon."

"It's still a long swim from South Island," Halstead said drily. Still, the possibility of amnesia wasn't just a far-fetched movie plot. Police investigations always covered hospital emergency department records and homeless shelters where a bewildered amnesiac might turn up.

He told Steph about Vern's suggestion.

"Oooh," she said. "How exciting, will you get to wear a gold chain?"

He grimaced. "Gold coloured, maybe."

"So, what did you tell him?" she asked. "Could be fun. I could get a big-brimmed picture hat, we could give teas." She crooked her little finger in mock elegance.

"Whoa," he said. "We're still on Middle Island, not Buckingham Palace. And I'm afraid you're going to be a policeman's wife for awhile yet."

11

The sun was sinking like a great blood orange into the horizon, leaking a red stain across the water. The line of cormorants were now just silhouettes, a row of exquisite black paper cut-outs, the work of some cosmic origami artist.

Ignorant of the beauty they were part of, exhausted from a day's fishing, the birds flew wearily over the rocky hump of South Island, headed for their own guano-smeared rock and the roost of home.

A little later, a light moved on South Island but there was no one to see it at this hour. Nobody to hear the trespasser but the small creatures who rustled and hid in the inhospitable clumps of juniper.

What could the trespasser be searching for in such a careless, loud, stomping manner? And with such angry, muttering.

All arrogance and no caution.

No wonder he'd tripped and fallen.

Such an inefficient way to hunt.

The creatures crouched and waited for the alien human to go away.

12

Ali opened the book *Treasure Island* and read aloud with zesty emphasis, Robert Louis Stevenson's description of a pirate.

"I remember him as if it were yesterday – a tall, strong, heavy nut-brown man, his tarry pigtail falling over the shoulder of his soiled blue coat, his hands ragged and scarred, with black, broken nails, and the sabre cut across one cheek, a dirty, livid white."

"Tarry?" Pete asked.

"I think it's pronounced like in tar," she said. "Apparently pirates dipped their pigtails in the stuff. No elastic bands in those days."

She made a face, "A handsome fellow. And then there's this part, we used to sing it as kids. Even though we never knew what it meant."

"Fifteen men on the dead man's chest –
Yo-ho-ho, and a bottle of rum!"

Pete chimed in on the rhyme, hoisting a laughing Nevra into the air, then dropping her into his arms.   "Yo-ho-ho, and ….
a ….bottle of rum!"

He threw the little girl up one more time, then tossed her, shrieking happily, into her crib.

Pete thought it was a great idea to include a pirate element in the lighthouse event. "The kids will love it."

"Actually it was Tyler's idea," Ali acknowledged. But she was adding all the details, starting by re-reading Stevenson's iconic book.

"This is *the* pirate book of all time," she said happily. "Long John Silver lives."

"I guess there were never any real pirates on Lake Ontario," Pete said. "Not the eyepatch and cutlass carrying type anyway."

Triumphantly, she pulled a photocopy from her Lighthouse Day work binder. "No but this fellow actually did burn a few ships. His name was Bill Johnson. He made a fortune smuggling tea and rum across the lake."

"He was Canadian?"

"There was no Canadian citizenship at the time. But Johnson was loyal to the British, at least until they called him a spy and confiscated his property."

"That would tick you off."

"Yes, well the British paid for it. He became an American privateer in the war of 1812 and set about attacking their supply boats. When they did catch him, juries refused to convict him. After the war he went back to his regular smuggling."

"Adding to the popular legend of the smuggler as hero."

"Yes," she said, "People do like to get around authority. Or at least to read about people who do."

She put the photocopy away in the binder. "I've found lots of interesting history about the lake. For instance, the route from the United States over Lake Ontario was part of the Underground Railway for runaway slaves. I'd like to do an exhibit on that, too. But it will have to wait till we can get the money to fix up the shed."

She sighed. "For now, I guess I'll have to go with old Bill's adventures but I'm not sure he'll fire the imagination of kids' expectations of pirates."

"Then just dress up in a pirate's costume yourself," he said. "A saucy red bandana, those pirate pants, you'd look great. *Avast me hearties.* and all that."

She grinned. "That would certainly be more fun than dressing up like a modern day smuggler - a middle-aged woman with an extra couple of dresses stuffed under her coat. Where's the excitement in that?"

"Agreed. So the pirate costume it is. You'll be a big hit."

"And I thought we could make foil paper doubloons to hide around the park. When kids find them, they can redeem them for a free ice cream."

"What's a doubloon worth in twenty-first century terms, anyway?"

She tweaked his nose. "Worth an ice-cream cone anyway, Mr. Smart Alec."

"Seriously though I suppose the storied chest of doubloons would be worth millions on the antiquities market today. No wonder people still keep looking for them."

"In the oceans maybe, but here in Lake Ontario we have Arrowheads looking for discarded government airplane models."

She shrugged. "It's the same impulse I guess. People looking for treasure, some for money, others just for something rare and unique to share in a museum."

Pete shook his head. "I doubt that Tice guy wants to share with the world."

"You said he had an expensive boat, that he was well-off. So it doesn't sound as if he needs the money."

"People with money still want money," Pete said. "But I think in this case, more than anything, Tice just wants to *win*, to be first to find those plane models. That's what drives that guy."

"Fame and glory then. Pretty much the same things that motivated Sir Walter Raleigh and Sir Francis Drake."

"Yeah, right."

She laughed. "Anyway, whether Mr. Tice is a modern day adventurer or merely a ruthless businessman, I can hardly hide miniature planes around the park. I doubt if kids would get the connection."

She pulled back the curtains so they could see the moon, a silver crescent hanging like a necklace charm in the summer sky.

"Beth Harrison says that the young couple who do the diving for Mr. Tice are his daughter and her fiance."

"That's right," Pete said. Though he hadn't know the couple were engaged. "And how did Beth find that out," he laughed. "Let me guess, she overheard it at the post office."

"Better than that," Ali said smugly. "Beth's great niece is working as a housemaid at Gus's motel for the summer. Miss Tice and her fellow are staying there."

"Not on the *Finders Keepers*? I'm not surprised." He whistled. "Wow I don't envy the fiance his new father-in-law."

"Now who's gossiping?" she teased.

"Just making an observation," he said. "It's all in my line of work."

He settled back against the pillows.

She eyed him admiringly. "Your days out in the boat aren't doing you any harm, fella. That tan, your steely, sea-scanning glance. That muscled, rippling back….."

"Read me some more of the book," he asked a while later.

She'd found that he enjoyed the treat. No one had read to him as a child.

But soon the anchor was short up; soon the sails began to draw, and the land and shipping to flit by on either side… The Hispaniola had begun her voyage to the Isle of Treasure….

"Yep, life must have been pretty exciting then," Pete said. "Living on the open seas. What would you think about getting a boat?"

"A boat?" she asked. "Gus said we're welcome to take out the canoe anytime we like."

"I mean a *real* boat," he said. "You know, with a cabin to sleep in and an inboard engine. We could take trips, take Nevra on a trip around the world. I've been looking at boating catalogues."

He reached down beside the bed and pulled up several glossy booklets and tossed them on the bed. "Here, have a look."

She flipped a few pages, while he enthusiastically pointed out a few.

"They're pretty," she said cautiously. "Pretty expensive too."

He grinned. "Something to save for, my pirate princess."

There was that restlessness again, as if Island life was proving too dull for an army man. She snuggled up against him, willing it away with her love.

13

Halstead sighed and tossed the weekend report sheet onto his desk. Storms and Jakes had laid twenty boating infraction charges. Ten for speeding, five for improper identification and five for drinking. Crime on the water wasn't much different or any more imaginative than crime on land.

There was no good news regarding Wes Sedore either. The search was getting downright frustrating. No one had heard from the man for a week now, not his government employer, nor either of the women in his life, nor any of his fellow band members. Computer searches had turned up no record of his credit cards or other I.D. being used.

No amnesiacs had turned up at provincial hospitals. If there had been any foul play, so far there was no evidence of that either. People were getting impatient and wanted an answer. As of this morning, Halstead had already fielded calls from the Ministry, from Bob Denyes and Vern Byers.

He looked wistfully out his office window. In a temperate growing zone such as Middle Island, close to the southernmost point of the country, a farmer was lucky to get his corn into the ground by the first of May. In a wet spring, the planting date could be even later.

This spring though, had been a favourable season and the view from the window now presented a scene of graceful green corn stalks, rustling softly in the gentle morning breeze. If the view had been a painting, and it would make a dandy, he would call it *Peace*. Let Steph and her clients meditate away to their hearts' content, for him it was a corn field on a summer day.

Usually, anyway. But not today. He had calls to answer. First though, he would have to sneak into the lunchroom and turn up the air-conditioning. It was a continuing battle in the station -- Jane didn't like it as cool as the men did and objected to wearing a sweater all afternoon. A trim grandmother, she spent money on attractive summer clothes and as she put it, didn't feel 'like dressing like a polar bear in the office.' She caught Halstead as he was reaching for the control switch and waved a small sheaf of paperwork at him.

"Some wrist exercise for you," she said. "Start signing."

"I thought you usually signed everything for me." he complained.

She smiled sweetly. "Only my own pay cheque." She looked up as Jakes appeared at the cubicle door. He'd been carrying out his morning review with Wes Sedore's credit card company, checking for recent transactions on the missing man's card.

"Did I hear something about pay cheques?" he asked.

"There's a line-up," Jane said. "Wait your turn." Actually the pay cheques came from Vern at the municipal office. She rifled through her papers, asking

"You fellows hear about the big smuggling bust up Cornwall way last night?"

Halstead snorted, "I was waiting for you to come in. We get all our news from you and your network of relatives." He knew that between them, Jane's many and various family members had the Island police station, Bonville hospital, the flower shop and two funeral parlours covered.

Jane sniffed and answered huffily. "Actually I just heard about it from Greg Jackman. I met him at the post office. He heard it on his boat radio."

But yes, of course Halstead had heard, he and Pete had already been discussing the report. The sting had involved a dozen arrests, and several million dollars worth of drugs seized. Apparently large amounts of marijuana, and ecstasy were now being produced in Canada and carried over the lake to the States.

"Interesting switch, I guess," he commented now. "Usually we like to think that all the bad influences come from the other guys. And the public attitude doesn't help the police any either. Your average citizen doesn't think there's anything wrong with beating the government out of a bit of tax on cigarettes or booze. They figure they pay enough as it is."

"But it gets a lot worse than that," Pete said. "Drugs, guns, human trafficking."

"True, " Halstead agreed, "And the coast guard probably catches only about twenty per cent of the action."

"Remember that case a few years ago?" Jane said, "When Canadian and U.S. border officers broke up a ring that was smuggling baby hawks and eggs. That's sick," she said disgustedly. "They said that most of the poor creatures died before they arrive."

"Makes drug smuggling look downright wholesome," Pete said. Then raised his hands defensively. "Joke. Just a joke."

Jane gathered up her papers. "In the old days it was rum, now it's drugs," she said when leaving. "All those miles of empty, unguarded lake. I guess it's always been a big temptation."

Her words lingered in the room, like some kind of dire pronouncement. The two men looked at each other.

"Could Wes Sedore be involved with smuggling?" Pete asked. "Is that possible?"

"Doubtful," Halstead said reluctantly. "The American border is a lot closer at the end of the lake where it joins up with the river. We're kind of away from the action down here. Too bad though, it would make a good story and Sedore's government job did give him the perfect cover for being out there on the lake."

Pete nodded. "And even if Wes Sedore *was* smuggling, he doesn't seem to have been getting rich on it. His bank account just shows the usual activity — rent, some bills, regular child support payments. Unless he's been stashing the money away somewhere to finance his breakaway."

Halstead looked incredulous. "Breakaway with who? You mean he might have had another woman stashed away – a third one? That doesn't sound like the guy you've described."

He considered, "Though such cases do turn up every few years, a man who has a secret life with another whole family. One case in England, the guy's two families lived only twenty miles apart. The wives looked similar, each household had four kids. It was only a matter of time till they ran into each other."

"But in this case," Pete objected, "Sedore would have had three women, and three separate households. We'd be talking polygamy."

"Bigamy, polygamy," Halstead scoffed. "You'd think all that would be pretty much in the past now that people can just live openly together. The tax department is the only place that cares nowadays. They don't give a hoot about your morality, they just want any money owing."

"So, no smuggling?" Pete asked.

Halstead scowled. "Not unless Sedore's got something the martians can't get at home."

Jakes was looking at him expectantly. "Ah go off to your boat patrol with Storms," Halstead said. "There's not much more we can do about Sedore except wait."

No contemplating the corn field for the chief though. He turned reluctantly to his computer screen. Jane had been badgering him all week to get to work on the ad for another constable recruit.

Wanted: Full-time police constable
Graduate of Ontario Basic Constable Training
Experience preferred

Halstead's ad was just one of several in the Ontario Police Directory. It wasn't an easy task to recruit constables. He'd got lucky with Jakes and his lovely wife, who had decided to make the Island their home. But most young people were looking for a lot more action than the tiny Island force could provide. His last recruit's posting had ended before Christmas, over six months ago.

"Having fun?" Jane asked over his shoulder.

"No," he said grumpily. "Listen to some of the other job postings on this website. *We are a modern, progressive and dynamic organization looking for people who are energetic, empathetic and committed to making a difference.*"

"Gee," Jane grinned. "Makes you wonder how you ever got your job, chief – this description doesn't exactly fit you to a T."

He ignored this and continued reading. "*We provide our employees the opportunity to grow and develop in a diverse community.*"

"We've got a diverse community," Jane laughed. "All kinds of crazy folk."

"What about this one?" *We are noted for our small town charm with a historic and vibrant downtown.*" I'd hardly call the Island Grill either vibrant or historic."

He groaned. "Of course the nitty gritty is the salary and pension package that a big city can shell out. I've done enough grovelling before Vern and council this year. I won't be squeezing out any more dough for awhile now."

She patted his shoulder. "We know you go to bat for us chief and we appreciate it."

He twisted frustratedly in his chair. "The whole thing is ridiculous, hiring someone through a Web site."

"You're just weeding out the chaff, chief" Jane consoled and left him to it.

Diligently, he filled in the blanks.

Please describe your station operations under the following headings.

Traffic Volume – as many as five pick-up trucks at a time on Main St.

Traffic Safety – watch out for deer crossings particularly in November.

Intelligence – good as most

Staff Morale – happy as a bunch of clams

Field Operations – mostly corn and tomatoes.

Crime Stoppers – lots of nosy neighbours

He scowled. Not nosy enough apparently. Other than the martian and flying saucer sightings, no one seemed to have been spying on South Island on the night of July second. Or at least no one was saying anything. He could only hope that something would break soon.

14

Keri Tice stood up in the canoe, threw her arms in the air and shouted out for the sheer joy of it.

"What a wonderful gorgeous day! Sunshine, water, picnic – and a whole day free of Grouchy Dad! Could it get any better?"

"Careful" warned Josh, as he grabbed at the gunwales and moved to accommodate the canoe s fragile balance.

"Oh I don t care if we do fall in," Keri laughed. "I don t care about anything today – we're free. A whole day to ourselves."

"O.K. But please sit back down."

She settled onto the seat, determined to let nothing spoil her mood. All week she had to listen to Josh's complaining about her dad, then her dad complaining to her about Josh. And the ridiculous thing was that they were in some ways quite alike. For instance when either man wanted something, he went right after it, single-mindedly and taking no detours.

In Josh's case, it was Keri he wanted. And he won her, but male-like didn't realize that was what she had wanted all along, as well. He didn't know that she had taken his diving class two winters ago, with a dual purpose in mind. One, to get instruction from a highly-recommended instructor and two, to get to meet said handsome highly-recommended instructor. Catching two fish with one net, so to say.

Now he wanted to marry her, which would made him even less popular with Dad. When she told Dad, which she hadn't as yet. Things were tough enough this summer with all three of them spending long days out on the boat. Dad fully expected her to carry on with her degree studies in lake currents and she fully expected to do so, but it didn't mean that she couldn't be married at the same time.

Josh certainly had no problem with her academic plans, or anything to do with water. That was his element and now hers too. They shared a love of exploring the magaical world below surface. This winter they were going to take a trip to Australia to dive at the world-famous coral reefs. Maybe it would be their honeymoon.

She mentally crossed her fingers that her gamble of joining Dad on the *Finders Keepers* for the summer, would work for the best.

"Dad needs experienced divers for the project," she'd told Josh. "Besides," she teased, "it's good money and there's the fringe benefit that we'll be together."

In the end, he'd also been swayed at the opportunity to dive in the clear cool waters of an inland lake, rather than the murkier Bahamian waters where he taught in the winter. Now though, he seemed to regret the decision. He paddled a few savage strokes, complaining as he pushed the canoe swiftly along the shore.

"A couple of months on the *Finders* Keepers you said. It will be a holiday" He spat into the water. "Not with your old man as the captain, Keri – it's like taking a holiday with a moray eel."

"I'm *sorry*," Keri said, turning to look at him. "How many times can I say it?

But why ruin today? It's a beautiful day, we're together. And my father is nowhere in sight. Can't you please just enjoy it?"

Earlier in the week, while returning from another unproductive diving day (by her dad's reckoning at least) she had spotted the perfect place for a picnic. A little cove tucked away on the rocky eastern shore of Middle Island. The *Finders Keepers* could never get safely into shore but the canoe they'd rented from the nearby Marina would get them in close enough to wade the rest of the way with the picnic cooler.

Keri smiled. thinking how Josh would be pleased with the contents. A whole cooked chicken, a bag of barbeque potato chips and a sixpack of his favorite brew. Plus herself of course in a new electric blue swimsuit.

He grinned too, "O.K. For a change though, let's stay on top of the water today. No diving."

The sneaker should have been the first unpleasant clue. Keri spotted the shoe as they were towing the canoe up onto the pebbled shore. She looked hastily around, thinking oh phooey we're not alone. But she saw no sign or trace of another boat. The sneaker was probably just a piece of beach debris washed up by the lake water.

There was actually quite a lot of driftwood here too, and some kind of icky seaweed. The cove must be one of those spots where the lake current swirled in to regularly dump debris. A few feet up from shore though, the round white stones glittered cleanly in the sun. Not as comfortable as a sand beach perhaps but that was the price of privacy and they'd be fine with the canoe cushions and a blanket.

She dropped her knapsack and took off her sunglasses. "Paradise," she enthused. "I'm going to explore."

"Be my guest," Josh said beneficently. He had already heard the cool clank of the sixpack. He cracked one open and lay back on a cushion, lazily watching Kerr's slim figure as she mooched along the shore, bending here and there to pick up a shell or a stone to examine. She wouldn't be going far, the shore got narrower that way, eventually being swallowed up in a big clump of spiky bushes that grew right down into the water.

He was just indulging in a pleasant fantasy of watching Old Man Tice sinking in his scuttled, leaking boat, when Keri screamed.

He ran up the beach towards her, his pounding feet scrabbling in the stones.

She was standing by one of the spiky bushes, looking up a little inlet that ran up from the shore. White-faced, she pointed to some largish crumpled thing, like a sodden canvas rucksack that lay in the shallow water. It seemed to have caught on a snag of a partly submerged tree trunk.

"I think it's a person, Josh," she whispered shakily. "Oh my god is it a dead person?"

He moved cautiously past her, intensely aware of the sound of the gently gurgling water. The rucksack thing was a couple of feet out into the muddy water, bobbing against the tree snag. There was an awful smell too, hovering over the scene.

He started into the water, hearing Keri gasp behind him.

"Josh, you're not going to touch it!"

He shivered and looked around for a stick. Not finding anything appropriate, he moved closer. Then felt sick.

"It's a man," he called over his shoulder. "He's dead, in bad shape."

"What can we do?" she asked desperately. "What can we *do*?"

"Nothing for that guy," he said, hastily splashing back out to her. "Have you got your cell phone?"

* * *

The scene had a déjà vu quality, Halstead thought, echoing the discovery of Mel Todd, two weeks ago. The blue and gold police launch was back, the bright yellow water ambulance with its red flag and the coroner's speedy sleek boat from Bonville.

All bobbing gaily from their anchors out on the water, as if attendant at some weekend regatta. Boats just looked cheerful, he thought, despite the circumstances. Maybe it was because they'd been featured in so many famous paintings through the ages with their bright colours and sails and the promise of escape from the everyday cares of life on land. It seemed downright incongruous to associate boats with murder.

But murder this was and a sad, definitely uncheerful business.

He looked assessingly at the two young people who stood before him. A good-looking pair in their twenties, both in great shape from their diving work. The boy was dark-haired with an open frank face, the girl a tall, fine-featured blonde. She'd got her looks from her mother Halstead supposed, rather than Tice's pugilistic build.

The boy had made the 911 call on their cell phone. They were a bit pale under their tans but otherwise looked O.K. and up to answering questions calmly and intelligently.

Officialdom hadn't arrived until an hour after their call but they had waited as told to, on the stony beach. Halstead noted a couple of empty beer bottles but said nothing, they obviously weren't anywhere near intoxicated. The booze could even have proved medicinal. Unlike police personnel, few people had much exposure to dead bodies and probably never to the sight of a man who had been in the water for a week.

So the kids were alright, and much better behaved than that sensation-seeking fool of a woman who had discovered poor old Mel Todd. He'd already got a preliminary account from them on arrival. Just the bare details and directions up the beach to the inlet where the girl had discovered the body.

They hadn't much more to tell. He sent them to wait with the ambulance crew.

"Ask them to give her some tea," he advised Josh. "She's had a bad shock."

The young man seemed to want to stay and watch the police but Halstead sent him off too.

He turned to rejoin the little crowd of professionals by the body. The inlet ran only about thirty feet up on to the land, a narrow trench dug out by succeeding storms and lake currents. An old cedar tree had teetered into it over time, finally toppling over altogether. In its turn, the tree had trapped some of the incoming water into a stagnant pool behind its waterlogged branches. It had also trapped a body.

The search for the searcher of bombs was over. Unfortunately for Wes Sedore it hadn't ended up with a mermaid in some tropical paradise but here, in a lonely cove on a northern lake.

Jakes looked grim. "Pelly has something to show you."

Pelly had obviously been interrupted on his day off and nodded brusquely at Halstead, from under his baseball cap. He wore shorts and had taken off his sandals to wade into the water.

With the help of the others, the coroner had moved Sedore onto a tarpaulin spread out on the stones. Halstead had looked earlier at the face for a quick identification. It was only barely possible and he had been relieved to look away. Now Pelly thankfully had covered the face with a fold of the tarp. Sedore had been wearing jeans and a t-shirt, with a picture of an owl and the logo of the World Widlife Fund organization. The coroner had tugged the soggy jeans up past one of Sedore's ankles. He didn't have to point, the blue stripes of rope burn marks were obvious.

"Tied up and weighted down," Halstead observed. He felt pretty grim himself.

"He would have already been dead though," the coroner said. "His skull is dented badly at the back."

"There's a mercy," Halstead said. "Hit with what?"

"I'm not sure. Maybe Roger Huma will get a clue back at the lab."

"How did the body come back up?" Halstead asked.

Pelly shrugged. "Must have worked loose somehow from whatever was weighing him down. Might have been tied in haste."

Halstead's mind veered away from the thought. This story wasn't getting any better. He looked the short distance back down to the stony beach. Whatever had been anchoring Sedore down, it had probably been left far out in the water. Somewhere where the water was deep and concealing.

"This is the pits," Jakes said. "He seemed like a nice guy. A good dad too."

Halstead nodded glumly. "We know one thing anyway. Now it's a murder investigation." He looked at the coroner, still bent over the body in his orange baseball cap. "You going to be much longer, Chris?"

Pelly stood up. "No, the rest of the work will be done at the lab. We'll get him on the stretcher and out to the ambulance.."

Halstead stepped out of the way and motioned to Jakes, "And I'm thinking we'll be hunting up the skipper of the *Finders Keepers* to have a little chat."

Pete too, was thinking of the tense argument he'd broken up last week at South Island.

Halstead headed up the beach, "Let's go talk to that pair for a minute."

Keri Tice was sitting in a fold up chair on the beach, both hands wrapped around a cup of tea. She was twenty-two or three Halstead guessed, but looking much younger now with her blonde hair pulled back in a ponytail and her eyes wide with anxiety.

"I have a few questions," he said gently. "If you're up to it."

She nodded and said in a surprisingly strong voice. "I'm O.K. thank you."

He took her again through the circumstances of finding Sedore. He didn't really need to but wanted to lead gradually up to his real question.

"I'd like to talk to your father," he said. "Do you know where I can find him? Is he on the boat?"

"He's gone to Brockville for the day to check out some equipment," the girl said. "But I already phoned and told him what happened."

"Do you know when he'll be back?"

"He anchors the boat at night at Lakeside Marina. He sleeps there," she added and blushed. "Josh and I are staying at the motel in the villlage."

Belatedly, she asked, "Why do you want to talk to Dad?"

"Just routine," Halstead said. "We'll be talking to anyone who has been out on the water the last few days, to see if they've spotted anything unusual."

The girl looked suddenly wobbly and no wonder. She'd certainly spotted something out of the ordinary.

* * *

The young couple left the cove first, pulling away silently and soberly in the canoe. Halstead had advised that they tow the canoe and come back to the village in the police launch but Keri had just wanted to get going. Besides, as she said a bit wanly to Josh, she didn't fancy any of the other choices much.

"There's the police boat, the coroner's, or the ambulance with the body," she shivered. "No thanks!"

Once on the water, she looked back forlornly at the little cove where her plans for a romantic picnic had been altered so drastically. Now the pretty curved shoreline, the sparkling water, the very sunshine, merely looked sinister. She shivered as if she would never feel warm again, then looked suddenly stricken.

"Oh my god, Josh, " she gasped. "Dad had that big argument with Mr. Sedore last week. That's why they want to talk to him. The police think Dad killed the guy!"

"I wouldn't be surprised if he did," Josh said mulishly.

"Josh! How can you say such a thing!"

"It's true Keri, you know as well as I do how he is about finding those damn plane models. It's his effing mission now. He's no fun to be around, he likely couldn't get anybody else to ship with him. Nobody but us, anyway," he added bitterly.

"He's not that bad," she said, but she looked worried.

Josh pushed the canoe savagely ahead. "Yes he is. If he went back to that island and that government guy tried to stop him …. Who knows? He's gone over the edge, Keri. He'd have us out diving at night if he could find enough light. Face it, your old man is crazy enough to do anything."

Peterson's *Lakeside Marina and Bait Shop*, read the lettering on the bleached piece of driftwood. If you squinted up your eyes, the wood was roughly the shape of a fish. The lettering was faint but had never been touched up, at least in Halstead's time. It didn't matter, most folks seemed able to find the place.

The Petersons lived next door in their green frame house but in the summer months spent most of their time at the shop, a rustic structure that housed an always intriguing mix of fishing gear and sundry camping goods. There were sets of fishing rods and fly assortments, rain ponchos, plastic mess kits, candles and boxes of matches, and some basic grocery items such as cans of beans and soup. When Halstead was a kid there'd been soft drinks and a few comics. Now there were tourist brochures and bottled water for cyclists.

A yellowing poster tacked on the wall over the cash register, offered useful advice.

Always wear your lifejacket.

Don't drink and boat.

Be Prepared – check gas – check weather conditions - notify someone that you're going out.

At the docks out back, there were two gas tanks for the boating traffic on the lake and mooring for a half dozen craft.

Halstead always enjoyed stopping in to say hello to Ralph and Edna. Now seventy-plus, Ralph had hired his grandson to work the pumps this summer but he and Edna were generally still to be found behind the store counter, exchanging gossip with their customers. Even today with a grimmer purpose in mind, Halstead took care to observe the Island amenities.

How's it goin Edna, Ralph?
Pretty good – how's that new wife of yours working out?
Pretty good – I'm thinking I might keep her for awhile.
Keeps you busy, does she? You're lookin' fit.

.

Edna opened the cooler and handed the two policemen cans of lemonade, beads of cold gleaming on the shiny aluminum.

"Here, you go boys. Set yourself down for a minute and cool off."

They sat at the picnic table out back. There were sailboats on the lake, shimmering like a fleet of butterfly wings in the heat haze. Halstead noticed there were only a couple of boats currently tied up at the two docks and neither was the *Finders Keepers*.

"Weather's been good," he commented. "Looks like a busy Island summer shaping up."

"Yepper," Ralph said. "We're selling lots of gas, and Edna's been busy at the store." He nodded toward Pete. "Your army pal has been here a couple of times, getting gas for that boat he rented. Says he's looking for treasure."

Edna cackled, "I don't know about any treasure out there. Ralph said maybe I should dump out my change jar by the dock, so the man won't be disappointed."

Pete laughed. "It's just good that Tyler can get out on the water, where he doesn't have to use his foot."

"I heard that Arrowhead guy is mooring here," Halstead said. "Do you see much of him?"

Edna sniffed and pursed her lips.

"Edna doesn't like him," Ralph laughed. "She makes me or Jimmy go and pump his gas."

"You boys practically fall all over yourself to do it," Edna said scornfully. She turned to Halstead to explain. "Ralph is going to have a heart attack one of these days, watching that Arrowhead girl get into her wet suit. Her birthday suit is more like. Look at him blushing like a baby just at the thought."

Ralph did look a bit pink.

"Think they'll ever find any of those airplanes?" Halstead asked.

Ralph chuckled. "No more than they're likely to find a bomb on South Island." He looked out over the water, lying innocently and impenetrable in the sunlight. "I told that Arrowhead feller, nobody's found those darn planes yet, after fifty years of looking. Doesn't look like good odds to me. But he wasn't much interested in listening to an old codger's opinion."

"If the models are there, they might still be intact," Halstead said. "Cold lake water doesn't corrode like salt water. That's the hope anyway, that keeps all the nut bars going."

Edna bristled. "I hope that jerk with his fancy boat finds a whole lot of nothing. He was downright rude to Ralph. Not nice at all."

Ralph shrugged. "If the man wants to dock at the Marina and buy his gas and food here, I'll take his business."

"So are they out there on the water most days?" Halstead asked.

Ralph nodded. "Every day for the past three weeks. They arrived just as soon as it got warm enough to dive."

"They come in at night?"

"He brings the young ones in, I think they're staying in town. But he stays in the boat. I think he's got a pretty nice cabin rigged out for himself below decks. It's a nice boat, altogether," he said admiringly

Edna snorted. "The best you can get for a half-million or so. *That* one doesn't need to find himself any treasure."

Halstead chuckled. "Would you know if he ever stays out later in the boat – or takes it out again at night?""

Ralph frowned. "I suppose so." He turned to look at his wife.

She shrugged. "We go to bed pretty early these days. But why would he go out again in the dark when you can't dive? He was away in Toronto for a couple of nights, " she added helpfully. "I wouldn't know what he'd take it into his mind to do there."

"Do you remember which nights?" Pete asked.

Edna rolled her eyes. "One day is pretty much like another around here. But he pays by the week. I could look it up and at least tell you what week it was."

Ralph looked shrewdly at Halstead. "That's a lot of questions, Bud. What's the guy done?"

"Just curious, Ralph."

"Does this maybe have something to do with the ambulance boat roaring up the bay a little while back?"

"It might."

"And does this maybe have something to do with that government feller that disappeared from over South Island the other day?"

"It might."

Edna crushed her straw. "I heard it was those extra-terryestrial creatures that got that man."

"Well now we've found him with his head bashed in," Halstead said. "And it wasn't any little green men who did it."

* * *

Halstead jawed some more with Ralph while Jakes did a bit of quick research into Tice's background on the cruiser computer. When he returned to the picnic table, he found that the Petersons had gone back to their store counter, while the chief had stretched his long length out on a conveniently-placed lounge chair.

"What have you got?" Halstead asked, opening his eyes from what looked suspiciously like the beginning of a nap.

"He's well-off, like we thought." Jakes said. "Made his money from the salvaging business like he says. The last few years pumping oil from wrecked tankers."

"There's a growing business," Halstead said drily.

Pete nodded. "Tice's company has a couple of rigs working on that. He also buys and sells boats that were wrecked in hurricanes."

"Better and better. It's heart-warming to know that disasters are positively good for some folks."

Pete read on from his notes. "Tice began searching for the Arrow as a hobby I guess, though now it seems more like an obsession. A couple of years ago, he was part of a group that lobbied the federal government for permission to buy salvage rights to wrecks. They didn't win."

"I don't imagine he was too happy about that." Halstead frowned. "So who would own the plane models even if Tice or some other Arrowhead *did* find them?"

"The Canadian government, I guess," Pete said. "Maybe the glory would be enough for Tice, he doesn't need the money."

He continued, "He's a widower as of ten years ago – that was the daughter's mother. And there's a record of a dispute with a patrol man who was giving him a speeding ticket. The patrol man said Tice threatened him. It took two men to get him into the cruiser."

"Was he drunk?"

"No, apparently just really angry about the ticket." Pete checked his notes. "The judge ordered a fine and sentenced him to take an anger management course."

"It didn't take," Halstead said drily.

"Other than that, no police record."

Halstead yawned widely. "So what have we got here? An obssessive, belligerent jerk who threatened the victim."

"In the sight and hearing of two policemen," Pete added.

"Certainly enough for questioning," Halstead agreed. "But realistically what do we think could have happened out there? And exactly when?"

He sat up and replaced his cap. "Sedore never called in to the Ministry on July second, after the Canada Day holiday."

Pete nodded. "He played an outdoor gig with his band on the afternoon of the holiday but Fran Reilly said he was headed back to South Island for the night. He didn't call into work on the second or third of July. And by the morning of the fourth, we were tramping over the Island looking for him."

"So whatever happened, must have taken place sometime on the first or second."

"Only the evenings," Pete said. "I doubt that Tice or anybody else would chance being seen there in the day."

Halstead looked out towards the small hump of South Island. "So, what the hell happened out there?"

"Why don't we ask Tice himself?" Pete suggested. "Looks as if he's coming in now."

16

The *Finders Keepers* slipped smoothly into its berth at the far end of the dock.

"Ahoy there," Halstead called out. "Police. Permission to come aboard."

Tice appeared at the stern, his brow butting out aggressively under a baseball cap. "Don't suppose it would do much good for me to say no. Have you got a warrant?"

"Nope," Halstead said. "But if you'd rather drive into the village we can talk at the station."

Tice grunted and waved them onboard with an unwelcoming hand.

When they reached him, he was ostentatiously lounging in a chair at the stern, open beer to hand, a stack of charts before him. He wore cargo shorts, a yellow t-shirt that clashed with his big sunburned face, and a pair of expensive deck shoes.

He raised the beer in a mocking salute, "It's O.K. officers, I've read the signs. The boat isn't in motion."

Halstead ignored this. "Too bad you were away today. You missed all the excitement."

Tice nodded towards a cell phone on the deck seat and gave an exaggerated yawn. "Oh I heard all about it. My daughter phoned me because she was upset, but it wasn't anything to concern me. It seems some fool got careless and drowned himself -- it happens all the time."

"You seemed mighty concerned about the fellow that day on South Island," Halstead said easily. "When you were arguing with him, that is. You two were going at it hammer and tongs. As I recall, we had a hard time getting you to leave the place."

Tice grimaced. "I disagreed with the man, yes. But I've disagreed with the government before and no doubt will again." He shrugged. "It's frustrating but what can you do?"

"Maybe you thought you *could* do something," Pete said. "Maybe you *did* do something. Your daughter wouldn't have known that there was a big dent in the back of Mr. Sedore's head. Or that there were rope burn marks around his ankles, as if he'd been tied to something heavy, to weight him down. It's pretty difficult for a careless fool to manage a trick like that."

Tice took a swig of beer. "No, she didn't mention any of that. Like I said, she was a little upset, but she'll be O.K. once we get back to work tomorrow."

"And where's that?" Halstead asked, moving over to look at the chart.

Tice hunched his body protectively over the chart, like a hawk protecting a rabbit kill. He was obviously not keen to have Halstead looking over his shoulder.

"Don't worry," Halstead assured him drily. "I'm not going to steal any of your precious underwater secrets. I can confiscate the whole damn file, though if you'd rather. So show me where you're working."

Tice ungraciously moved back and indicated an area on the chart about a kilometre southeast of Lighthouse Point. "We've been diving there about a week now."

Halstead forbore from asking if they'd found anything.

"And mooring here at the Marina at night?" Pete asked.

Tice gave him a 'duh' look. "What else? Can't dive at night."

"Can't dive," Halstead agreed. "But you never know - you might have decided to take a moonlight cruise some night. Or maybe you got a sudden a whim to go to South Island and visit your old brawling pal Wes Sedore. Say on the night of July first or second."

Tice rolled up his precious chart. "Nope, no moonlight cruises for me. Early to bed, early to rise in this work. We have to use all the daylight we can get."

He looked with irritation at the still bright sky. "We would have been out there today, if Keri and Josh hadn't quit on me. My daughter should know better -- there's only so many diving days in the Canadian summer."

Pete was amazed the pair had got the day off at all.

Halstead kept to the point at hand. "You got anybody who can vouch that you didn't take the *Finders Keepers* out on either of those nights.?"

Tice shrugged elaborately. "The kids are staying in the village at the motel. I guess you could ask the old folks who run the marina but they seem to go to bed even earlier than me."

"Actually, the Petersons say you were away for a couple of nights."

"That was in June," Tice said. "When we were getting set up. I had to go to Toronto to pick up new sonar equipment I'd ordered from the States." He grinned smugly while he rummaged in the drawer of the chart table.

"Here's the credit card record for the Sheraton Hotel, for June twenty-fifth and twenty-sixth. A whole week before the time you've been talking about."

"So, otherwise you say you've been moored nights at the Lakeside Marina?"

"In bed by ten and sleeping like a baby," Tice said. He adopted a phony bright look. "Say I guess this means that bomb hunting program will be cancelled and we'll get to dive around South Island sometime soon.."

"This isn't going to get you any closer to South Island, Tice," Halstead warned. "Now the place is doubly off-limits. This is a murder investigation."

Tice picked up a chart and shook it out. "Can't last forever," he said cheerfully. You'll   all leave eventually."

"Oh, we'll still be here," Halstead said. "We're not going anywhere. And neither are you. That's an order."

"Not a likeable guy," Pete stated the obvious, as they walked back up the dock.

"At least he knows we're watching him," Halstead said.

Pete opened the cruiser door. "He didn't look very scared."

"Let's just hope that Roger Huma can narrow down the time frame for us."

"Do you think there would be much difference in water-logging damage whether it was six days or seven days that Wes Sedore had been in the lake?" Pete sounded dubious.

"Probably not," Halstead said sourly. "And Tice hasn't got much of an alibi. Maybe nobody noticed that he was gone, but nobody can vouch that he was there either. It doesn't sound as if Ralph or Edna take much notice of the comings and goings of their customers. They would have in the old days but their memories aren't as sharp any more."

"What about Jimmy, the grandson?"

"Ralph said he only started there this week."

Jakes pulled out of the Marina parking lot and took the road towards town.

Halstead looked musingly out at the water.

"So, say that suppertime on July second, Tice drops the kids off at the Marina and goes back to South Island. He's either planning to sneak around the shore in the dinghy to check out his charts, or he figures what the hell, he'll just park openly at the dock and have another try at bullying Wes Sedore. Whatever, he runs into Sedore, Sedore objects again and this time, they do come to blows. Tice hits Sedore too hard - giving him the benefit of the doubt, which I guess we have to allow the jerk - and Sedore goes down."

Jakes took up the story.

"Tice realizes the guy is dead. He panics, thinking we won't believe him and he's facing manslaughter charges at least. What's he going to do? He couldn't risk dumping the body in the day, and he could hardly have stowed Sedore on the *Finders Keepers*.

There were no hiding places on the boat, Keri or Josh would have found him."

Halstead nodded. "He would have had to act quickly and dump Sedore that night. And come back late into the Marina."

"Now all we have to do is try and prove it," Pete said. "We could start with Keri and Josh again, to see if they confirm Tice's movements."

"The daughter's not likely to say anything against her father."

"Well Josh, then. He hasn't any reason to be protective of his future father-in-law."

"And it looks as if he might be having some change of heart about that plan too," Halstead said drily.

"Wouldn't you?" Pete said. "Imagine that Tice guy as an in-law. Still, we don't know yet that he's a murderer."

Halstead looked with a proprietary air out at the passing scenery. "I know my Island folk, Jakes. They're as nosy a bunch as you can find anywhere. If a boat stopped at the dock on South Island last Wednesday evening, some bored busybody with a telescope saw it. We'll set out up a crime hotline for calls."

He added grimly, "*Somebody* out there saw *something*. And sooner or later they'll tell us all about it."

17

A bit of a pall hung over the Save the Lighthouse group, faced as they were with another local tragedy, even worse a murder. They'd met at Miranda's house where a discussion of the news threatened to dominate the agenda. Beth Harrison and others feared there would be unfavourable publicity that would keep people away from their event.

"Nonsense,' Miranda said. "Murders happen somewhere every day but the lighthouse still needs saving,"

And there was some exciting news to lighten the mood. A historical association hoped to put together a documentary on heritage lighthouses across Canada. The film crew had heard of the Middle Island group and would be adding the Norris site to the project.

Treasurer Joan Stutz reported that the event committee were still in the black, chiefly through community donations. Benny Sorda was lending them his mobile catering truck and cooking equipment, and the local grocery was contributing burgers.

"Now we just have to pray it doesn't rain," she added.

At the mention of the R word, everyone hissed.

"It's supposed to be a dry summer," someone said. "Look at the cedars. They're already browning up."

This was true. Ironically, though Middle Island was surrounded by water, the few inland water courses had almost dried up by June. Normally the committee members would welcome rain – just not on the day of their planned fund-raising picnic.

With this rather dubious comfort and when Beth, in her drill sergeant role, had allotted out the tasks still to do, the ladies headed out into the afternoon.

Ali fetched Nevra who was watching a video in the sunroom, while Miranda dumped out the tea pot in the sink.

"I'm going to have some wine," she announced. "Beth Harrison drives me to drink. Honestly, you'd think the whole project was her idea the way she takes credit for everything. I'm the one who wrote to that historical association for heavens sake. I'm the one working on the grant proposal."

She held up the bottle but Ali waved no thanks. Miranda poured herself a healthy dollop of red and took an appreciative swallow.

"I shouldn't go on about the woman. She's a hard worker and she knows how to badger folks for money! But I've never had much to do with that bunch. I wanted to travel, and teaching allowed me to do that. I guess Beth and the others who spent their lives here, have always thought me a bit of a rogue."

Ali laughed. "You were just ahead of your time, Miranda. Nowadays most young people want to see the world. I wanted to teach too," she added. "But sometimes I think I just wanted to have an audience! I could only rarely attract Nuran's attention so I was constantly trying to get it somewhere else."

As the only child of a brilliant globe-trotting woman sociologist, Ali had spent much of her teenage years in boarding schools. When she added in Pete's estrangement from his father, she sometimes felt that the pair of them were virtually orphans. Hence, she was determined that their daughter would grow up in a home with two loving, involved parents.

Miranda looked affectionately at Nevra. "Times have changed and for the better as far as women are concerned. Maybe she'll be prime minister of the country some day. Or go to Mars."

The little girl smiled and clapped her hands.

"She must like that idea," Miranda said.

"Not to Mars," Ali said. "That's too far away -- I doubt that Skype can reach that far!"

Although she had to admit that the computer video connection was a marvellous device. Even Nuran used it regularly to keep in touch. Since the birth of her granddaughter, Nuran had become much closer to her own daughter and intent on making amends for some of Ali's lonely years at school. She practically demanded daily Facebook pictures of Nevra.

Miranda began to clear the coffee table. "I see that Mr. Cotes didn't come to the meeting."

Ali frowned. "No, he had a doctor's appointment in Bonville. Just as well really, he's so negative about our efforts. I doubt that he'll be very involved in our little event."

Miranda seemed surprised at her tone.

Ali felt she had to explain. "Look at the way he went on at our last meeting when we talked about the estimate to fix the staircase. He pretty well said it was a hopeless case."

Miranda frowned. "He was just pointing out that $10,000 is a lot of money. And that's true enough."

"Sure it is," Ali said, "but that doesn't mean we won't be able to raise it. If we were going to be frightened about money we would never have taken on the lighthouse project in the first place."

She added angrily, "And what about his suggestion that it would be better to knock down the lighthouse, set up a smaller model, and sell ice cream. He doesn't respect at all what we're trying to do!"

Miranda smiled gently. "I'm sure he wasn't serious, my dear. Of course nobody wants to tear down the lighthouse." She chuckled. "Though maybe it's not such a bad idea to sell ice cream. It would give people a reason to stop and look around the place."

Ali looked abashed. "I suppose you're right but tell me, do *you* like Tyler – I get more fed up with him every time I see the man. Sometimes I think he wants to convince Pete to sign up again in the army."

Miranda nodded judiciously. "He seems like a nice enough fellow to me, but I've had that happen with certain people, even people I've just met. I think then we get the same reaction as Emily." She patted the dog's soft ears. "Our hackles go up. Literally. There must be some instinctual alarm."

"And maybe the dogs are right," Ali said soberly.

"Nevertheless," Miranda smiled. "We still can't go around barking and biting at people my dear. That would be most frowned upon in polite circles."

She frowned though, thinking of Beth, "Much as I wouldn't mind doing some biting in that quarter. Did you ever see such a silly old flirt. *She* certainly dotes on Mr. Cotes."

Ali laughed at last. "At least Tyler has *one* fan. Oh, I'm sorry to go on about the man, Miranda, he just gets on my nerves. And of course I don't dare say anything to Pete. I wouldn't hurt him for the world. What would you do?"

Miranda smiled ruefully, "I doubt that a confirmed spinster like myself is the most informed person to give you marital advice my dear."

After Ali left, Miranda poured herself another glass of wine and read aloud her own words.

The earliest attempts to guide sailors were simply bonfires at the ends of points or harbour entrances. These were eventually replaced by towers with fire beacons on top. By the 1800's, keepers were using oil lamps fuelled by vegetable, fish, seal and whale oils according to their location and available supplies.

She paused to look at the dog, who lay with paws crossed prettily on her plaid blanket. "Did you get all that Emily?"

In 1846 a Canadian in Nova Scotia invented kerosene which was used in cheap, reliable lamps. And by the end of the 19th century, electric light began to replace these earlier forms of illumination. However, the lighthouse keeper still had many duties, including keeping the light, providing radio communication and weather information, tending fog alarms and providing rescue services. There were now hundreds of lighthouses that had to identify themselves with a pattern of flashes.

She stopped for a contemplative sip. "O.K. I agree it's not wildly exciting stuff but for commentary accompanying the old photos, it will do nicely."

Emily yawned.

She hoped her human audience would be more appreciative. Elders like herself, the keepers of memory, were needed, to instill some respect for heritage into the budgets of those government bean counters. And the public as well of course. The past mustn't be let slip away like so much water through a sieve.

The lake waters have always been treacherous around these islands.

So many ships had been wrecked in the lakes, so many sailors had perished. The graveyard of the great lakes, they had called these areas once. And it wasn't only in the past, fishermen had perished in her own time. There was poor Mel Todd. True, he had been drinking, but still you couldn't get past the fact. The man had died with lake water in his mouth. It was almost Shakespearean in its aptness.

But ... I would fain die a dry death.

She shivered, despite the heat. "Come Emily, let's feed the chickens."

"Here chick, chicka. Here chicka, chicka."

She kept only a half dozen hens now. They reminded her of her long-gone brother and their farmyard childhood. Merely the conceit of a silly old woman, really, with eggs, milk and everything else readily available at the grocery in the village. Not like the old days, when a farmhouse and barn had to be a self-maintaining unit for several winter months at a time.

The pleasant clucking of hens was part of the background fabric of her childhood and feeding the chickens had been one of her earliest tasks. When she began, she had barely been taller than the bucket of seed she carried. Barely older than the Jakes' little daughter Nevra. Of course her father's chickens had just been plain old chickens, he would have been scornful of this flock. But the birds were pretty and she liked their odd pink and blue coloured eggs. She picked up two now, happily scraping off bits of straw and dirt. She would save the eggs for little Nevra's breakfast tomorrow.

She smiled thinking of how gently the little girl liked to hold the eggs. Then her brow puckered as she looked across the road towards the Jakes' house. She hoped things were going well and that the visit of Pete's friend wasn't going to be a permanent disruption in the usually happy household.

18

Ali drove into the Cedar Grove driveway, looking out warily for the blue rental car before Number Three cottage. It was only quarter to two so she was reasonably sure that Tyler would still be over in Bonville at his appointment. However, reason had little to do with her feelings. And worse, she was finding it more and more difficult to hide her dislike of the man.

The other night while over for dinner, he had gone on about the Island again. Asking the Jakes if they didn't mind having to go to Bonville for many services. Not to mention entertainment. He'd had a great time mocking a poster he'd seen at the Grill, advertising an old-time fiddling concert. He'd thought it hilarious to suggest that Pete consider taking up the accordion.

But Joan had asked her to deliver the minutes of the meeting and the new staircase sketches to Tyler, for his opinon. And because Ali could think of no plausible reason to refuse, here she was. Nevra was asleep in in her car seat and Ali had planned on just leaving the information on the step, but the flimsy screen door swung open at her touch. Tyler obviously appreciated at least one aspect of Island life --trust in one's neighbours.

She stepped in to grab at the door but once inside decided that she was being overly silly, so walked on in. She noted that the compact kitchen area was scrupulously clean and tidy. The half dozen cottages at Cedar Grove were originally fishermen's cabins that had been made more comfortable with indoor plumbing and better bed mattresses but the basic design remained the same. A simple, open concept, with a big picture window facing the water and a small bedroom tucked away at the back. The furniture was a colourful conglomeration of pieces collected over the years and this area too, was as tidy as a military barracks.

She could have left the envelope in the kitchen, but moved on into the living room, drawn towards the framed photo on the coffee table. It was the same photo that sat on the bookcase in the Jakes home. The picture of Pete and Tyler and their four other buddies, all in desert camouflage gear, arms draped across each other's shoulders and smiling into the camera. Six young men, looking as if they were having the time of their lives.

There were no other pictures visible, none of the former wife for instance. She looked for another long moment at the young warriors, then shaking herself, she turned to the pile of books on the table. Some were the books Miranda had lent Tyler, others were from the Bonville library. She picked up one, *Smuggling Stories from the Great Lakes* and leafed idly through it. There were grainy old photos of rum runners with shaggy hair and pirate-style mustaches.

"Darn," she exclaimed, as something slipped out of the book and floated to the floor. Probably a bookmark and now she'd lost his place. But it was a folded sheet of paper, a map of Lake Ontario. There were notations scribbled on the piece of paper – compass or nautical notations regarding a location, as far as she could figure out. Probably best just to leave the map out of the book, as if it had fallen out naturally.

She dropped it to the table, then froze, hearing a boat motor pulling into the cottage dock. It was Tyler, he was already tossing the rope up to moor the boat. She stepped back hastily from the picture window, then scolded herself. How ridiculous! She had a perfectly good reason to be there. She moved to the back screen door, pasted a smile on her face and swung it open.

Tyler obviously hadn't registered yet that he had a visitor. For a moment she stood stock-still and speechless as he stepped in one fluid and nimble movement onto the dock. No walking cast, no cane, no outward help at all. He was wearing a perfectly ordinary pair of sneakers, one on each foot.

Carrying fishing gear, he started up towards the cabin.

"Hello," she finally called out.

He looked up, obviously startled and almost dropped the tackle box.

"Ali," he said awkwardly.

She was still staring at his leg. Immediately he winced and almost lost his balance. She stepped forward and grabbed at the fishing rod.

.   "Thanks," he said. "Sometimes I forget my leg isn't what it used to be."

"Yes," she said, uncertainly.

They carried the equipment in. "I brought you the minutes of the Lighthouse meeting," she said. "Since you were busy."

The statement hung in the air.

He put down the fishing gear and dropped heavily into a chair, stretching out his leg.

"The doctor changed my appointment to next week," he said. "It was such a nice afternoon, I decided to play hookey and go out in the boat. I like being on the water where I don't feel so handicapped. I even take off the foot cast."

That hung in the air too. Ali could see the cast now, abandoned by the screen door. She hadn't noticed it before.

Tyler offered tea, but Ali expained that she couldn't leave Nevra in the car.

She left, thinking she must have imagined what she saw. She didn't like Tyler much but that didn't mean he was a liar.

* * *

Pete cut into the shiny green watermelon, slicing off a big piece for Nevra. It looked like a beautiful pink smile Nevra giggled and soon father and daughter were matching each other bite for juicy bite.

Ali was glad Pete was having some fun. The Sedore murder investigation would be making for tough days at the station. From the little Pete had said on coming home yesterday, she knew it had been a miserable job reporting to Wes Sedore's widow. Ali's whole womanly, protective soul shrank from the thought. And she knew that Pete felt just as badly.

She mentioned her visit to Cedar Grove cabins that afternoon.

"How did Tyler do with the doctor?" Pete asked, spitting out seeds to Nevra's delight.

Ali explained about the time change.

"I'm surprised that Tyler was limping so much the other night when he came for supper. I saw him getting out of the boat today and he seemed to put his whole weight on it, without any trouble at all."

"Well that's great honey," Pete said. "I'm glad to hear it."

"But a minute later, it seemed he could barely get up the hill."

Pete wiped his mouth and hands with a napkin. "I guess he has good days and bad days. Rehabilitation from injuries is like that. I went through the same process."

"This was different, " she said stubbornly. "He moved like a totally fit man."

He shook his head. "You must have got it wrong. He was just having a good day when you saw him honey – and I hope there are lots more for him soon. I'm sure you do too. He's desperate to get back on duty, he can't wait."

"Of course I want that," she said. *Then maybe he'll leave.*

Immediately she was ashamed and grateful that Pete couldn't read her thoughts.

19

South Island baked in the glaring sun, like a flattened cake in a too-hot oven. A snake had been moving along in the water, following Pete as he walked by the shore. Curious he guessed. Pete felt like plunging into the water himself, snake or not.

"So what do you think?" he asked Art. He and Storms had been searching the area again. Wes Sedore's campsite, the shoreline, the dock.

"Find me something," Halstead had demanded when sending them off on the sweltering expedition. "A weapon, a clue, evidence of a scuffle. Anything to nail this case down, No green men, nothing mysterious. Something *real*."

A weapon. The coroner's report hadn't been too specific, merely a confirmation that someone had killed Sedore with a blow to the head before lashing him to a heavy weight and dropping him in the lake. The blow to the head could have been administered by a rock, a hunk of wood, a hammer or myriad other things.

"I know," Halstead agreed when Pete suggested that finding the proverbial needle would be simpler. "But apparently that week in the water would have washed away any traces of metal or dirt in the wound, or any other handy clue."

There wasn't much left to find at the campsite. The police had scoured the place twice already when investigating Sedore's disappearance and had finally allowed a representative from the Ministry to come and fetch the government boat and UXO scanning equipment. There'd been no word yet whether the project would contiinue but the island was still off limits to the public.

Pete grinned, recalling the chief's conversation with the Ministry on the subject.

"*You* keep people away," Halstead had barked into the phone. "I haven't got men or boats to spare to run over to South Island every five minutes. Tell the Department of Defence to get some personnel over there if you're so worried. It's not my liability if anyone gets blown up over there."

Then he'd tossed the phone on his desk, muttering a final 'UXO's my arse. The lunacy!"

Once again, Pete hoped fervently that the chief was right. He and Art had spent the morning covering the area in ever-widening circles around the campsite. Had found no blood-stained two by fours, no wayward hammers. By now they were back at the shore.

Art wiped his brow. "I'm getting too old for this kind of thing. I'd rather be out on the water."

Pete could understand the appeal, especially when contrasted to this sort of hot work. He was enjoying the summer on the lake, and the work was important as well, keeping the waterways safe for both man and critters. Last week there was that daredevil jet-skiier, a real goon who had plowed into a family of swans, terrorizing the birds. It had been at least some satisfaction to slap the guy with a thousand dollar fine, under new wildlife protection laws.

"Can you go back to the coast guard?" he asked.

Art grimaced. "Too late now to build up the pension. I have to stick with this."

Pete knew that Art was long divorced with grown children who lived down east, where he usually spent some time in the winter. This summer he was renting an apartment in Bonville.

Art poured water from the plastic bottle over his neck and popped another piece of nicotine gum into his mouth. He chomped on the gum, then swore and grabbed at his cheek.

"Damn but I don't know if this is worth it. I'm always chewing my mouth up.".

He looked resignedly around. "Ah well, better get back to this wild goose chase. But I don't know what Bud thinks we're going to find. The fight might not even have happened on land. Tice could have beaned the guy on his own boat."

"So you're pretty sure that Tice did it?" Pete asked.

Art nodded. "You bet. From what I've heard around the marinas, that guy is a real nut about finding that airplane. He's one of those super-competitive types. By now, he'd do anything to find it, bulldoze over anybody who got in his way. And I guess when Sedore told him he couldn't search around the island, Tice blew his stack."

Pete looked at the stubborn landscape that so far had yielded no secrets. "Sure, I guess it could have happened that way."

"Who else might have bumped off Sedore, then? You said the guy hadn't any enemies."

"I've been thinking about the smuggling angle," Pete said.

Art looked amused. "Exactly what smuggling angle is that? You think that this Sedore fellow might have been in the smuggling racket?"

Pete shrugged. "It's just an idea. The chief doesn't think there's ever any action in this part of the lake. What do your contacts in the coast guard think?"

"In the old days, sure," Storms said. "During Prohibition, there were booze shipments every night and there was a smuggler's cove marked on every island in the lake. But these days – I doubt it. The big action is farther east, up Cornwall way."

Pete looked out over the calm, unruffled surface of the lake. He pictured a century's worth of activity, and from what Ali had told him, even more before that. Sailing schooners, big and small, involved in all sorts of endeavours and not all of them legitimate by a long shot.

The life must have seemed exciting, probably irresistible to an Island farm boy who faced a summer of nothing but hard work at hoeing corn or breaking sod. Even if the boy hadn't actually read

Treasure Island, he'd be familiar with stories of boys who had run away to sea, seeking adventure or just an escape. It was a similar impulse that had moved a younger Pete Jakes to run away and join the army. He'd been unhappy at home, there was no reason not to go.

He gave himself a shake. But he was all grown-up now and a policeman to boot. And smuggling wasn't much like that anymore, not a kid's fantasy at all — if it ever had been. Today it was run by syndicates and ruthless gangsters. He wondered if even Robert Louis Stevenson could manage to glamorize that world.

It would take a hefty stretch of the imagination to cast a decent, ecology-minded father like Wes Sedore in a plot featuring a gang of modern day pirates. It was much more likely that he had died unnecessarily at the hands of a bullying jerk. Which was tragic indeed.

* * *

"Hot out there was it?" Halstead asked. He was nice and cool himself, had flicked the air-conditioning up a notch while Jane was out at the post office and she hadn't noticed the change when she returned. Sometimes paperwork was quite a bearable pastime. Jakes, grimy and dust covered, didn't bother commenting. He'd already told the chief that the day had been unproductive as well.

Halstead looked resignedly at the cup of stale coffee on his desk. "So, lots of motive but no proof, no evidence of Tice's movements either of those nights."

"Not unless one of your special corp of Islander spies turns up with the news that they spotted Mr. Tice in the vicinity of South Island that night. Preferably with pictures."

"Humph," Halstead said. "What else have we got?"

Pete forced himself to concentrate on the discussion rather than the cold beer waiting for him at home. "We've already decided that it was highly unlikely that either of Sedore's women organized a boat over to the island to carry him off somewhere. It's even more doubtful that they could have murdered him and carried the body off to dump it in the lake."

"Unless they were working together," Halstead suggested facetiously.

Pete looked the question. "So they can split the guy's pension – more likely his debts?"

"Joke." Halstead sighed and kicked his chair back. "Someone wanted his job at the Ministry office? One of the band members thought Sedore was hogging the spotlight at a free charity concert?"

Jakes shook his head. "Nope, and nope, so far Tice is our best bet. How did the interview with Keri Tice and Josh go?" he asked. "Anything helpful there?"

Halstead had gone early that morning to the motel, intending to catch the young couple before they left to go diving for the day. He had no qualms about irritating Gerald Tice but he didn't want to be asking the daughter questions under her father's bullying glare.

"Keri Tice seemed pretty anxious – she's no dummy and must have known why I was asking the questions. But I doubt that she was hiding anything. She said that she and Josh got off the boat those nights like always and drove to the motel. That she assumed her father spent his evenings at the mooring site. She says he's always tired after a day's work and goes to bed early."

"What about Josh?"

"He says that Tice likes his rye at night. But much as he would have liked to say otherwise, he had to admit that he wouldn't know whether Tice went out again that night or not. So, no help there. He did mention how crazy Tice is getting about finding the plane models."

"And did either of them notice if Tice was behaving any differently around that time?"

Halstead grinned sourly. "You mean other than being the huge pain in the butt he always is. But no, it was apparently just an ordinary day of covering a grid on the site, with the sonar. Josh said that Tice was maybe a bit grouchier than usual – he called it a level two grouch, apparently he has his own ranking system."

Pete laughed. "Can't blame the guy."

Halstead agreed. "The issue of the day was that Tice was teed off because they were short a couple of diving tanks. But it didn't matter because they weren't diving that day anyway."

"What happened to the tanks?" Pete asked.

"Josh didn't say, just that they seemed to be missing."

They looked at each other. Pete said it first. "Diving tanks are pretty heavy. Can they sink?"

BONVILLE PRO DIVING SUPPLY AND TOURS
Come with us or plan your own day.
We carry all you need for a perfect diving experience.
Tank Rentals – Air Fill Station – Fill your scuba tanks here.

"Can I help you, officer?"

The girl was young, blonde and buff, reminding Pete of Keri Tice. A closer look showed that she was likely in her thirties. Diving workouts obviously made for good health. He wondered if the exercise gurus were on to this yet.

The Diving Shop was no California beach shack with a selection of day-glo surfboards, but a serious supplier of professional diving equipment. The wall shelves were stacked with displays of wetsuits, breathing apparatus, and an impressive choice of underwater camera equipment.

Pete pointed to a diving tank display. "I have some questions about diving, thanks."

The woman looked at him with frank interest, her smile as healthy looking as the rest of her. "Were you thinking of taking up the sport? You look fit enough to handle the challenge."

He grinned, "Maybe sometime, it looks like fun. For now though, I just need some information."

She snapped to mock attention. "Right you are officer, what do you want to know?"

"Basically, how heavy are diving tanks, will they sink and for how long?"

She was smart and looked curious, but addressed herself to the question.

"Maybe we should start with the kind of tanks that are available." She led him over to a display.

"We have two kinds of tanks. These twelve litre aluminum tanks cost $250 each. They're more buoyant than these steel tanks which cost $600 each. The price in each case includes eighty fills of air here at the Diving Shop."

"How long does a fill last?" Pete asked.

"About an hour," she said. "Depending on some factors."

"He approached the tanks. "O.K. if I pick one up?"

She nodded.

He chose a steel tank and hefted it to his shoulder. It was heavy. "About thirty pounds?" he guessed.

"Close," she said. "That's the dry weight. Of course it's easier to manoeuvre underwater with the air buoyancy," she pointed out. "We get kids as young as twelve on the tours and they take the lighter tanks.."

He put the tank down. "So, what do they weigh underwater?"

"More, as the air is used up."

"And would an empty tank sink if let loose?"

"It could sink even with air in it," she said.

He looked thoughtfully around the store. "This is a nice looking place. Business is good?"

She laughed. "In the summer, anyway. My husband and I head to Florida in November. But yes, it's a good business. Divers and boaters have found out about us – they can fill up their tanks here without driving all the way to Kingston. The air storage tanks are out back."

"So, how many tanks would an expedition use say in a day, or in a week?"

"Depends what kind of an expedition," she said. "We can accommodate up to a dozen guests at a time on our own diving tours, plus the instructor. So, say twelve tanks to give everybody an hour underwater, and then a few extra tanks for safety."

She added, "But most folks who are just up here for a week or so, would only need a couple of tanks a day. They would likely just rent the tanks."

She tapped a ledger book on the counter. "We keep track here of clients and their air filling needs. How much they require, when they will need to fill up again."

"I'm wondering if you've rented any tanks to some people who are diving over Middle Island way."

"Sure," she said. "Boaters from there come to the shop all the time."

"This particular group is looking for Arrow plane models."

She rolled her eyes. "There's somebody every summer. Nobody's found any planes yet but they keep spending money to look." She shrugged, "Like my husband says, if they want to buy our air, that's fine with us."

"This year, it's a Mr. Gordon Tice." Pete said. "A big fellow, fiftyish. A loud guy, likely rude."

"Oh yeah, *that* jerk," her face reddened at the memory. "He was in here last week, giving us a hard time about some tanks."

"What was the problem?" Pete asked.

"He said we had short-changed him two tanks but there was no way. I always mark the tanks out in the book. Look," she pointed to an entry. "You can see right here, we gave him ten filled tanks, the same order he's been getting for the past month. But he paid no attention to the register or the invoice, wouldn't look at them. He just kept saying that we had made a mistake."

"So he said he only had eight tanks?"

She nodded and grinned. "Yeah but he didn't get anywhere with us. He had to rent two more and Paul my husband said if Tice couldn't find the tanks, he'd have to pay us for them. Of course that made him *really* mad. That was the best part, made my day."

"So what could have happened to Tice's tanks?"

She shrugged. "He was probably just trying to score a couple of free tanks."

"He's not hurting for money," Pete said. "He's got a nice boat, lots of time to spend on his crazy hobby."

She grimaced. "You'd be surprised. Rich people are often the biggest cheapskates."

"If he did lose the tanks somehow in the water, will they turn up?"

"Maybe – unless they're snagged on something."

* * *

"So our number one suspect was missing a couple of diving tanks," Halstead said. "That's interesting."

Pete was sceptical. "Maybe. But then why would the guy make such a big fuss at the Diving Shop? It would be more likely that he would just go to Kingston or Toronto and quietly replace the tanks."

"Maybe he didn't have much time. Josh had already noticed that they were missing tanks. He had to give the kid the story about the store short-changing him."

Jakes still looked doubtful.

Halstead grinned. "Here's some news to cheer you up. I've got a witness who says that Tice's boat was out the night of July second and didn't come back till almost dawn."

"When did this witness crawl out of the woodwork?"

"He's been sailing on a trip to the Gaspe. He only came back yesterday to the Peterson Marina and heard the news from Ralph."

It was often that way in police work, Halstead reflected. Jakes and Storms comb the terrain of South Island for two days and find nothing. Then new information turns up by pure chance.

"Did Ralph ask him specifically about the second?" Pete asked.

"He didn't prompt him, if that's what you're worried about. It just came up in conversation. I gather it was the usual kind of rambling chit chat, and then the light dawned kind of thing. I talked to the guy, he came into the station."

"And he remembered Tice and his boat?"

"Yes, and so does his wife. Hard to forget, I imagine. Tice wasn't exactly a friendly mooring buddy, no surprise there. No boat parties for him. Apparently he barely said hello."

"Yeah, well I guess now we invite him to a party at the station. This is one conversation he can't get out of."

Gerald Tice didn't improve on acquaintance, Pete noted. And of course being questioned in a murder investigation might put anyone on edge. Still, Pete's advice to Mr. Tice would be that it never hurt to be civil, especially with the police. Not that the guy was listening.

Tice was one of those types who figured that if he just yelled louder than everyone else in the vicinity, he would win. And now that his strategy was clearly not working, he yelled and blustered louder than ever.

"The chief would like you to come into the station to answer some questions," Pete explained quietly and for the second time.

Tice waved his arms in dramatic exasperation. "I'm here, you're here. Ask your damn questions. I've already told you idiots I didn't murder that Sedore guy."

Pete glanced at Keri Tice, huddled shocked and wide-eyed by the wheelhouse.

"Come on," he said, appealing to Tice's paternal instinct. "It would be better to do this at the station. Let's just go out to the cruiser."

But apparently Tice didn't have a lot of paternal feeling. "We've got a day's diving work planned. What if I won't go?" he demanded.

Pete shrugged. "If I have to return to this boat to pick you up, I'll have backup, a warrant and a set of handcuffs." He looked at Keri again. "Is that the way you want to play it?"

Maybe it was the mention of the handcuffs. Tice turned to Josh, who had been avidly watching the scene. "Get the equipment ready," he said savagely. "It'll be a short day goddammit, but we'll be going out this afternoon."

I wouldn't be too sure about that, thought Pete. *This boat might not be going out treasure hunting for quite awhile.*

* * *

"How about I start with a little story," Halstead began.

Tice, meaty arms crossed across his chest, shrugged. "Go ahead, suit yourself. As long as it doesn't take too long – I've got a diving operation to run."

Halstead glanced at the calendar, and began, "Once upon a time – say on the evening of July second, say about five o'clock – you came into Peterson's Marina and dropped the kids off as per usual. Normally, and as per usual, according to your daughter and Josh, you would pour yourself a rye and water, then spend a couple of hours with your maps, then go to bed.

"Instead, you took the *Finders Keepers* back out again.."

He gestured to Tice who was looking ostentatiously bored. "You're welcome to stop me anytime, if you have something to add to the story."

Tice merely grunted and closed his eyes. "Wake me when you're done."

Halstead grinned. "Better stay awake, you don't want to miss anything."

He picked up the story where he'd left off. "Anyway, there you are out on the boat, it's a beautiful summer evening, perfect for your plan of taking a little tour around South Island. Because you've got some bee in your bonnet that those plane models landed somewhere in those waters. You want to get a good look from the shore."

"Maybe you've anchored on the other side of the island from the dock, and plan to use the dinghy. Or maybe you just don't care if you run into Sedore. He won't have his police escort and you figure you can outyell him."

"You anchor and row the dingy in. But even though it's getting on for dusk, Wes Sedore sees you or he's heard the *Finders Keepers* arrive. Sedore's so mad after telling you to stay away, that he jumps you unexpectedly and catches you off guard. He's likely mad as hell. The two of you get into a scuffle and somehow Sedore gets hurt bad."

Tice didn't actually begin to snore, but looked as if he might.

"You should have called us," Halstead continued. "That was big mistake number one."

He started to count off on his fingers. "Big mistake number two – you should never have decided to get rid of Sedore's body."

"And big mistake number three -- if you were going to stash the body, you should have done a better job, like making sure Sedore would never drift free of the diving tanks you tethered him to."

Halstead leaned back in his own chair. "So what do you think of my little story?"

Tice opened his eyes lazily. "It's got a crappy ending. You called me in to hear this?"

Pete moved forward from the window where he'd been standing, "We thought you might be interested in the diving tank angle...."

Tice shrugged.

".... seeing as you were missing a couple of diving tanks last week."

"Those people at the diving shop short-changed me," Tice said, showing a reaction at last. "They tried to cheat me out of a couple of tanks of air that I'd already ordered and paid for."

"That's not the way the shop manager and her husband see things," Pete said. "And they have the records to prove it."

"Records!" Tice snorted. "Anyone can write up a fake record."

"They would have had to copy out a whole new book with records going back to last July," Pete said. "Seems like a lot of work, just to cheat you out of a couple of tanks."

"There's no figuring some people," Tice said.

"Just to be clear," Halstead asked, "Is that your explanation for the missing tanks? That the people at the Diving Shop cheated you?"

"Yes!" Tice thumped the arm of the chair and stood up. "Is that all you wanted to ask me? Can I go now?"

"Not just yet," Halstead said. "You say you didn't like my story, so my question is, what's your version?"

"What do you mean?" Tice asked trucently, but sinking back down into his seat.

"It's pretty straight-forward. My question is, if you didn't take the *Finders* Keepers over to South Island the night of July second, where did you go instead?"

Tice grimaced, "I told you the other day, I didn't go anywhere that night. Just had a drink and went to bed like usual."

"Yes you did say that. Trouble is," and at this point Halstead paused just enough to see the flash of wariness in Tice's eyes. "The trouble is that I've got a couple of witnesses who says you did go out that night. And you didn't come back till nearly five in the morning."

"What witnesses?" Tice scoffed. "Just some more liars, like the people at the dive shop."

"I don't think so," Halstead said harshly. "I think you're the liar. So stop fooling around and tell us where you went that night."

Tice paused, thinking. Then took a deep, resigned breath. "O.K., I did have the boat out that night. I was checking out a dive site."

"At night?" Halstead scoffed. "I doubt it."

"I wanted to check the locale out myself. I might have been noticed in the day."

"Might have been noticed dumping a body, you mean," Halstead said grimly.

Tice shook his head angrily. "I told you I didn't kill Sedore."

"Where is this imaginary site then?" Halstead demanded, "Tell me that."

Tice shook his head. "It's taken me two years of research and a lot of dough to get this information. I'm not nuts enough to hand my data over to anyone else. I'll just tell you that it isn't anywhere near South Island."

"You got anyone who can verify this story?" Pete asked. "Your daughter, Josh, anyone else who was with you that night?"

Tice sighed. "No, I was on my own."

"Why did you lie and say you weren't out that night?"

"I just told you, I didn't want anyone finding out about the site. The people looking for these planes can be a bunch of jackals."

You got that right, Halstead thought. *Or jackasses maybe, in your case.*

Aloud, he said. "Without some corroboration, your story is just that – a story."

He leaned forward confidingly. "We're reasonable people here, Tice. Why don't you just fess up. You were over at South Island that night, you and Sedore got into a scuffle and it went wrong. You hit him too hard, or he fell down, somehow Sedore ended up dead. Anybody can see it wasn't premeditated murder, things just went wrong. But it will go better for you, if you come clean. This lying about where you were isn't helping your case at all."

But Tice wouldn't change his story, nor would he tell them the location of his mysterious 'site'.

They left him to stew in the room for a half hour.

"I don't know," Pete said. "He stayed pretty cool. The only time we got a reaction out of the guy was when he was griping about the diving tanks."

"We've got enough to book him," Halstead said.

Tice was livid when he was told the news. "You've got nothing. No proof for your stupid story. Search my boat, you'll find nothing."

"We intend to," Halstead promised. "And meanwhile you'd better call your lawyer."

Tice was still protesting when they cuffed him and drove him across the causeway. Destination, the district detention centre on the outskirts of Bonville, where the bullying salvage dealer was about to do some time in dry-dock.

AVRO HUNTER TAKEN INTO CUSTODY
IN SOUTH ISLAND MURDER

Halstead grinned and tossed the *Record* on his desk. Poor Bob! The fun was over. No more martians to report on. Just a plain old human vs human murder. The rest of the story was a straightforward account of the arrest and a rehash of the original story of Wes Sedore's disappearance. No details of diving tanks had yet been released to the press.

"Heads up!" Jane called from the front counter. "Incoming."

The Vern signal. Heads down, more like, or Head out, but there wasn't time.

The County Clerk seemed downright peppy this morning. After a bit of witty repartee with Jane (*Going to be hot as Hades out there this afternoon.*) he sallied into Halstead's office and sat, exuding benevolence.

"Good work, Bud," he said, picking up the *Record* and surveying the headline with satisfaction.

"Just doing my job, Vern. I guess some other nut is going to get the glory for finding that airplane."

Vern snorted. "If there's anything left of those models after fifty years, which I very much doubt." He turned to the back pages of the newspaper which were full of advertising for cottage rentals, sailing lessons and a half page notice of the August holiday celebrations and fireworks display at the end of the month.

He sighed contentedly, "At least the waterways are safe again and we can get on with the business of summer."

"It was hardly a *Jaws* situation," Halstead protested. "People weren't staying away because they were frightened of being chewed up by a giant shark. I bet we had even more people than usual coming to see our X-files island mystery."

"You're not responsible for public relations," Vern said, his mood darkening a little. "You don't have to meet with that Bonville waterfront events committee. It's a big headache."

Halstead laughed. "As you keep telling me. Never mind, Vern you can handle it. You and that mayor's hat are a fine fit."

"*Acting* Mayor," Vern corrected. Still, he left cheerfully enough to face the lions of Bonville.

Halstead felt pretty fine, too. It was good to have made an arrest in the case and a complimentary headline in the *Record* never hurt the Island station's image either.

Of course anywhere else, the local story would have been eclipsed by the news that there had been another major international drug bust near Cornwall, the city up the river. The successful investigation had resulted in more arrests and more drugs seized. A police spokesperson had looked pleased about the arrests, though had added forebodingly,

"These criminals aren't using trucks as much any more. Trucks are too easy to stop at borders. Instead, boats are obviously being utiilized to avoid points of entry to the United States. Criminals using boats don't know borders. That's why you see more and more of these joint Canada-U.S. operations."

"They'll never get them all," Halstead said to Jane. "Nowadays people can set up grow-ops anywhere. In the cities, they just look like regular houses. It's like trying to put out a whole lot of forest fires, there's always another one starting up somewhere else."

"I'm glad we don't live in the middle of it," Jane said.

"Right on," Halstead said. "We don't need that kind of trouble on the Island. He folded the newspaper under his arm, to take home and savor over supper.

* * *

Steph tilted her wineglass for the last deliciously cool sip of pinot grigio and contemplated the silver band of moonlight that led like a shimmering pathway across the dark water.

"Kind of weird," she said. "To be celebrating finding a killer."

"It's part of my job." he reminded her gently. "Luckily not too often. And if we're glad about anything, it's that our Island is a safe place again."

She smiled ruefully. "Lesson one in my mother's manual, 'How to Handle Men," – ask them about their business." She put the glass down, "And I had to marry a policeman."

She softened the words with a kiss. "Sometimes I think I don't know my own community any more, though Bud. What's happening here?"

He put his arms around her, and she leaned back against his chest. "This is a good place," he said. "People live and die anywhere."

She twisted around to face him. "And I suppose you're going to say they get murdered anywhere too."

He tweaked her nose. "Don't get sassy with me,missy."

"Could be fun," she said musingly. Then more wickedly, "Fancy a skinny-dip?"

He laughed, "I haven't had one of those since I was twenty."

"Then you're long overdue for another one," she said, kicking off her sandals and holding out her hand invitingly.

He looked nervous. "I don't look like a twenty-year old anymore. Steph. Heck, I don't look like a forty-year old anymore."

She laughed and started to pull off her tank top. "Neither do I."

"I'm a grandfather!" he said desperately.

"Come on, Bud, it's only me. What's the good of having the kids grow up and leave, if we can't have a little fun?"

He looked dubiously up towards the guest cabins, one of which was still lit with a lamp behind the screen. When he looked back at the shore, Steph was just a slim white shape entering the water. She laughed and splashed at the cold. Great way to stay unnoticed, he thought. With his luck one of those nosey Islanders would be using a telescope tonight.

With a sigh he started to step out of his shorts.

* * *

Edna Peterson moved restlessly in her bed. The room was stifling hot and her nightgown was sticking to her back. But Ralph said he didn't want an air conditioner giving him pneumonia. She glared at him, lying peacefully on his back in the other twin bed. If the summer heat continued like this, Mr. Peterson might just have to put up with pneumonia. That or move out to the shed.

She thrashed about mightily in her sheets, dislodging Fred the giant orange cat.

"Shoo sweetie," she said, unceremoniously pushing him to the floor. Fred was a lovely source of purring heat in the winter, but not welcome in July.

Phooey! Now she had to go to the bathroom. She knew from long experience that the urge wouldn't pass. Oh well, she was awake now anyway, might as well sit in the kitchen for a bit and have a glass of ice water. It might be cooler there. She picked up her paperback mystery book from the bedside table to take with her.

Marinated Murder. She liked the cooking genre mysteries. Except they always made her hungry. One of those chicken legs left over from supper would go well with the ice water. Fred followed her, likely thinking the same.

Soon they were settled in the rocking chair, Edna deep into her book.

From somewhere out on the lake came the quiet hum of a boat motor, but Edna didn't notice. Her hearing wasn't that great lately.

* * *

A cat and mouse game they called the smuggling trade.

The players scooting in and out of the coves and inlets all along the lake.

Virtually undetectable.

A solitary night heron hunting in the marshes, heard the sound too, but didn't look up.

The heron had his own game. It involved a night's dinner. And frogs.

23

Ali Jakes sneezed mightily, disturbing several decades worth of dust.

Wayne Jessup, Joan's carpenter son-in-law, said with the satisfaction of someone whose opinon has been aptly demonstrated, "It's a heck of a mess up here."

Undeterred, Ali looked excitedly past a dust-smeared window at the birds-eye view of the open sparkling lake. The lighthouse tower may have been only twenty-two feet tall but poised on a rock shelf over the water, the effect was quite splendid. Like being in the wheelhouse of a ship.

"Can we open up any of the other windows?" Steph asked Wayne, looking at the nailed-up boarding. "It would be nice to air the place out."

Jessup, a sturdy young fellow, wearing t-shirt, jeans and construction boots, had already looked askance at the women's capri pants and sandals. "Watch out for rough wood and nails," he'd warned them.

Now he sighed, "Lots of broken panes," he said. "That's likely why they're boarded up. To keep the rain and snow out – and the birds."

Swallows swooped busily under the lighthouse eaves, darting into the gourd-like mud nests to feed their young. Hundreds of the small, graceful birds moved effortlessly past each other. Like tiny airplanes that needed no air traffic controller but their own sense of each other.

Ali smiled and said brightly, "It's not raining now. Help me open this window at least."

Steph rolled her eyes. They'd been coaxing the fellow since they first cracked open the lighthouse door. It was obvious that Jessup hadn't much optimism about the project but Joan said that he was looking for extra work. His wife was expecting their first child and they were hoping to put a down payment on a house.

He moved reluctantly to the window, easily pushing it open with his strong arms. The summer day rushed into the tower space, bringing heady scents of lake water, sweet grass and wild raspberry.

Ali clapped her hands delightedly. "Thanks!" she said. "That's wonderful."

Steph looked back down the staircase they'd come up. "So, what do you think?" she asked Wayne." Can you do something about these steps for us?"

He shook his head, as if faced with the reconstruction of the Panama Canal.

"The whole durn stairs should be yanked out," he said direly. "You might better start all over again, if you want to do the job right."

Clearly it would be fine with Jessup to knock the lighthouse itself down. Apparently he didn' t share his mother-in-law's passion for preserving historical landmarks. Still, she had vouched for his carpenter skills.

Steph nodded. "I appreciate what you're saying, Wayne. But I think Joan told you we don t have enough money for that just yet."

"We were just hoping that you could shore up those supports a bit for now," Ali added, "so that we can organize the ceremonial lighting of the lamp up here at the end of the month."

He looked at the two eager faces. "I could put in some two by fours," he said grudgingly. "Won't do for crowds but for a couple of people at a time, it should hold up."

"That would be great!" Steph said. "Plus we need you to fix those four window panes on the lake side."

"I'll need some cash up front for materials," Jessup warned. "Wood for the supports and some new glass for the windows."

"Just tell Joan what you need," Ali said. "and she'll get you the money."

Jessup got out a tape measure and moved to the windows to do his figuring. The tower space was circular, only about five feet in diameter so Ali and Steph moved against the wall to keep out of his way. Ali grinned and made a thumbs up sign.

Jessup made more measurements on the staircase, jotting numbers down on a crumpled notepad that he jammed back again into his jeans pocket.

"When can you start?" Steph asked. "I know you've got other work, but we haven't much time before the picnic."

"I'll pick up that stuff at the lumber yard," he said. "Be here tomorrow morning, shouldn't take me more than a day. " He shook his head again, "But I'm not giving any guarantees out."

The three of them stood in contemplation of the perfect morning at the Point. The sky was an arc of deep July blue above a softly waving expanse of small lemon and white flowers. Past the old tower, the lake lapped gently at the stone-scattered shore.

A splat of swallow crap landed on Jessup's baseball cap. He swore and looked up, "You ought to get rid of all them birds while you're at it."

Lucky Miranda isn't here, Steph thought. As far as her aunt was concerned, the swallows were staying. "The birds have been here since the tower was built," she'd insisted. "It's probably their mud nests that are keeping the place glued together after all these years."

To divert Jessup, Steph asked what he'd thought of the recent events at South Island.

He was batting his hat against some grass to clean it but gave up. "My granny was disappointed. She liked the UFO idea. She watches all the television programs about those things."

But he had no opinion or much interest whether Gerald Tice was guilty or not. Neither the murdered man nor the accused were

Island folk and therefore barely worth comment. He did know about the other story though, the big smuggling bust.

He nodded knowledgeably. "It's not all up Cornwall way either, there's drugs in Bonville if the kids want them, maybe even here."

They walked Jessup to his pick-up truck. Ali gave him the extra key they had made for the tower door. "Thanks for coming. We appreciate your helping us to save this wonderful piece of our heritage."

He grunted non-committedly and drove off.

"What do you think?" Steph asked.

"We can hope," Ali said.

Steph looked back at the tower, its peeling and scabbed boarding showing the years. "The whole thing needs a good scraping and a coat of paint," she lamented.

"All in good time," Ali consoled. "In the meantime, think how neat it will be to light the place up, even just for one night."

"And is Pete still available to help us put on our little light show?" Steph asked.

"He wouldn't miss it," Ali said. "He's as keen as we are to light the tower up."

"What about Tyler? Is he coming?" Steph asked.

"I'm not sure," Ali said. "He seems to be out in his boat a lot these days."

"Too bad," Steph said wrily. "Beth will be disappointed."

Not me. Ali thought.

Aloud she said, "I'm going to pick up Nevra at Tracy's and then we're off to Bonville. It's Nevra's eighteen-month check up with the pediatrician."

"Ouch!" Steph winced. "Those booster shots are the pits!"

* * *

Nevra had passed her check-up with flying colours. Hadn't even whimpered when she got her booster shot, she'd been so dazzled at the prospect of the green sucker the nurse was holding out to her. Sugar-free of course. Ali thought they tasted awful.

The receptionist waved good-bye. "See you next time, cutie," she said to Nevra.

Ali packed Nevra into her car seat, thinking about what to get Nuran for her sixtieth birthday. Her mother wasn't an easy woman to buy for. She had long ago efficiently organized all her travel needs and the small apartment she occupied only occasionally in Vancouver was almost scarily spartan. So, it would have to be a new photo of her granddaughter in a corny grandma frame. Ali was certain Nuran would make room for that.

Stopped at a traffic light, she drummed her fingers impatiently on the car dashboard. It seemed she had hit every red light for blocks now. And these Bonville four way red lights lasted so long! Then she had to laugh at herself. She supposed she was truly a Middle Islander now, a hick from across the causeway, where the only set of traffic lights in the village was at the intersection of Main Street and the causeway.

Still, this stop, where the traffic flow was limited to one lane because of construction, was longer than most. She'd already seen two light changes.   Luckily Nevra didn't mind the delay. She sat quietly in blissful concentration with her treat.

Idly Ali watched the sidewalk passersby, half wishing she had the time to check out the book store. Then her eyes widened, as she caught sight of Tyler Cotes walking with two other men along the street. Tyler moved without cast or cane, taking easy strides along the pavement. As he approached the intersection, she scrunched down into her seat, feeling foolish. Why did she do that? She wasn't the one hiding anything.

Was Tyler hiding something? Why was he pretending to the Jakes that his foot hadn't healed yet? She felt like jumping out of the car and accosting him, right there on the street. But of course she couldn't, not with Nevra in the car. And there was nowhere to park either. Tyler hadn't noticed the Jakes' SUV. The three men had stopped at the entrance to a downtown restaurant and Tyler seemed to be talking animatedly. He wore slacks and a short-sleeved shirt, the others were in suits. Ali wondered who the other men were, she couldn't remember Tyler ever mentioning that he knew anyone in Bonville.

It was very mysterious altogether. What the heck was he up to?

When the light changed, she moved reluctantly on with the traffic.

24

⁶⁶**A** *ll Rise."* The bailiff called. The judge entered the courtroom and took his seat on the dais. *"Court is in session."*

Halstead had always approved of the century-old Bonville Court House, with its long echoing corridors and massive gloomy windows that darkened even the sunniest daylight. When eventually reached, the dim, high-ceilinged court room gave some weight to the concept of justice he thought, and impressed the young louts who were brought there for petty crimes. On the way into the building, they lounged disdainfully on the front steps, laughing cockily and grinding their cigarettes into the concrete balustrades. But on the way out, they were chastened and silent and hopefully full of resolve to straighten up, rather than to come back again.

Yeah right. Oh well a pleasant fantasy anyway.

He was there to attend Gerald Tice's bail appeal and curious to see what effect a couple of days in the lock-up had exerted on the bullying salvage dealer. Tice had pleaded not guilty at his arraignment but despite the work of his high-priced lawyer brought for the purpose from Toronto, the judge had not granted bail. First-degree murder was the most serious of charges and Tice, with residences in both the States and the Bahamas, had been deemed a flight risk.

Less than half a dozen people sat or slouched in the dark wooden benches that had been worn smooth by a succession of anxious, restless occupants. Halstead idly assessed the day's crop. The solitary woman looked young, poor and frightened. A shoplifting charge he guessed. The man with the bruised face had likely been involved in a squabble in a bar. The two skulking teen-age boys probably broke into a convenience store. No doubt looking for money to buy drugs. A century ago, they'd have been excited to find a bottle of alcoholic cough medicine. Nobody had heard of or even imagined the cornucopia of designer drugs available today.

The other supplicant before hizzoner was Gerald Tice. Dressed in a dark suit, white shirt and tie, the salvage dealer seemed a bit thinner but his bearded chin stuck out as belligerently as ever. Halstead assumed the soberly suited man who sat next to Tice was the big-city lawyer. On the table before the two men was an open briefcase and a fat file folder.

At this bail hearing, the lawyer probably wouldn't need it. Not a lot could happen here today. If a defendant pleaded guilty, say in the instance of a minor charge such as disturbing the peace, a judge could set a fine on the spot. Even in the instance of something more serious, such as the bar squabble, a plea bargain could often be negotiated. But murder was a major charge and Gerald Tice was pleading not guilty, which guaranteed there would be a trial.

Today the judge would merely be setting a preliminary hearing date which would be of crucial interest to Tice. The way things were going in the Ontario Court schedules these days, that could mean up to two months of waiting.

The lawyer spoke briefly, but Carl Kurneck the crown attorney reiterated the seriousness of the charge and the flight risk. Not surprisingly, the judge again denied bail. Tice spoke hotly with his lawyer who was obviously trying to calm him down, then was led away by the bailiff.

Halstead was curious whether he would receive a phone call at the station any time soon. Now that the salvage dealer was facing weeks more in the detention centre before even a preliminary hearing, he might be more inclined to give up his so-called secret diving location. He doubted the information would prove to be much of an alibi at any rate.

* * *

Carl Kurnek took a swig of courthouse coffee and grimaced. "So far the evidence is all circumstantial, Bud. You've got to get me something better than that before the trial."

Halstead, wise from experience, drank canned ginger ale from the vending machine. The weighty dignity of the upper floors of the old building didn't seep down to the basement level. The small luncheonette provided little more than weak coffee and shrink-wrapped egg salad or tuna sandwiches.

He shook his head. "I'm damned who else looks good for it, Carl. We can't even find a grudge against the victim, let alone a motive for killing him."

"We've all got enemies," Kurnek said, glaring at his cup. "For instance, someone down here has been trying to poison me for years."

Halstead explained about Sedore's wife and girlfriend. The glowing testimonials from his workmates, bandmates and friends.

"Then get me more on your suspect, this Arrowhead guy," Kurnek said.

"You've got motive, opportunity, his bogus story about the diving tanks," Halstead protested. "You've got a previous assault or interrupted assault on the victim."

He went on, ticking off points on his fingers. "We've got a witness who says Tice lied when he said he'd been moored at the Petersons that night. And we've got Tice himself who won't say where he was. The judge agreed that was enough to keep Tice in custody."

He looked over at the rack of plasticized sandwiches, decided he would pick up a burger on the way out of town. "What more do you want? We're not saying the guy is a serial killer or a psychopath, but he does have an uncontrollable temper. He needed more than an anger management course to handle that."

Kurnek had given up on the coffee. "It's a start, sure, but I'd feel a lot better if one of those diving tanks turned up. Or if there was some evidence that the victim had been on Tice's boat."

Halstead nodded reluctantly. "We went all over that boat. But Tice had lots of time to swab the deck down. He can't produce or explain those missing tanks though, other than his ridiculous accusation against the diving shop people."

"It's a big lake out there," Kurnek said. "Those tanks might never turn up."

Halstead grimaced. "If I was Tice, I'd been praying that they never do."

Kurnek looked at the clock above the vending machines, and pushed back the cheap vinyl chair.

"Keep working on it Bud. You say he won't tell you where he actually was that night. But he's bound to crack. And I don't need the defendant coming up with a surprise alibi in the middle of the case."

"He doesn't have any alibi," Halstead reiterated. "Just that cock and bull story about finding a lead on those planes. It's all a crock."

"Nevertheless," Kurneck said soberly. "I want to know where he was. Don't leave me out on a limb. No surprises."

Halstead headed for the causeway. He stopped for the light on the Bonville side and looked out over the bright scene of colourful sails and sparkling water. The area was becoming more popular every year. Maybe Steph was right, maybe there were too many strangers coming to the Island. But what could he do, build a moat? Erect a toll gate? That would be a heckuva friendly attitude.

Besides, he didn't want the Island to stagnate. The world didn't stop with folks his age. There were young people who had work to find, marriages to make, lives to live. They needed to be part of what was going on in the big outside world. He didn't want the Island to become some sort of elephants' bone yard.

He'd left himself, when he was younger. Steph's daughter Livy was out there now, studying at university in B.C. That was right, the way things should be. So if a bully like Gerald Tice came along once in awhile that was just the unfortunate down side of change.

Still, it was a real down side. He hadn't handled many homicides in his tenure on the Island, fewer out and out murders. Bad temper often had a lot to do with it. Booze too, but that wasn't a factor here. Just sickening, bullying greed.

He thought over his conversation with Kurnek, and wished the prosecutor was more certain of a conviction. He punched the steering wheel and moved the car forward. Goddamn it though, he thought, this one looks right. No matter what kind of fuss Gerald Tice or his fancy city lawyer kicked up, he couldn't see what could possibly upset this particular applecart.

25

Jane hailed Pete cheerily as he came into the station. Jakes was such a quiet, polite young man. And handsome too, when he lit up that so sober face with a smile. A poster picture policeman.

She handed him the mail to take into Halstead. "How is that army friend of yours doing?" she asked.

"Tyler's doing well, thanks," Pete said. "He's coming along."

Jane nodded approvingly. "That was a good suggestion of yours, that he come here to recuperate. The Island is good for everybody.``

The suggestion might have been good for Tyler, Pete thought ruefully, but he was well aware that Ali wasn`t exactly crazy about his buddy. At first he'd been hopeful that her dislike would pass. Sure, Tyler had some rough edges – professional soldiers didn't spend a lot of time in polite company. And all-male humour could seem crude at times. But there was a lot more to Tyler than that. Tyler was a good man to have at your back, who knew better than Pete?

He was glad that Ali didn't know that Tyler had asked to use Pete's name as a reference for a bank loan for ten thousand dollars. He meant to tell her but there was never a good moment. Whenever Tyler's name came up, she seemed to get upset. He had been a bit surprised at the amount but figured Tyler was good for it, once he got back on duty. The guy was probably a bit short from being on disability for all these months.

Halstead was just ending a phone call, a puzzled frown on his face. He nodded abruptly at Jakes' entrance.

"We're going over to Bonville. I just got a strange call from Roger Huma. Something about Todd's autopsy but he wouldn't tell me over the phone."

Halstead noticed a difference the minute they walked into the lab. Roger Huma wasn't his usual unruffled self. A slight-bodied neat man, dapper even in his white lab coat, he normally projected a cool, scientific confidence in his findings, whether or not the conclusions pleased his law-enforcement colleagues. His job might not have been cheery but presumably he enjoyed doing thoroughly professional, good work.

Huma had a dry sense of humour and usually was glad of the opportunity for some chit-chat to relieve the coldness of his surroundings. Today though, after hemming and hawing for a minute, he came out with his unpalatable news.

"There were some anomalies in the Todd autopsy report."

"You're just finding this out *now*?" Halstead asked. "Todd's been in the ground for three weeks."

"A combination of errors, " Huma said tersely. "A new lab clerk in Toronto sent the postmorten results to the wrong address. Then they neglected to send it on to us."

Pete felt sorry for the careless employee. Sounded like a reason for dismissal, for sure.

"So, what is it?" Halstead asked. "Don't tell me, he's risen from the dead."

Huma doggedly talked them through the new findings, concluding with the main point, that there was no evidence that the fisherman had suffered a heart attack before falling into the water.

"So he had a stroke," Halstead said.

"No stroke either. We looked into that, too."

"So, he was blotto with booze, like he was every night. Too blotto to save himself."

"Oddly, he hadn't drunk that much," Huma said. "Maybe he just hadn't got around to it yet, but for an alcoholic, his blood readings were not that high."

"So he hit his head on something."

"A couple of minor abrasions from bumping against the shore. Nothing to knock him unconscious."

"Any wounds?" Halstead asked Huma. "Evidence of a blow?"

Huma snapped the file shut. "No and no."

"But he did drown? You got that part right?"

"Yes," Huma said drily. "The man did drown."

"So, what are you telling us, that now you think that somebody might have *killed* Melvin Todd? For god's sake, maybe the guy just fell *asleep*, did you think of that?"

"Asleep, isn't unconscious," Huma said. "Most people would wake up once water started to enter their orifices." He added pointedly, "I m just correcting the previous report. Mr. Todd did not suffer a heart attack nor a stroke. Neither did we find any evidence of an injury to his person."

Halstead scowled. "Other than a gallon of lake water in his lungs."

He shook his head. "This has been a real barrel of laughs, Roger. A mystery death, that's all I need. Thanks a bundle." He picked up the file, "What am I supposed to do with this crap?"

Huma shrugged. "I just give out the bad news, Bud. It's your baby now."

* * *

"This is one for the books," Halstead muttered, as he and Jakes left the building. So much for his applecart analogy. Maybe the entire applecart cart hadn't tipped over but it looked as if a few stray apples might have rolled off the top.

"We don't know that Todd was murdered," Pete said.

"We don't know that he *wasn't*."

"What are you thinking, that maybe somebody held him down in the water?"

"No, whatever Huma says, I'm still hoping that Mel just fell asleep. But if we were looking at possibilities, what do you remember about that beach?"

Pete tried to visualize the scene. "Rocky. Like all the beaches on the Island. The water's edge was stirred up a bit. That tourist guy had been back and forth a few times, calling to his wife. Then we arrived."

Halstead scowled. "If there had been proof of anyone else being there, it's long gone by now. You'd better go talk to some of Todd's old cronies. Maybe one of them was drinking with him that night and hasn't fessed up that he was there."

Pete was sceptical. He'd seen the three old fishermen who gathered at their regular table at the Island Grill to play euchre.

"I doubt if they remember what day it is, let alone something that happened a month ago."

Halstead tossed the offending file onto the car seat. "Use your boyish charm. All those old guys like to talk."

26

Pete bumped the cruiser along the rutted track that followed the curved shore of Fishermen's Cove. The area was one of his favourite spots to birdwatch. There was a swamp at one end of the cove where great blue herons had established a rookery. The elegant, long-legged birds, about fifty of them, had settled in the network of dead trees that rose up starkly from the rich green swamp water. It had been a wet spring, with lots of peeper frogs to eat and grow on, so an ideal spot to raise their young. By now though, the swamp waters were low and rank and the fledgling herons spent the days out flying with the adults.

Pete was always glad of a chance to visit the cove, so he'd welcomed the assignment to call in on Jim Gill, one of Mel Todd's old fishing buddies.

"Gill is a funny old coot," Halstead cautioned. "He must be seventy-five at least, but see what you can get out of him."

Most of the time things were pretty quiet at the cove, and quieter than ever the past few years, since the government had cancelled the few remaining commercial fishing licenses. In earlier times, the herons had shared the cove with a dozen fishermen who lived for the season in small cottages or shacks near their boats. Now the last of the boats were beached and the few shacks that remained had fallen into disrepair. A pair of Canada geese and their half-dozen fuzzy feathered young poked about in the uncut grass of Gill's front yard.

Pete parked the cruiser on the side of the road and got out to the barking of a small, stiff-legged brown dog. It was only an obligatory warning however, for her tail was wagging and she came up eagerly to sniff at his trousers. The shell of a once fine boat lay permanently beached on the overgrown lawn. Another boat which Pete recognized as Mel Todd's battered old outboard, was drawn up on the sand under one of the mammoth old black willows that graced most of the Island shores. Even fallen down as this one was, there were entire new trees growing out of the broken limbs and cool shade in the lapping water beneath.

There were a couple of rickety lawn chairs on the shore and an orange plastic cooler sitting in the water. Pete felt an overwhelming temptation to take off his hot shoes, dabble his feet in the lake and dip into that cooler for a cold one. He thought as he often had before, that the old fishermen lived in a paradise that beat any crowded Hawaiian resort. In the summer, anyway.

But the chairs were empty, and he was an on-duty policeman.

He turned to the shack, a listing construction of plywood and tarpaper, and caught a glimpse of a whiskered, screwed-up face in a small, open window. Jim Gill was home, but he didn't look particularly hospitable. Pete had called to say he was coming but maybe the old guy had old-timers's disease and had already forgotten it.

Pete waved, "Howdy Mr. Gill, Pete Jakes here, from the station."

He walked as he spoke, keeping Gill in sight. By the time he'd finished his question, he was practically nose to nose with the fellow at the window. It was like talking to a gnome.

"Can I come in?" he asked.

"Looks as if you're gonna anyway."

The place was a dark cool den. Coming in from the bright outdoors, Pete couldn't see much. There was the clutter of living but no stale or bad food smell, that was often the mark of neglect.

Gill wore a faded sleeveless t-shirt and baggy shorts that showed his stringy legs. His hair was yellow white and his beard looked like a permanent project.

He rapped the table, "You might as well sit down," he said. "Want a beer?"

Pete reluctantly shook his head. "Maybe some water, thanks"

Gill shrugged. "Suit yourself." And drew a glassful from a plastic jug in the fridge.

Gus had commented that Jim hadn't been around the Grill much lately and wondered if the old man wasn't well. But Pete thought the old man looked pretty spry, despite the standard rheumy eyes and swollen nose of the committed alcoholic. When Gill had served the drinks, he sat cowboy style on the other chair, waiting for Pete to speak. He seemed nervous, on edge.

"I just wanted to ask you a couple of questions about Mel Todd," Pete said. "He was your friend I know. I was sorry to hear that he died." This sounded a bit odd, when he had last seen Todd face-down in the lake but it would have to do.

Gill nodded, "I worked with Mel's dad. Then Mel and me was partners, fished these waters for thirty years." He looked out the little window towards the old willow.

"That's Mel's boat down there by the water. Bud Halstead, when he was looking for a place to tow Mel's boat, he told them to bring it here. So here it came."

Pete nodded. He would ask about the night at the camp in a minute. Let the old man take his time.

"I never even looked at the boat till the other day," Gill said. "Didn't want to. It made me feel old." He shook his grizzled head. "The old days are gone and soon we'll all be gone too."

He seemed about to fall into a reverie of reminiscence.

"About the boat, Mr. Gill," Pete prodded. "If you want to know whether you can keep it or not, you could ask a lawyer." Though he doubted there would be any contest over the thing.

Gill turned back to the table. "Mel's boat is staying here," he said with reedy forcefulness. "I know that's what Mel would want." He hesitated, sighed. "I guess you're here about the money. I shoulda known I'd have to report it."

Pete blinked, but was wise enough to stay quiet.

Gill turned in his chair and pulled at a kitchen drawer. It was sticky in the humidity and he had to jiggle it a bit. Then he drew out a plastic grocery sack and tossed it on the table. The open end gaped to show a stack of twenty dollar bills.

Pete pulled the bag over, looked in.

"There's five thousand dollars in there," Gill said. "I found the bag in Mel's boat. In the locker under the seat where he kept his flashlight and rain gear."

Stunned, Pete hazarded a guess, "He didn't like banks?"

Gill snorted. "That would be a lot of cashed pension cheques. Anyways, like the rest of us, he drank up most of those." He looked regretfully at the bag and sighed, "I gotta be honest, I thought of keeping the money. And if I wasn't about to meet my maker so soon, I probably would have."

"Maybe he's left it to you with the boat," Pete said, but his thoughts were racing.

Gill shook his head. "Mel showed me a picture once of his grandson out west. A cute little tyke, he must be about sixteen now. If that lawyer says the money is mine, I'm going to give it to that boy. He could use the money to go to college."

Maybe to buy his books, Pete thought. Old Jim was a bit out of touch. But it was a nice thought.

If the money was his to give.

The burning question was, where had it come from?

Pete leaned forward, his voice intent. "Jim, is there anything else you haven't told us? Like whether you or any of the other fellows were drinking with him the night he died. Do you know anything about what happened at Mel's camp?"

"Never went out there," Gill said. "Too old to be sleeping out. Saw Mel a couple of days before though at the Grill, at our euchre game."

"And you never saw him again after that?"

"Nope, that was it. I remember Mel was talking about getting a new motor for the boat. He was always having trouble with that old Evinrude. But he was finally going to do it, go over to Bonville and buy a brand new motor."

He shook his head. "The other guys said that was crap, how would he ever pay for the damn thing. But Mel said that was no problem. Bought us all a round too. First time ever."

Gill looked owlishly thoughtful, "Maybe he knew somehow that was the last time he'd be with us. Stranger things have happened."

Pete concentrated on the other strange occurrence. "So he was flush and bought his friends a round – where did you think he was getting the money for all this?"

Gill shrugged. "I thought it was just drinker's talk. You know -- what would you do if you won the lottery talk." He laughed roughly, "I didn't know he had a bag of dough in his boat."

Pete looked around the tiny quarters where Gill lived. Neat as he kept the place, it wasn't much bigger than a boat cabin. The furniture was shabby, there was an old wood stove. This place and his knobbly-knuckled old hands were all that the man had to show for his years of hard work. There was the government pension at least, to buy his beer for comfort.

Presumably Mel Todd wouldn't have been any better off. He didn't even own a fishing shack, since the government had cancelled the lease. He would normally have been stretching out his few dollars to last to the end of the month. Instead, and improbably, he had been buying rounds at the bar and talking about getting a new motor for his boat. And, most tellingly, he had five thousand dollars in unexplained cash stowed away in a bag in that very same boat.

"Had Mel been doing anything different in the weeks before he died?" he asked Gill.

Gill looked puzzled, "Like what?"

Pete shrugged. "Anything different in his habits. Or was he just doing everything as usual. What was his mood, how was he feeling?"

"How was he *feeling*?" Gill snorted.

"Sure. Was he cheerful, was he miserable, was he uptight?"

Gill sighed and thought, wrinkling up his forehead in exaggerated effort. "Mel was generally pretty miserable, anyone would tell you that. But like I said, he was downright cheerful that day, the last time I saw him. And now that you mention it, he hadn't been coming in regular to the Grill for the euchre game."

Pete leaned forward. "Did he say where he was going instead?"

"No, he never said."

Pete could glean no more useful information from him. Either Gill was hiding something, or more likely, he simply didn't know.

"If you think of anything, please give me a call." He looked around the place, saw there was a cell phone on top of the fridge.

Gill followed his glance. "Yep, my daughter got me that cell phone for Christmas. I stay with her in the winter but in the summer I like to be here."

He stroked the little dog's muzzle. "We both like to be here. She's stiffened up now," he said, "but she used to hop on and off that boat like a little mountain goat."

He scratched behind her ears, "They was good days weren't they old girl? When the fish were running."

He looked at the bag on the table. "So, what should I do with the money for now, officer? Take it to the lawyer?"

Pete nodded. "That might be a good idea."

He left, stooping at the low door. Outside, he lingered for a minute, enjoying the breeze. The family of geese had moved to the water and squawked and splashed noisily as he approached Mel Todd's beached boat.

Jim Gill had covered the motor with a piece of tarpaulin but the rest of the craft seemed in even worse shape than when Pete had last seen it near Todd's sprawled body. The paint had continued to flake off and the aluminum sides were dented as an old cooking pot. The metal locker, about the size of a tool chest, was still there under the back seat. Pete flipped open the lid but the locker was empty. The boat was empty too, and stilled. Like the motor, like Mel Todd.

He stood there under the old willow looking across the water to the smudge that was South Island. Two men found dead in the lake, one murdered, another under unexplained circumstances. Was there a connection? If so, the answer was out there on the lake.

But when Pete voiced his thoughts to Halstead, the chief was sceptical.

"Old Jim is likely just confused. I imagine that one afternoon runs into another around that euchre table."

"Mel Todd didn't buy his buddies a round of drinks every day," Pete persisted. "And what about the money in the boat?"

Halstead chuckled, "I think you hit the nail on the head with your first guess. Maybe Mel didn't like banks. He was pretty paranoid, especially after the Ministry cancelled the fishing licenses. He thought the system had it in for him."

He sighed, looking at his own pile of paperwork. "Most of us feel that way at least part of the time."

He knew Jakes wasn't going to let it go though. Once he encountered a puzzle, he was on it like a dog with a bone. A trait that could sometimes be valuable and at other times, a pain in the butt.

"You mentioned a connection – well what is it? What connection could there possibly be? I doubt that Wes Sedore even knew Mel Todd by sight, and vice versa."

"Their deaths could be connected," Jakes said doggedly. "You're the one who taught me to be suspicious of coincidences in police work."

Halstead acknowedged the compliment, if it was one. "Todd died two weeks before Sedore," Halstead pointed out. "And nobody's saying that he was murdered."

"Nobody's saying it yet," Jakes objected.

Halstead sighed and leaned back in his chair, "O.K. so saying that Mel was murdered, who's the killer – one of his fishing buddies?"

Jakes shook his head. "It would be a real stretch to cast one of them as a killer. Even in a drunken, stumbling brawl, they'd be lucky to lay a punch by accident. And Jim Gill at least is a nice old guy. I can't see him leaving a pal to die. He'd known Mel all his life. Mel left him his boat – and his money, it turns out."

"So who else? Gerald Tice? He didn't know Mel from a hole in the ground. They hardly ran in the same circles."

Jakes stood up and stretched, "I say it's got something to do with the money Jim Gill found in Todd's boat. Solve that mystery and we might solve the whole complicated mess."

27

"Howdy Miranda, checking that you're still alive?"

Vern was merely making the standing post office joke among the older crowd, whose first stop when getting the mail was always to check out the black-edged funeral notices in the glass-fronted case.

Miranda responded in kind. "No Vern, actually I was looking for your name up there in the notices."

"Still alive and kicking," he said, opening his own post office box.

His father used to say the same thing, Miranda thought. Vern looked just like him too, skinny and somehow his clothes never hung properly on him.

"I'm glad to catch you," she said. "I wanted to have a word with you about how difficult it is to find a parking spot out front."

Vern looked pained, "Now Miranda, you know it's tourist season. We all have to make some allowances."

"Fine then, I'll take your parking spot at the municipal office."

"Har de har har," the clerk departed on the run.

The Island post office was really just a section in the back of Patty Moore's gift shop. For a government stipend, Patty gave space to mailboxes for village residents. She also sold stamps and posted letters. Miranda's mail like that of other rural residents, was delivered by the mail lady to the box at the end of her driveway but when she was in town, she always popped in to Patty's to check the funeral notices.

The notice for Mel Todd had been removed and replaced with a card for the woman who had taught Miranda and her brother six decades ago in a one-room schoolhouse. The teacher had been ninety-eight. A good run. Miranda didn't bother doing the arithmetic. She had no illusions that she would be around forever, but saw no point in dwelling on numbers.

"Hi there," came the cheery voice of Jane Carell, looking spruce as always in white slacks and a tailored linen blazer. Grandmothers never used to look like that, Miranda thought, trying to picture Jane rocking on a porch and shelling peas. Hooray for modern times.

"How's the lighthouse campagn coming?" Jane asked. She had already contributed her twenty-five dollar membership.

Miranda held up a large brown envelope. "I'm sending off the grant application today, and our Lighthouse Day picnic is shaping up nicely. Now as long as we don't get another drowning or murder," she added drily, "we might actually attract some people to the event."

"The chief's doing his best," Jane said brightly. "He's made an arrest and hopefully things will go back to normal."

"Oh yes that man who's been searching for the Arrow planes." Miranda frowned. "Why can't these people just enjoy the beauty? Instead of always wanting to roar around and do something expensive?"

Jane shrugged. "Maybe that Tice fellow wants to be famous. Have his name on a plaque somewhere."

"*Glory is like a circle in the water*", Miranda quoted the Bard, "*it disperses to naught.*"

"And what about the supposed bomb threat," she continued. "What's going to happen out at South Island, now that that fellow who was looking for the bombs is dead? Is the government planning to send someone to replace him?"

"The island is still off-limits to the public," Jane said. "I'm not sure what the Ministry will do now."

She didn't mention that the chief was actually still battling the Ministry over who was responsible for keeping the public away. The department of defence hadn't decided yet whether to put another man on the Island. Understandably, employees were reluctant. Halstead's best offer was that Jakes and Storms could swing past once or twice a day on their patrol. Greg Jackman and his rescue training crew could also go by occasionally. But that was it. If the Ministry wanted the place patrolled, they would have to maintain some kind of presence themselves.

"Courting couples and camping teenagers have been stopping at the island for years and nobody's been blown up yet," was Halstead's attitude. And Jane was inclined to agree.

Miranda's next stop was the Middle Island library, a tiny frame structure squashed between the municipal building and the Wool Shop, which sold knitting supplies. The library, staffed entirely by volunteers, was only open three afternoons a week. Today, Monday, was Miranda's shift.

As she dug in her carryall for the key, she was surprised to see Tyler Cotes coming up the steps, leaning on his cane.

"Sorry," she said. "Were you waiting to come in?"

"That's O.K." he said. "I had some other errands in town anyway."

He was really a very good-looking man. A clean and crisp type in his short-sleeved shirt and cargo pants she thought they were called. And sporting a marvellous summer tan, or perhaps the tan was permanent as he'd spent so much time in the Middle East. His foot cast and cane only emphasized the muscular, tanned fitness of the rest of him. No wonder Beth Harrison had practically drooled over the sight of him.

Luckily at her age, Miranda was immune, which didn't mean she minded looking. But there was a library to open. She wrested out the key, struggling with her assortment of bags.

"Let me help you with that," he said, grabbing them up.

She always enjoyed entering the dim, quiet building and turning on the lights to reveal the neat shelves of books. There wasn't a huge collection, and many of the books and magazines had been donated, but the library represented a real achievement and the efforts of many people dedicated to fostering the importance and pleasures of reading.

It was a cause to which Miranda had devoted many years of her life, both in her teaching career in Canada's North and now here on Middle Island. When she thought of what Ali had told her about Cotes' opinion of Island life, she bristled, ready to defend this little gem against an outsider's comments.

But he actually looked approving. "I've been curious to see the inside of this building. What a neat place."

She smiled. "We try."

She headed for the check-out desk. "Is there anything in particular I can help you find or would you just like to browse?"

"I enjoyed that book you gave me about the rum runners," he said. "Are there any more? Also are there any historical maps of the lake from that time? The writer mentions coves and inlets with all sorts of local names. I don't seem to be able to find them on the regular navigation maps."

She nodded. "And you're not likely to. Folks around here have always had their own names for places. Just ask for directions and see how far you get."

"I hear you," he laughed. "When I asked the cleaning lady at the cabins how to get to Fishermen's Bay, she told me to drive till I got to the old Perkins house, then turn left. Then keep going till I got to the government sign and turn left again."

"Did you get there?" Miranda asked.

"It might have helped if she'd told me that the Perkins house wasn't there any more."

Miranda sat Tyler down at a table where he could keep his bad foot out straight and brought him the big historic atlas of the Island and surrounding area. She opened it to a page showing the lower shore of Middle Island.

"There's Paris Cove," she pointed to a tiny inlet. "Named after my great-grandfather, the lighthouse keeper."

There were also names such as Tea Cup Cove, Wreck Bay and Dogleg Inlet.

She left him poring over the page showing South Island. It was odd how many people were interested in that little scrap of land this summer. When it had been sitting out there all along, a nondescript bump on the water.

"Thanks so much," he called after her. "This is just what I was looking for."

Such a polite fellow and seemingly truly interested in the Island history.

Whatever could Ali find so objectionable about the man?

28

Keri Tice rolled out of bed and crinkled her sun-tanned forehead in a frown. She'd been thinking of something just before she woke up, something important. Something about a boat, though that wasn't surprising since it seemed she had spent half her young life living on boats and around water. Her dad used to say that she should have permanently webbed feet.

That made her smile, and then it made her sad. Thinking that Dad was right now, on dry land and boxed up in a jail. And that thought she'd had, if she could only remember it, might have been something that could help free him. But frustratingly, the thought was gone, it had floated away in the fog of half-waking.

"You're in a heckuva mood today," Josh said. "What's bugging you?"

"Gee, I don't know," Keri said sarcastically. "My Dad's in jail, we don't know what's going to happen to the stupid project, what are we going to *do*?"

He looked embarrassed. "Sorry," he said. "I guess it was a pretty dumb thing to say."

"My Dad's in *jail*. People think he murdered someone. It's like we're living in a nightmare."

Josh said nothing.

She looked up at him. "I know you think he's guilty. Josh, how can you think that?"

He shrugged helplessly. "I'm sorry Keri, but it looks bad for him. Your dad is a big, tough guy and he's got one hell of a temper."

"That's just the way Dad talks," Keri said. "It doesn't mean anything. He's a gentle, kind man really. I should know, he brought me up."

Josh reached out his arms, trying to hug her but she hit out at him.

"You're wrong!" she cried through tears. "You're wrong!" And she ran away.

Later, when she'd walked around the village and settled down a bit, she went over it all again. There was nothing else on her mind, the nightmare filled her days. It was true that Dad had lied to the police about being at the Marina that night. And now he wouldn't tell them where he'd actually gone.

She'd visited him at the detention centre, told him it wasn't worth being locked up for murder, nothing was. She'd tried her best to convince him to change his mind, but he wouldn't. He just kept saying that the preliminary hearing would come up soon and then they'd have to let him out.

She wasn't so sure about that, though. Most people just seemed to assume that dad had killed that man. And then that darn newspaper headline made it even worse. She wondered if the police were even looking for any other suspects. When she thought of dad going to prison for the rest of his life, she got such a feeling of panic in her chest, she could hardly hold it in.

She had to do something! She would go out to the *Finders Keepers*. She was always happiest on the boat, it was a lucky place for her. She would search through Dad's records and charts and find the secret place where he'd been that night. He might be mad at first, but he would thank her in the long run.

* * *

She thought that Josh would be too negative about her plan, so she waited till the next afternoon when he left with some fellows he'd met to go to a baseball game in the city. Then she'd driven out to the Marina. She waved to Mr. Peterson who had always been nice to her when she popped into the store. She didn't linger though, it was awkward talking to people these days. Even the nice ones didn't know what to say.

It was strange being on the *Finders Keepers* without Dad there, sitting in his accustomed spot in the stern. She'd only been back on the boat once since he was arrested, when he'd asked her to gather up some toiletries and his shaving kit. That was pretty weird too, weird and sad.

Now she rifled guiltily through her father's desk, looking for his I-pod. He hadn't been allowed to take the pod to the detention centre and it had occurred to her that there might be a clue to his mysterious journey on it. Finally she found the thing, not in his desk but in the cupboard where he kept his rain gear – slicker, hat and boots. The pod was in one of the boots.

She hauled it out triumphantly and saw that it still held a charge. Feeling guiltier still, she pressed the on button. But she forced the guilt away. If her dad wouldn't help clear himself, she would have to do it. She had to guess a bit at the password, which Dad kept hidden even from her. But that didn't take long. They were probably the only two people in the world who knew what Mom used to call a famous breakfast cereal.

She tried the photo section first. One thing to be grateful for, she thought as she flicked through the files, her dad was a neat freak. All the photographs were labelled by date, even by the minute. He must have bought an app to do that.

She scrolled quickly through the files till she found one marked July 2nd. The evening when Mr. Sedore had been killed, the evening when her father said he'd been somewhere else on the lake, scouting out the new site.

There were about forty photos in the file. She moved slowly along through the pictures, looking for clues to identify the site. Not an easy task when you were looking at water, water, and more water, broken only by what seemed to be random bits of rocky shoreline.

However, she was a diver and could glean information even from the colour of the water. And judging from several of the photos, they had been taken at a place where the water was unusually deep for this part of the lake. She might be able to find a match in the daily records Dad kept. She could look for depth and other details and get the co-ordinates.

Conscientiously though, she first continued to scroll through the remaining photos on the I-pod. Water, rocks, water. The pictures were getting darker now as evening advanced. Wait, here was something different, something breaking up the monotony. A buoy! Now that could be a big help, if she could only read the number.

She zoomed in excitedly. Yes, there was a number on the buoy, 243-629. She wrote it down. In the distance, behind the buoy, she could now make out a thin finger of rocky shore and a bit of cove. And what seemed to be two tiny boats, moored together, there in the water. It seemed a strange empty place to stop.

Ah well, it was the buoy she was interested in, not a couple of unknown boats. She could call the National Buoy Centre and find out its location. That should be interesting information for the police. She gathered up the photos and the piece of notepaper she'd been scribbling on. At least now she had something to do! Some way to help. She patted the side of the *Finders Keepers* affectionately. If there was an answer in these photos, something to clear her father, she would find it.

The police would then have to find another suspect who might have killed that unfortunate Mr. Sedore. But that wasn't her problem.

29

Nevra chuckled as the tiny white butterfly hovered over her fingers. She moved though, and the pretty creature fluttered away. She turned to other delights – splashing water happily, as her father rowed the boat along the shore.

"More, Daddy. More."

The little girl wore a bright orange children's safety vest but Ali still kept a steady hand on the vest belt. Dragonflies, bright as jewelled brooches, darted through the shore weeds. A dozen of the white butterflies settled on the water, bobbing like a flotilla of miniature sailing ships. Pete put up the oars as they drifted under an old willow whose hanging branches brushed their faces. Heavenly, Ali thought. No noisy ski doo machine could offer better treats.

The rowboat came with the Cedar Grove cabin. Tyler was up at his cabin now, firing up the barbeque.

"To thank you guys," he said when he'd issued the invitation. "I'm making you dinner for a change."

The menu was to include fresh grilled perch and summer vegetable kebobs. Hard to resist, and Ali could think of no plausible reason to refuse. So here they were. Tyler had offered the Jakes the use of his rental speedboat but Pete had politely declined, saying that Nevra would have more fun under oar power. And he was right. Ali looked fondly at the tableau of husband and daughter and resolved to try and enjoy the evening. She had so much to be thankful for, surely she could be pleasant to Pete's friend for a few more weeks.

Dinner was delicious, the fish grilled to perfection, fresh potatoes, corn and tomatoes on the side. Tyler limped from grill to the picnic table, serving up the food with a flourish. There was wine for Ali, beer for Pete and a pink creamsicle for Nevra.

Ali, a smile pasted on her face, had to acknowledge that Nevra certainly liked 'Uncle' Tyler. And children, like dogs, were supposed to have good instincts.

Maybe she should have brought Emily along too, she thought wryly.

Pete started thumbing through the pile of books on the coffee table. He read out some titles. *"Smuggling on the Great Lakes," "Drowned Fortunes" "The Booze Bonanza."* Planning your next career?" he joked.

"I wish," Tyler laughed. "The area was a goldmine, especially during Prohibition. There must have been tons of booze dropped in the lake, maybe scuttled cash boxes too."

"Think you'll find something? Next you'll be telling me you're becoming an Arrowhead."

"You never know," Tyler laughed. "But what the hell, I need something to take my mind off my foot."

Oh yes, his poor foot, Ali thought

In the kitchen, having carried plates and cutlery there against Tyler's polite protests, she wondered whether to mention seeing him in Bonville. Pete and Nevra were playing catch on the lawn, it was a good opportunity.

She watched him hopping around, fetching the coffee things. Her heart beat rapidly. If Tyler did lie, would she have the nerve to challenge him? And how to begin? Even if he flatly denied being there, even if she said that she must have been mistaken, he would know that she *knew.*

And what would that mean? She could never take it back. Tyler could tell Pete that Ali was acting unpleasantly and then what?

Still, she was angry at the pretence, at the fact that he would try to fool Pete.

She took a deep breath, and blurted it out. "By the way Tyler, I saw you in Bonville the other day. I would have said hello but I was in my car."

He carefully finished rinsing a glass and handed it to her. "What day was that?" he asked.

"Wednesday," she said. "You were walking along the street with some other men. Then you went into a restaurant."

He put another glass under the tap. "Oh yes, I'd been checking out the Bonville gym. My doctor suggested that I drop in there to supplement my therapy program. He thought I might be able to try some of the easier equipment. But that won't be for awhile yet."

She put the clean glass in the cupboard. "You were moving along so well, I'd think you had already graduated to the advanced equipment. You didn't even have your cane."

There it was out. She'd said it.

For a moment, he looked taken aback, then he smiled sheepishly.

"Heck, you've caught me out."

He looked quickly out at the lawn, then leaned confidingly towards her.

"I've been working on a surprise for Pete. I thought maybe sometime soon, I could just casually challenge him to some push-ups. Then I'd drop to the floor and do a couple before he could say anything."

He grinned and looked at her expectantly. "What do you think? Kinda silly I guess, but I can't wait to see the look on his face."

She didn't answer. Did he expect her to believe *that*? What a lame, hastily concocted explanation.

He looked embarrassed. "I guess it sounds like a stupid stunt to you. Shows the state I've got to, sitting around here with nothing to do."

She was considering how to answer, when Pete came into the kitchen, carrying Nevra under his arm. "Diaper change," he said cheerfully, then stopped on the threshold as if he sensed the tension in the air.

He gave her a *What have you said?* look.

Gave his wife that look, she thought. Not his buddy. She was hurt.

Later, at home, Pete whistled cheerfully as they got ready for bed.

"That was a nice day," he said. "And a great meal. Ty's a good cook."

Ali, unpinning her hair, agreed through a mouthful of pins. "Better than I am, that's for sure."

"Thanks for coming," Pete said. "It meant a lot to Ty. I know he rubs you the wrong way sometimes, some of the things he says. But he doesn't mean anything by it. It's just soldier, macho talk."

"I know." She shook out her hair as it fell in a soft curtain to her shoulders. "Though you have to admit, he is inclined to embroider his stories sometimes. That one tonight about being surprised by an enemy patrol. You've told me all about that same incident and it wasn't nearly so dramatic – they were only a couple of kids."

He dropped a kiss on the top of her head.

"They did have machine guns. Besides, everybody dresses the details up to make a better story. I do it, even you do it my sweet."

Ali laughed. "What? You mean you don't believe my every word about our darling little daughter?"

"Not when you tell me she can read at a year and a half."

"I said she knows the letter N, the first initial in her name."

"Whatever you say – but it sounds a bit like embroidering to me," he teased.

She didn't even want to get into telling Pete about seeing Tyler in Bonville. Walking along just fine and chatting with those other men. What on earth had he been up to? And why did that expression seem so apt.

She studied her own face in the mirror. Saw a sceptical woman, unconvinced. She certainly didn't buy that dumb story about surprising Pete. So, why would Tyler hide the fact that he had pretty well recovered from his injuries? Why wouldn't he be proud, be happy? Instead he was sneaking around, concealing his activities, acting really like some kind of criminal.

What would he have to hide, she wondered. Not a romance. He had no ties, he was free to date whoever he wanted. Maybe he was buying drugs! Yes, that could be it, she'd been naïve. Pete had told her that a lot of the solders had smoked dope in Afghanistan. Well, that wasn't so bad. Possessing small amounts of dope wasn't even considered much more than a fining offense in Canada. And who knew, maybe the stuff had even been helping in Tyler's recovery. It was being used medicinally now.

She was glad she hadn't said anything more to Pete. He was a steadfast man and she loved that about him. So she shouldn't be surprised that he was a steadfast friend.

Her mind relieved, she turned out the light.

30

All cities have their sleazy sides, most towns do too. At some imperceptible point on the main street, the storefronts and buildings start to look run-down, alleyways more forbidding, as if the sun never shone there. Bonville was no New York, with entire city blocks harbouring the unfortunates and those who prey on them, but it did have its homeless and mindless, its streetcorner and doorway drug merchants.

Trouble was, Officer Pete Jakes was no undercover Serpico and a clean-cut appearance was only a disadvantage when seeking out drug dealers. Not to mention an actual police uniform. He'd been sent to make inquiries. Turned out that the chief and Art Storms had been too optimistic about the extent of the drug smuggling activity to the east. New information revealed that the smuggling operation had actually spread its tentacles far down to their end of the lake.

Detective Anderson, Halstead's contact in the Cornwall detachment, had sounded philosophical.

"Sure we've broken up one smuggling ring, but there's always another operation cropping up somewhere else. We'll never put them all out of business."

According to Anderson, the drugs were being manufactured or grown in grow op houses in Ontario, then driven to contacts in various local marinas. The drugs were then taken by boat in a run across the lake to any of innumerable hiding places on the States side. In fact, it was possible that some of the product was originating from farms north of Bonville and being trafficked through the city marinas.

"How often are they making these runs?" Halstead had asked. "And how big are the operations?"

They could hear the shrug in Anderson's voice.

"Getting bigger all the time, that's for certain. It's no longer the nutty kid heading out into the lake with his waterproof pack full of weed. We're working with the police over there, trying to find where the boats land and make contact with the U.S. dealers. But it's a never-ending job."

No one yet had found a connecting link to Bonville and environs. However, this time when Pete brought up the question of where Mel Todd got his money, the chief was willing to listen. Armed with a photo of Todd, Jakes had started out, trying a couple of downtown bars. It seemed a logical place to begin.

Passing by the Barista, he stopped outside for a moment, thinking of Fran Reilly. The last time they'd met, he had been the bearer of very bad news. The visit to Cathy Sedore had been even more difficult. At least Wes Sedore had left good insurance policies, a good father and provider to the end.

Now Fran winced when Pete came into the café.

"You got more bad news for me officer?"

He shook his head. "I'm surprised to see you back at work."

Fran shrugged. "I have to do something. And it's worse just hanging around at home with the cat. She isn't a whole lot of company."

She waved the pot in her hand. "Are you staying for coffee – it's fresh."

"No, but thanks." He opened the brown envelope he'd brought with him. "Actually, I'd like you to look at a picture for me and tell me if you've ever seen this man."

The photo wasn't great – a copy from a *Record* story three years ago, about the cancelling of the commercial fishermen's licenses.

Two hundred years of family livelihood ends, read the front page story headline. There was an interview with Mel Todd and the photo, a grainy shot of a grizzled sixty-two year old man in a battered Maple Leaf baseball cap.

Fran wrinkled her nose. "Looks as if he could use a session at the dog grooming parlour up the street. They'd trim the hair and nails and perfume him up right smart."

"Afraid that wouldn't help him now." He explained, saying only that Todd had drowned in an unfortunate accident.

She gave the picture another look. "There's a few rummies who hang around Main Street. It's hard to tell them apart. But I'm pretty sure I never saw this man. Why do you ask?"

"He might have been selling drugs. Crystal meth, ecstasy, some dope. Nothing big, just small bags."

She bristled at that. "And you think I would know about that? What kind of a dive do you think this is?"

"All kinds of people take drugs," he said mildly. "You know that. What about Wes and the other band members. Ever sniff a little coke?"

She frowned. "I thought you caught the creep who killed Wes. I hope he gets put away forever. So why are you still sniffing around asking questions?"

"Just chasing up some loose ends," Pete said.

She shrugged. "Maybe a couple of the band members might smoke a little dope," she said. Who doesn't these days? – it's even legal in some countries you know. But Wes would be the last guy to be into those other drugs. He was always interested in eating healthy, hiking in the woods, nature stuff."

She paused, tearing up. Then she swiped her eyes and turned abruptly to the coffee machine.

"Was there anything else?" she asked over her shoulder.

"Thanks for your time," he said.

He wondered if she would still go to Spain.

* * *

The Bonville waterfront was a lively sight in the summer sunshine. The various marinas bobbed with yachts and smaller craft, and sailboats skimmed merrily across the Bay waters in an obliging breeze. A string of bright yellow and blue pennants announced the August Waterfront Festival while across the causeway, the Canadian flag rippled on the flagpoles at Middle Island.

Pete parked the cruiser in the shade of a newly-planted maple and scanned the dock till he spotted the boxy green shape of the auxilliary coast guard training boat. Kids seemed to be swarming all over it. When he got closer, he could see that the young people were carrying paint cans and brushes. There were four boys and two girls, all in their late teens, all in t-shirts, shorts and baseball caps.

"Hi," he called out. "Is Mr. Storms around?".

One of the boys looked over his shoulder towards the shore. "Art's at the shop getting some stuff —no here he's coming back now."

Storms swung along the dock, carrying a roll of plastic sheeting and a gallon jug of paint thinner.

"Hey Jakes," he hailed Pete. "What brings you over to the big city?"

"Have you got a minute?"

"Sure. Just let me unload this stuff and check out my faithful crew. Make sure they haven't painted over the wheelhouse windows." A couple of the kids groaned at the joke.

After a minute, Storms joined Pete on the dock. They walked a bit away from the boat to talk. "So what's up?" Storms asked curiously.

"Nothing probably," Pete admitted. "I've just been checking out a crazy idea I had."

"A lot of police work, amounts to checking out crazy ideas," Art said. "So, shoot."

"I was wondering if Mel Todd ever brought his boat over here."

"Mel?" Art shook his head. "Maybe long ago. But I doubt that he'd been over this way in the past few years."

"Did Todd have a car? Did he ever drive to Bonville?"

"Na, he had a truck once, but Bud ordered that off the road a couple of years ago. It was a public menace," he laughed, "Held together with baling wire."

A blast of rock music came from the dock, scaring away a couple of seagulls. Storms winced and looked back toward the painting crew. "I swear every time I leave that boat, the volume goes up on those speakers. But why all the interest in Todd?"

Pete shrugged. "He'd come into some money before he died. Transporting drugs is one way to earn money quickly."

Art laughed, a big guffaw. "You're barking up the wrong tree there, Jakes. A drinker like Mel Todd could barely organize a trip into Middle Village from the Point, let alone run a drug operation."

He slapped Pete on the shoulder. "Come on up to the Inn for a beer. You look kinda hot."

A fit, middle-aged couple in sailing whites waved and said hello as they took a table on the outdoor patio. "They came in from Rochester yesterday," Storms said. "Asked me over to their boat for a drink."

He ordered a couple of beers and popped one of his nicotine gums. "Yessir, I do like summer life on the boats. People are friendly, it's a different life than on land. We've all got something in common, we love boats."

Pete looked out at the vibrant harbour scene and couldn't help contrasting it to his own lonely city-bound summers. He wished he'd had a father or an uncle like Art, a boat man, living outside in the open air. Rather than drying up in a government office as his own father had done. They could have travelled every summer on the water, relied on each other, got to know each other. Instead, after Pete's mother died, they lived as two lonely satellites in a cheerless apartment. Until Pete left.

* * *

He spent the afternoon diligently showing Mel Todd's photo to the staff at twenty-odd other likely Bonvillle establishments with no results. Wearily, he returned to the Middle Island station, his clothes and hair redolent of stale beer, burger grease and fried onions.

Halstead, comfortable in his swivel chair and air-conditioned office, wasn't encouraging.

"I'm with Art on this one," he said. "I can see Mel Todd doing a bit of bootlegging down at the Point, the fishermen always did some of that. But I can't see him handling drug runs on some kind of regular basis. He just wouldn't have been that reliable."

Pete wasn't convinced. "I doubt these big drug guys can afford to be that picky. It's not as if there are a lot of honest, reliable, stand-up types to choose from."

"They still have to be careful," Halstead pointed out. "Loose lips sink ships as they said during the war. And loose tongues can lead to an unhealthy interest from the police."

"What about the money?" Pete asked. "Mel Todd didn't find that money in a bag on the street. And he was expecting more to come his way."

Halstead nodded, acknowledging the point. "Keep at it, then. Maybe somebody else heard about Todd's recent wealth, and it was a robbery gone wrong. But it's unlikely that there's any connection between Todd's death and Sedore's murder. Tice killed Sedore and the crown won't have any trouble making the case."

Pete sighed and got to his feet. "It must be tough on the daughter," he said. "She lost her mother and maybe now her father. I hope she's got some family left, somewhere to go."

Halstead nodded. "Yeah, well at least she's got a mighty fine boat to get her there."

31

"Ten dozen burgers, ten dozen buns, ketchup, mustard, relish," Stephanie Bind counted off items on her list.

"Five cases of canned lemonade," Ali continued. "Five cases of bottled water...." She broke off. "Do you think we're actually going to get that number of people Steph?"

"Sure we will. Beth's done a great publicity blitz. We've got posters out all over Bonville and announcements on all the radio and tv public service listings. We're going to be a big hit."

Community support from their fellow Islanders had been heartening. Foremost was Benny Sorda's donation of the use of his catering unit for the day. Powered by its own generator and equipped with a cooking grill, water well and freezer, the truck would be an essential part of the day's activities. A local farmer was donating several bushels of his newly ripe corn crop. Steph and the others wouldn't even pick the corn till the night before the picnic, then have a husking bee to get ready for the next day.

When they'd stored the meat in the Retreat's big freezer and stacked the non-perishable items into boxes for travelling, the two women sat with glasses of iced tea on Steph's pretty patio.

Steph noticed Ali looking at her watch and smiled indulgently. "It's barely two. Another hour to go."

"Caught me out," Ali said, looking embarrassed. It was Nevra's first full day at the sitter's. They were trying the arrangement out, in preparation for Ali's return to teaching work in the fall.

"How did Nevra like being there yesterday?" Steph asked.

Ali sighed, "She loved it. Tracey is wonderful and there were the other kids to play with."

Steph, laughed, "You sound disappointed."

"Not really," Ali smiled ruefully. "I'm glad that Nevra likes the change. She's ready, I just don't know if I am. But don't worry, in my other moments, I know I'll be glad to see my students again. I'll be fine."

She stretched her arms, shaking off her motherly anxieties. "I know you're busy with bookings, are you and Bud going to get any time away this summer?"

"Probably not till the fall," Steph said. "Summer is always a busy time for policemen – as you know! Most people are good, but there are always some idiots out there too."

"Lots of bad people too," Ali said. "Pete told me about all the drug smuggling that goes on."

"Of course that's wrong," Steph said, "but I wonder what Bud would think of some of my shopping sprees in the States."

She laughed guiltily, "When I was in highschool, my friends and I would always come back across the border, wearing a couple of extra sweaters or hiding a pair of new shoes in our backpacks. I'm sure that the guards knew. Why else would Canadians be rushing over to the Syracuse Mall on the day they've advertised a big sale?"

Ali didn't comment. Only three years ago she had been living in a war-torn country where crossing a border could mean the difference between life or death, and she was still amazed at the Canadian cavalier attitude towards crossing the U.S. border.

Conversation returned to details of the picnic. Steph and Joan would be serving burgers at the truck, while Ali, in her pirate outfit, supervised the children's fish pond. Beth's two teenage granddaughters were running the ring toss and other heritage games. For those who preferred to sit in a cool spot, there would be a canopy tent where people could ask Miranda questions about the project, buy a raffle ticket on the painting, a membership, or make a donation to the project.

"Maybe next year people will be able to climb the tower," Steph said. "But at least Wayne's shored up the staircase well enough so that you and I and Pete will be able to scoot up there and light the lamps."

Perhaps someday, it would be possible to find and purchase an original fixture for the lighthouse but for now they had decided to go ahead with the hurricane lamps.

"It's symbolic of our dream," as Steph said. "There will be a light in the tower again, if only for that night. I'm sure the people down below will be impressed."

"As long as it doesn't rain," Ali said. The Island skies had been a clear, blazing blue for nearly two weeks, but Beth had gloomily predicted that it couldn t last. Apparently her aunt's rheumatism never lied.

"It won't rain," Steph said decisively. "Phooey to Beth' s aunt."

She picked up her event binder. "So," she summed up, "we'll get there about eight a.m. and set up the tables and awnings. Tyler said he'd spell Joan and I at the food truck."

"If he actually arrives," Ali said. "He hasn't exactly kept up with the meetings."

"He told Beth that his physio appointments always conflict," Steph said. "It was the only time the therapist could slot him in."

Ali's shrug was eloquent.

Steph gave her a keen look. "I notice that you aren't exactly crazy about your Mr. Cotes."

Ali smiled weakly. "I should try harder to hide my feelings. It's getting difficult to hide them from Pete." She made a face. "What a mess, I can't stand my husband's best friend."

Steph smiled wryly. "You're not always going to be thrilled with your husband's friends, sweetie. For instance, it's fine with me that Bud likes to go on his own for morning coffee down at the Grill. He's welcome to his 'man' time as far as I'm concerned."

"What do you think they talk about?" Ali asked. "When I ask Pete, he just says 'stuff'."

Steph laughed. "Bud says he's keeping his finger on the pulse of the community but I know he loves to natter with Gus and the old fellows about the hockey or soccer game or whatever other boring sport that's on the TV."

"But that's not really the same," Ali said. "You don't dislike the Grill fellows, you just don't want to spend your time talking sports."

Steph frowned, and said seriously. "Tyler hasn't acted improperly has he, made a pass at you?"

"No, nothing like that," Ali said hastily. "He's always polite, nothing remotely close to flirting." She laughed shortly, "He probably doesn't like me either."

Steph patted her hand. "The good thing is that Tyler Cotes will actually be leaving at some point – going back to the army. So your problem will be going away."

Ali nodded and tried to sound convinced. "Yes, my problem will be going away."

* * *

Humming as she drove, Ali wasn't paying much attention to the radio. She was looking forward to seeing Nevra, and getting that special 'here's Mommy" smile. At least she could laugh at herself and her fretting. She might as well be one of Miranda's mother hens fussing over a chick.

The news came on and she reached to change the dial. Maybe it was just superstitious but she didn't want to hear the weather report. Or maybe it would be better if it would rain now, she thought, at least it would be out of the way.

Then she paused, her attention caught by the newscaster's words. He was talking about a new development in the recent smuggling case. The police now suspected that some of the drugs in question were coming from somewhere north of Bonville, then being moved by boat over to the United States. Pete had mentioned that possibility too, something about a local connection, but she had been busy bathing Nevra and not really listening.

A chill settled on her shoulders, despite the warmth of the afternoon. She switched off the radio but the words kept resonating in her head.

A local connection. A Bonville connection.

Could it be Tyler Cotes?

The thought had leapt full-blown into her mind.

Because it was already half-way there, she realized. Lurking in some part of her mind. She just hadn't acknowledged it.

Tyler had a boat, he had constant, unexplained 'appointments' in Bonville.

No one was keeping track of his movements. He could pretty well go or be anywhere he wanted, at any time.

Tyler was a perfectly fit man, and had been for some time. Yet for some reason he'd been hiding the fact.

She shook her head violently, as if she could physically rid herself of these thoughts. She mustn't let her dislike of the man taint her judgement.

But the pictures wouldn't go away.

She felt dizzy for a moment and pulled the car over to the side of the road. She was sorely tempted to drive back to the Retreat and confide her suspicions to Steph but pushed the thought away. She needed time to think. Besides, Steph would probably think she was crazy.

No, if she was going to talk to anyone, it would have to be Pete. It wouldn't be fair if he heard from someone else that she had been gossiping about his friend. But how could she tell him, would he believe her?

The thought that he wouldn't, the thought of how hurt he would be, made her stomach lurch. She would have to wait until she was absolutely certain. She would have to have undeniable proof.

* * *

Pete had made a treasure chest for the doubloons, modelling it on one of the illustrations in Stevenson's book.

"How's this?" he asked, proudly bringing it into the living room. He'd painted the chest black, with bands painted in gold-metallic paint.

"That's wonderful!" Ali said. "You're getting kind of handy."

He was new to carpentry, had never been anywhere long enough in his nomadic army days to collect the tools. But now through birthday and Christmas presents, in addition to his own happy prowls through the hardware store, he was gradually building up a workshop in the shed behind the kitchen.

He liked the tangy smell of cut wood, the precise work. And as Ali said, he was rapidly getting the hang of it. She still treasured his first carpentry job though, a bird house he'd made for her when they were expecting Nevra. The roof tilted a bit but the winter juncos didn't seem to mind.

She'd experimented with different ideas for the doubloons. In the end, she'd cut cookie-sized pieces of cardboard and wrapped them in gold foil that she got at the dollar store in Bonville. She'd made about fifty, and now piled them up on a piece of purple velvet in the chest.

"Pretty neat," Pete said as they admired their joint project. "Long John Silver himself would be impressed."

Each coin was marked with a number. They were going to be hidden about the picnic ground and could be turned in for ice-cream cones and small prizes.

"Tyler said he would give me a hand hiding them," Ali said. "But I doubt it's going to happen. He was all gung-ho at first but he hasn't been coming to meetings lately."

Pete, checking the clasp on the chest, said absently. "I guess he's too busy."

"You mean he's out in his boat a lot. Does he talk to you much about where he goes?" she asked.

"Not much," Pete said, satisfied with the chest. "Like me, I think he just likes being out on the water." He smiled. "It's all that time patrolling out on the desert, makes us thirsty."

She decided to take a different tack. She had finished sewing her pirate costume and now tried it on. Baggy striped pants, puffy sleeved blouse, suede vest, a red kerchief tying back her hair. The final touch, a foil-covered cutlass that she tucked in at her belt.

"Well, what do you think?"

He whistled, "You can shanghai me any time, madame pirate."

She dimpled. "I think the term shanghai came along later."

After a fun interlude that involved some adjusting of her new outfit, she sipped wine and asked casually how the smuggling investigation was going.

He frowned. "It's tricky," he said. "Not straightforward work at all. And we'll probably never even get near the guys at the top of the chain anyway"

"But the Cornwall police have already broken up a ring," she said. "They've made arrests, there will be charges. What kind of penalties will those people get?"

"Oh the sentences will be pretty stiff," Pete said. "Years anyway. Sometimes as much as ten or fifteen."

She whistled. "The smugglers must start out thinking it's worth the risk. – I guess there's a lot of money to be made, even for the lower levels."

"Maybe not so much for them. But for the big risk takers, millions." Pete said.

"What percentage of drug dealers get caught, do you think. Most of them?"

"Only about twenty percent. But don't let the news get out." He grinned. "Why all the questions? Are you thinking of getting into the business?"

She raised her brows, "You never know. Nevra might be an aspiring pianist and need a baby grand to practise on. Or she might want to go to Oxford University, which might be a bit rich for parents on a policeman's and a teacher's salaries."

"She'll get a scholarship," Pete said. "And we can save our money to go and visit her."

She laughed uneasily, thinking of what he'd said about the drug dealers. It was only logical that the biggest risk takers would get the biggest rewards. And from the stories he told, it sounded as if risk-taking had been a hallmark of Tyler Cotes' army career.

32

"Hello, can I help you?" Jane Carell asked kindly.

She recognized the Tice girl, who was unfortunately well talked about in the village. She was a foreigner (not an Islander), she was pretty, and apparently her father was a murderer. Your basic, unbeatable combination of gossip material.

Regrettably, Jane had indulged in some of the gossip herself. Perhaps to make up for that, she widened her smile and tried to make the girl's visit to a police station as welcoming as possible. Miss Tice wore a denim skirt and a light blue tank top that contrasted nicely with her all-over tan, and she didn't look much older than Jane's own twenty year old neice.

"Can I help you?" she asked again.

The girl looked hastily around the room, as if regretting coming in, then crossed to the counter.

"My name is Keri Tice," she said, "and I would like to speak with a policeman."

* * *

Halstead looked at the photos spread out on his desk, then looked quizzically past the girl to Jakes.

Pete leaned forward. "You say you took these photos from your father's I-pod."

"Yes," she nodded eagerly. "They wouldn't let him take his I-pod into the jail but I got to thinking there might be some evidence there to help him. I went to the boat and I found these."

The pictures were taken from a boat deck, presumably the *Finders Keepers*. Some showed merely the green treetops of a shoreline in the distance. But a half dozen of the photos showed a large buoy tethered in the water. There was a number stencilled on the buoy and time and date notations at the bottom of the shots.

Keri looked at the two men with hopeful brown eyes. "I checked with the National Data Buoy Centre and found the co-ordinates for that buoy. If you look it up on their map you'll see it's not anywhere near South Island."

She pointed to the time and date notations. "And these show that Dad was in the area for several hours that night. So it's just as he's been saying, that he wasn't at South Island at that time. Josh and I are going to take the *Finders Keepers* out there and look for the actual spot."

Halstead winced. The girl didn't seem to know that Tice could have killed Wes Sedore almost any time during that night. The autopsy of Sedore's water-logged body couldn't be any more accurate than that.

But he hated to rain on her hopes. Let her have them for a night at least. He thanked her for coming in to the station and said they would confirm her identification on the buoy as soon as possible.

She stood, nervously clasping the strap of her denim knapsack. "My Dad would hate for me to be doing this," she said. "He was even mad that I let you interview me without having his lawyer there. But I wanted you to have this information."

Her face lit with passionate conviction. "I know that you're just doing your job but I also *know* that my father wouldn't kill anybody. It must have been somebody else. It *must* have been."

"Well?" Halstead asked, when Jakes had ushered Keri Tice out. "She seems a nice kid but I'm afraid there's not much we can do for her. Do we even believe her about these photos? She'd do anything to point the murder away from her father."

"The photos look genuine," Pete said. "I'm sure they're O.K."

Halstead scoffed. "I thought you could fake anything on a computer these days."

"I'll check her information on that buoy with the National Data Buoy Centre," Pete said. "That's straightforward enough."

"And what will that prove?"

"Maybe that Tice has finally got a lead on those plane models," Pete said absently. He had picked up a magnifying glass and was studying a couple of the other photos.

"This is interesting," he said. "If you look real hard at these pictures of the distant shoreline, you can see a couple of boats sitting just off shore."

"So?" Halstead asked. "There's lots of boats out on the water this time of year."

"I don't see any cottages or homes on the shore there," Pete said. "Could be that the buoy is a meeting place."

Halstead leaned over his shoulder to look. "Probably just folks fishing. Can you make out any identifying marks? Registration number, anything like that.".

"It's all pretty small," Pete said. "But looks as if one of the boats has a wide blue stripe along the bow."

"Could be the 98 SpeedCrest," Halstead said. "It had a big blue stripe."

Pete looked up. "No kidding? That could be useful"

Halstead shook his head. "Not really. The SpeedCrest is a very popular boat and that was a popular model. What about a registration number – can you make that out? Should be on both sides of the prow."

"No, nothing."

"Like I said, probably just folks fishing."

Pete straightened up. "I downoaded the girl's pictures on our computer. I'm going to work on them and see if can get a better magnification."

Halstead gave the photos a last dismissive glance. "Sure, you can check out that buoy number, but it's not going to help Tice any."

Jane couldn't hear anything through the interview room wall and had to wait until Keri left to get the scoop.

"Well?" she asked, carrying a file into the room, though neither man was fooled about why she was there.

"Pete's going to call a man about a buoy," Halstead said.

But Pete meant to do a little checking on boat registrations too.

* * *

A peaceful Wednesday night supper at the Retreat. Steph had spent the afternoon planning the *Coming Home to Your True Selves* arrangements for August but the Retreat was quiet this week, apart from the regular morning tai chi classes. Over dessert, newly-picked raspberries from the garden, they watched the evening entertainment at the shore. A family of swans foraging in the cattails, the cygnets comically gawky with unkempt shaggy heads.

Halstead should have been content, but found he couldn't leave the day's work behind. "I don't like this drug stuff coming near my Island, Steph. What's the matter with kids today, isn't the discovery of sex exciting enough to last for a couple of years anyway?"

She laughed. "Come on, Bud. We had our diversions too, still do." She looked pointedly at his beer mug and her wine glass.

"You know what I mean, Steph. Now booze isn't enough for these kids either. They're going to be burnt out by the time they're twenty. Can you imagine a kid these days who would get a kick out of stealing an apple?"

She laughed and patted his shoulder. "Only if it was the latest I-pod gadget!"

* * *

Nuran had sent Nevra a new bedtime book. In the story, a little bunny talked of running away from home, but the mother bunny always found ways to keep him safe. Nevra didn't understand many of her books yet, but she liked to turn the pages and look at the pictures. Ali kissed her goodnight and turned on the night light. She hoped it would be a good long time before Nevra got any ideas about running away from home to seek new adventures.

Downstairs Pete was loading the dishwasher.

"I thought you were dropping in on Tyler tonight," she said.

"He s away, remember. He s gone to the city to deal with something about his rehabilitation leave compensation."

That s what he says, anyway, she thought. *Heaven knows what he's really up to.*

Pete mentioned Keri Tice's visit to the station.

"Poor girl," said Ali. "How is she doing?"

"About as well as you could expect, under the circumstances. I imagine it's pretty tough for her."

"Why did she come in to the station?" Ali asked curiously.

He explained about the pictures.

"That sounds interesting," she said. "She sounds like a smart girl. Will the pictures help her father's case?"

"I don t think so," he said. "Unfortunately Keri Tice has nothing concrete to help her father, no corroboration other than her loyalty." He handed her a plate. "And that's not enough."

It's enough for you, Ali thought. *Enough for you to hear nothing bad about Tyler.*

But she merely said mildly, "I'm off to Miranda's, we've got some more picnic day details to go over."

She left Pete starting up a video featuring Sly Stallone as a cop. It was one of his favourites, with lots of gunfire, car chases and explosions. Not exactly cheery fare for a summer night, but Pete actually found these movies funny. And oddly helpful, when he was working through something puzzling such as the recent case. He said it was comforting, if fanciful, that the police always triumphed.

As she walked down the driveway in the softly enveloping dusk, the sounds of a screeching, careening car chase came drifting from her living room window. She smiled affectionately. Runaway bunnies, cops who always win. We all need our stories.

And what about Ali Jakes, she thought more soberly. So far the story of her love and marriage had been as pretty as a fairy tale. But what to do now about that lurking huntsman, Tyler Cotes? Was she, like the over-curious princess in the tale, about to bring about her own doom?

But enough of this dreadful indecision. Pete had said that Tyler was away in the city. Tomorrow she would stop at the Peterson's Marina to ask a few pertinent questions. Then she would drive to Cedar Grove and search the cabin – for those nautical maps, for the discarded foot cast, perhaps even for hidden drugs or cash. Tomorrow, for better or worse, she would find the information to make her case.

33

Edna Peterson sat on a lawn chair in front of the Marina, a copy of The Record on her lap and a big orange cat on top of both. Luckily, she had a biggish lap. She wore a fraying straw hat and a sleeveless shift dress in bright tropical colours that displayed her large freckled arms.

"Howdy Mrs. Jakes," she smiled. "Hot enough for you?"

"Just about," Ali agreed.

Edna patted the chair next to her, and reached into the cooler by her feet. "Take a load off. Have a cold one."

"Thanks, Edna. I will. I'm just going to put one of our Lighthouse posters up in the window first if that's O.K."

"Sure, honey. If there's no room left, just yank down that one about the lost dog. He came home a couple of weeks ago."

The window was so crammed with flyers and posters, some of them months out of date, that barely any light came through to the store. Ali cleared a spot and taped her poster up, glad that Beth had chosen a bright fluorescent green paper that caught the eye.

She reached into the cooler for a lemonade drink and joined Edna on the lawn. The view of the lake, with attendant wheeling gulls, was idyllic as usual, broken only by the grey green smudge of South Island. Ali kicked off her sandals and wiggled her toes.

"You don't have to retire, Edna," she said. "You've got it all right here."

Edna nodded contentedly and lazily stroked the cat. "I could do with a shorter winter," she said. "But other than that, I've got no complaints. I don't see how Sam and I could retire anyways. Most of the folks at this end of the island get their boat fuel here."

"So the summer is going well?" Ali asked.

"Busy as we want to be. Busier. The young lad's a big help with gassing up the boats. He'll probably take over the place someday but that's a ways off. He's still in high school now."

She smiled affectionately as the boy approached, wiping his oil-smeared hands on a rag. He was a lot skinnier and taller than either of his grandparents, Ali noted.

"Hey Grandma," he greeted her, from under his baseball cap.

Ralph came out of the house to join them. His doughy cheeks were creased and his white hair tufted, unmistakeable signs of a recent nap.

"How's it going down there, Jimmy? I see you selling lots of gas. What are the folks saying – are the fish biting today?"

The boy nodded. "Yeah, the walleye are good over in the Bay. Some guy got a ten--pounder this morning."

Ralph whistled, "I hope he took a picture."

Ali laughed, "He probably put it on You Tube."

Jimmy made a face. "Grandma and Grandpa wouldn't know about that. I've been trying to teach them but it just don't take."

Ralph tousled his grandson's hair. "You see the sass we get?" he said to Ali. "Enjoy your little girl now before she gets old enough to give you the lip."

He cast an experienced eye at the docks. "I asked the fuel truck to come a day early, Jimmy. You're going to need more gas by tomorrow."

"I think that friend of Pete's probably gets his gas here," Ali said. "Do you know him?"

"Sure," Jimmy said. "That guy from Cedar Grove. He comes by a lot."

"He sure uses a lot of gas," Ralph mused. "I told him where the good fishing is by Harrison's Inlet but he wouldn't use up all that gas just going there."

"Likely thinks he's found a better spot," Jimmy said. "You can't tell these city fellers anything. They always got to know better."

Then, realizing who he was talking to, he looked embarassed. "Sorry, ma'am".

"That's alright," Ali said. "I know what you mean."

I know exactly what you mean. said her little inside voice. *That describes Tyler perfectly.*

"I don't think Mr. Cotes is fishing much when he goes out," she added. "Pete says he's got some book on the old smuggling days and he's checking out the sites."

Edna snorted. "Looking for treasure, likely. I know that book and the story about the rum smugglers tossing bags of money overboard. And I know the feller who wrote it. He's long gone now, but I bet he's laughing up his sleeve, thinking of all those people he set to searching for that bag of money."

Ralph laughed. "I lost a toonie down by the dock yesterday. That's about the only money anybody is ever going to find in that lake."

"So Tyler goes out in the boat a lot?" Ali asked.

"Most every day," Jimmy said.

Probably meeting with his connection from up the lake, she thought.

Aloud, she asked."Is he away for a long time?"

Jimmy shrugged. "Sometimes. Other times only a couple of hours."

She wanted to ask if Tyler ever took the boat out at night but Ralph was already beginning to look at her oddly.

She laughed weakly instead, "Hey Ralph, exactly where did you drop that toonie?"

* * *

Tyler's blue Honda rental was parked at Cedar Grove. So he was back from the city. That kind of put a crimp in her plans.

She had an excuse for the visit, to put up a copy of the new picnic poster on the communal bulletin board, but she could hardly go in and search the cabin if Tyler was there. Perhaps he was out in the boat though, she could at least find that much out.

Still, she lingered in the car. If Tyler was at home in the cabin, she didn't feel like running into him. She doubted she could hide her suspicions much longer and if he actually was this drug connection the Cornwall police were looking for, he could even be dangerous. That was a very unpleasant thought.

But he could be dangerous to Pete too, said her little inside voice. *You can't just leave it like this. What are you going to do?*.

Then she jumped, literally, as a voice sounded at her window.

Tyler! Leaning chattily into the car, his tanned, smiling face only inches away.

She was so panicked for a second, that at first she couldn't make out what he was saying. She smiled inanely, nodding her head.

"Hey there," she heard. "Lucky you caught me, I just got back about an hour ago. How's everything going with the Lighthouse group?"

Numbly, she handed over the poster.

"Looks great," he said, scanning it quickly. "Sorry I missed the last meeting, I had to go to the city to do some army paperwork about my foot."

He lifted his sneakered foot up nearly as high as the car window and flexed the ankle, winking at Ali. "I still need a bit more practice before doing those push-ups – you haven't told Pete yet?"

She shook her head. He winked again, as if she should enjoy being a party to his dumb prank. In fact, he looked scarily fit to her and ready to go back into full combat action.

He gave the car hood a hearty parting thump, "Say hi to the old man for me. Tell him to come out some night soon."

He didn't seem to have noticed that she hadn't spoken a word.

Frightened, she drove away.

She *had* to speak to someone, she simply had to.

34

Halstead sat at his desk, his gaze drifting to the window and the cornfield with its Van Gogh colours of gold and green. From farther afield came the muted sound of a tractor, like the drowsy, hypnotic drone of a giant bee. He pushed aside the pile of government bafflegab on the desk, his eyelids getting droopy.

Jane's voice, calling from the front counter, broke into his reverie. "A visitor for you, Chief."

There followed a gentle knock on his cubicle window. "Chief?"

Ali Jakes. A vision always worth waking up for. Her hundred candle watt smile lit the room. Today she wore a lime green cotton shift that set off her honey-coloured skin and she'd gathered her long black hair up off her elegant neck. An eastern princess in a green baseball hat.

He scrambled to his feet and indicated the other chair. "Ali, what a nice surprise."

"Pete's not here," he said when she was seated. "Is there something I can do for you?"

She nodded and reached into the bag she carried. "I've just been to the Municipal Offices and picked up the permit papers for our Lighthouse Day picnic. Apparently you have to sign them too, if you don't mind."

"Not at all. Hand them over and I'll have a look-see. I don't imagine you're requesting crowd control."

"You never know," she said lightly. "We wouldn't turn away a crowd – we badly need the money."

"You and Steph and the others are doing a great job," he said. "If that lighthouse is saved, it will be because of your efforts."

"Thanks Bud." Her smile dimmed a bit. She leaned forward in the chair, her fingers playing with the handle of the bag she carried.

"Actually I wanted to speak to you about something else, if you have a minute."

He took note of her tense, determined stance. She seemed to be nerving herself up to something. He hoped fervently there was no trouble in the Jakes' household and if there was, he was reluctant to hear about it. He was fond of the young family.

"Sure," he said, hiding his own uneasiness. "What's up?"

Again with the finger twisting. "I feel terrible even talking about him like this ….," she began. "Even for *thinking* such a thing."

Now he was really worried. A policeman heard a lot of confidences in his career, some people seemed to think of a cop as a kind of priest. He knew the signs well.

He put up a staying hand. "I can see this is hard for you Ali," he said. "Maybe you'd prefer to talk to another woman. I'm sure that Jane …."

He got up as if to call her, but then Ali startled him with a small strangled laugh.

She tugged at his arm. "It's O.K. Bud, I'm not talking about Pete. It's someone else, his friend Tyler."

This was even worse!

She laughed again at the look on his face. "Please sit," she said. "I'll try to make sense now."

But after she'd explained, it was still pretty bad, though in a different way. He appreciated her dilemma.

"So, to sum up," he began. "You think that Cotes has been lying about his foot injury for some reason. That's he's actually able to move around just fine."

She nodded.

"More importantly, you think that he's been lying about his activities. He says he's been to physiotherapy appointments but instead he turns up unexpectedly at his cottage. You've seen books on smuggling and some navigation maps at his cabin. Apparently he's out in the boat a lot, supposedly looking for treasure."

She nodded again.

"And thirdly, you've seen him meeting with some shady characters in downtown Bonville."

She groaned with embarassment. "I didn't exactly say shady."

Then she said seriously. "I may be crazy, Bud. I hope I am. But I can't shake the idea. I have a gut instinct that something is wrong about the man. You must know about those instincts. Miranda says it's akin to a dog's hackles rising."

Yes he knew about that. The sort of instinct that had saved the life of many a policeman, and many a soldier.

She added plaintively. "Don't you think it's odd that he would have come to Middle Island at all? This is so definitely not Tyler Cotes' kind of place. I've even been wondering if it's possible that he had a smuggling connection already arranged."

"He knew Pete though," Halstead pointed out. "And he'd suffered a serious injury. That can affect even the toughest man's thinking, at least for a time."

"He hadn't seen Pete or been in touch with him for over three years," Ali reminded him. "No phone calls or even e-mails."

Halstead forbore commenting that men usually didn't maintain friendships in the same way women did. No cheery exchange of birthday cards and pictures of grandchildren. He himself had friends he'd met at various policing conferences in the U.S. They might not see each other for years, but picked up the connection easily enough to get together and chew the fat when they did meet.

"And if Tyler dislikes the Island so much why isn't he keen to get away?" Ali asked a little desperately. "Why is he hiding the fact that his foot is practically healed?"

She took a breath, calming herself. "I thought maybe you would have some way to do a little investigating Bud, without letting Pete know. Then if I'm wrong, and I pray I am, there's no harm done."

Halstead smiled reassuringly. "I appreciate that it was difficult for you to do this. I'll do what I can discreetly, but I'm pretty sure there's nothing for you to worry about."

She thanked him and left, looking relieved to have shared her burden.

Halstead sat for a while at his window. Despite his assurances to Ali, his policeman's antenna was on alert. He wondered just how sure Jakes could be of Cotes, an old buddy he hadn't seen for three years. And there was Ali's interesting idea that Cotes might have had a pre-arranged connection before coming to the Island.

He would have Jane run a records check.

35

"National Data Buoy Centre," said a pleasant female voice. "How can I help you?"

Pete checked his notes.

"A couple of questions," he said. "I'm interested in marker buoys at the eastern end of Lake Ontario."

"Certainly sir. But could you be a bit more specific? On the Seaway alone, we maintain ninety-nine lighted buoys. And there are many different navigational aids out there on the water. Coloured channel markers for instance. Green for the right side of the channel when leaving the harbour, red for the right side."

"This object is yellow," Pete said.

"Can you tell the size?" she asked. "Yellow is for special service markers, indicating danger or just to stay away. The weather buoys are usually bigger than the other markers."

"It's got a number painted on it," Pete added. "243-629."

"That's a weather buoy all right. You should call Environment Canada – they're responsible for placing and maintenance."

In his next call, Pete got a quick briefing on weather buoys which apparently were capable of measuring air temperature, wind speed, barometric pressure and wind direction. They also gauged water temperature, wave height and wave length period. They recorded all this information and then sent it via satellite to weather centres. No human intervention was required, other than setting up the system in the first place.

His informant, cheered no doubt by his interest, further told him that the buoys were yellow with a flashing yellow light at night. They were moored with chains and poly rope and were about a meter and a half in diameter. Moored weather buoys could also act as navigational aids. Interesting as all this was, Pete was by now chafing to check the identity and the location of his buoy.

"Yes," said the clerk when he had run the number through his computer system. "We've only got one weather buoy there. That's your 243-629."

He gave the co-ordinates, then added, "It's probably easier to say it's located just outside Hartland Cove."

Pete glanced at his map. Hartland Cove was about ten kilometers east of South Island. So that much of Keri Tice's information from her father's photos was correct. He doubted it would be as staightforward a task to identify the shadowy boat in the photos. He anticipated a long telephone wait. Better get a coffee first.

A half hour later, he reviewed his information.

In Ontario all pleasure craft powered by an engine 10 hp or more had to be licensed. The licenses were free and valid for ten years. The registration number allowed Search and Rescue operations access to information in an emergency. So, he'd headed resolutely on to the boat registry department. The premise sounded easy enough but was similar to checking for a car license plate with only part of the plate number. There were approximately two million pleasure boats registered in Canada, he learned, with an average of 100,000 new licenses granted annually!

There were strict rules regarding the numbering system. The number had to include the two letters of the province of registration, as in ON12345 for an Ontario owner, and the boat must be marked on both sides of the bow in block characters at least three inches high.

All reasonable requirements of a sensible system, that would work wonderfully if one did indeed have a number to work from.

Unfortunately, even after enlarging Keri Tice's photos and then poring over them with a magnifying glass, the best that Pete had been able to come up with with was a possible identification of the last two numbers as 04. Asssuming that the provincial identification letters were ON, that left three unknown numbers in the middle. Considering all the combinations available, that left a very big gap.

In the end the gap was insurmountable. He couldn't identify the boat, he just didn't have enough information. The SpeedCrest with its blue striped hull might as well be a ghost boat.

* * *

"There's the buoy," Keri said excitedly. "Stop the boat, Josh."

Josh brought the *Finders Keepers* alongside the bobbing yellow marker. It was about a metre high, floating on a circular base. Hanging over the side of the boat, Keri checked the buoy number with her notes.

"243-629!" she called back to Josh. "This is the one, this is it! This proves that Dad was telling the truth. This is where he was that night."

He didn't seem to share her excitement. "Now what?" he asked, when she straightened up.

She grinned, "Now we go diving, or at least I do."

He looked at the water. "It's a bit choppy."

"No it isn't," she said. "It's perfect."

"What's the depth?" he asked.

"Supposed to be about forty feet," she said. "No problem. Let me go down first and have a look."

He knew Keri well enough to know that there was no discouraging her when she was determined to do a thing. "O.K." he said, "but only for half an hour, then come back up and report."

"I'm taking the camera," she said determinedly. "If there's an answer down there, something that will help Dad, I'm going to find it."

She was in her gear of suit, tank and flippers in minutes. Then she flipped nimbly backwards off the boat rail. Twenty minutes later, Josh looked apprehensively at the spot where she had entered the water. Normally he was totally at ease both above or below surface, but this morning he found himself oddly spooked. He wondered why -- his surroundings couldn't be more familiar, the gentle rise and fall of the boat deck, the fresh smell of the water, the sun on his bare shoulders. The background setting of his life since his teens, ever since he'd discovered diving. No, nothing spooky there.

And he wasn't worried about Keri the water-baby either. She was as at home in the lake as he was.

Weather? His senses detected no danger there. The sky was clear, the forecast good. There wasn't much else to consider. The nearest land was merely a long strip of grey-green scrubby trees, a typical Ontario landscape. He couldn't see why people were always wanting to buy paintings of it. If the diving wasn't so good in the clear lake waters, he'd be just as glad to stay and work in the Bahamas year-round.

There were no other boats in the vicinity, the *Finders Keepers* bobbed alone in the water. But there was nothing strange about that. It wasn't as if they were floating in the middle of the ocean. Still, he couldn't shake the feeling, and looked around uneasily. Now he knew what was bugging him, he felt as if he was being watched.

But that was just plain dumb. Nobody was watching the *Finders Keepers*. What was there to see?

Keri resurfaced in exactly thirty minutes. As Josh pulled her into the boat, he saw that she was carrying something. It was a black plastic container about as big as a thermos.

She handed it to him, while she set about removing her mask.

"What the heck is this?" he asked. "Where did you find it?"

She pulled off the mask and took a big breath of air.

"Not down below," she said. "It was clipped under the weather buoy."

He turned the container over in his hands, looking for an opening.

"What about the plane models?" he asked. "Did you see anything?"

She shook her head. "I don't think so," she said. "I took some pictures, but I doubt that they'll show anything either."

He kept fiddling with the container, finally pressing a latch that popped open the top. Keri stood on tiptoe, peeping over his shoulder.

"Well, what is it?"

"Money," he said, pulling out a rolled stack of bills. "A whole lot of money."

"But what was it doing in the water?" Keri asked. "That's a dumb place to keep money. Haven't people heard of banks?"

Josh looked around at the distant line of trees, at the water now almost sinisterly quiet. "Some people don't use banks. Come on Keri, let's get out of here. It's not healthy to be holding this money. We'd better get this to the police as quickly as we can."

"Wait, Josh," she grabbed his arm. "Are you saying this is bad money?"

"It's not good money, that's for sure," he said impatiently. He headed for the wheelhouse. "It might even have something to do with that smuggling gang we heard about on TV. The buoy could be a drop-off spot and somebody could come by any time to pick the money up. Somebody dangerous."

Her face went white under the tan. "Maybe I should put the container back on the buoy."

"There might not be time," he said urgently. "Besides, if you didn't do it exactly right, they'd know somebody had found it."

Keri shivered despite the hot sun.

"Josh, I don't think we should tell the police at all. This will look even worse for Dad. They're likely to think that he was working with that smuggling gang. That he was out here to collect the money."

"Your father's been in jail for the past two weeks Keri, he wouldn't be picking up any money out here."

"I'm confused," she said, biting her lip. "I don't know what to do."

"Don't you understand Keri, if it's like you say and your Dad didn't kill that government guy, then someone *else* did. And we don't know who."

She started determinedly towards the stern. "I've decided. I'm going to put the canister back."

He looked at the dark line of trees. "Well hurry up about it. This is dangerous stuff to be mixed up in. I've got a feeling this is not a good place to be."

36

Stay away moon. Get behind those clouds. You're not supposed to be showing up tonight. Moonlight is not the smuggler's friend. Lucky it's not the old days with lighthouses all lit up on every point.

Best keep the boat motor quiet, at this part of the lake, coming near the buoy.

Where is it? That's the trouble with dark. It conceals you but also everything else.

Clouds darting like cormorants across the face of the moon.

Where was the other friggin' boat?

Tonight was different for some reason. Tonight he was imagining things, hearing things. A creaking sound coming from somewhere over the water. An eerie flapping of huge, wind-filled sails

As if one of those old ships was out there, what did they call them?

Yes, a brigantine. A brigantine full of pirates. That was a joke though, Because he was the pirate, as bad as any of them anyway.

Betraying friends, betraying trust.

He was glad he didn't have much farther to go to meet the other boat.

The shipments kept getting bigger, the runs more dangerous, than when he started out. He was glad he wouldn't have to do this for much longer. He'd have the dough he needed and he could kiss this job good-bye.

37

The mallard landed with a carefree splash in the water. Unlike the fish-seeking gulls, who entered the water seamlessly without disturbing a drop. Life on the water was so rich in the summer months. Pete had been a keen and diligent birder in the winter too, and it was always a pleasure to be greeted in a leafless and chilly woods with the chatter of chickadees or even the raucous warning of a jay. But there was no comparison with the sheer lavish abundance of summer birds living on and around the lake.

He now carried his binoculars with him at all times and today was rewarded with the spotting of a loon farther out on the water. But no, it was a cormorant. Just a cormorant, as the locals would say. It was the bird's misfortune, a curse even, to be considered ugly. At least on this side of the world, where sports fishermen annually demanded a cull of the birds.

But Pete had seen videos showing how Japanese fishermen had enjoyed a working arrangement with cormorants for centuries. The bird was venerated in poems and ceremonies for its fishing abilities. Now he chuckled as this fellow emerged, its feathers sticking up comically from the black head. The sight helped dispel some of the sinister water images that had filled his thoughts for the past few weeks.

"Duck stake-out again," was the chief's dry comment about Pete's bird-watching. "So long as you do it on your own time."

The term was apt enough, Pete thought. Basically you staked out a vantage point, then waited and watched for your subject to make an appearance. Of course the avian subjects weren't criminals. And he was eating a sandwich so he was technically on his lunch break. He'd been on police business this morning—somebody had stolen two five gallon containers of gas from a farmer's barn.

The farmer suspected his neighbour's son who had recently bought an old clunker car from a buddy and in the farmer's words 'was too damn lazy to make money to buy gas'. When Pete drove up the to the next farm to investigate, he found that the youth was also too damn lazy to hide the containers. His father said he would make the kid work his debt off before he drove the car again. Case solved and resolved. Pete only wished they were all that easy.

He'd parked the cruiser at one of his favourite bird-viewing spots, between the Petersons and the Cedar Grove cabins. Fisherman's Cove with its beached boats, was a few kilometers further south. Looking out over the water from this vantage point, he had a good view of all the usual suspects. The lake, both on surface and below was busy with life, which included rulers, predators, and victims. As in the world of humans. Because the lake wasn't always a bright, sparkling playground. At times it had much darker depths.

He scanned the far-off view of horizon and sky, then swung the glasses slightly to his left. And there it was. The small, rough-edged chunk of land that was South Island. Sticking up stubbornly alone in all that blue. Insignificant no longer, but a scene of mystery and now murder.

Sticking just as stubbornly in his own thoughts.

But Gerald Tice has been arrested, he could hear the chief say. *He's going to be convicted.*

Nevertheless, there were loose ends. The case was as complicated as the deceptive, cunning shoreline of the lake. A maze of inlets and secret concealing coves. But there was a trail running through all this, he was certain. And he would bet money that the smuggling connection was a part of that trail. He reached for the map on the car seat, the folds in the paper creased with much use. A map of the lake, the three islands and surrounding waterways, coves, bays and inlets. Because the water was where it all began and where this case was being played out.

Starting with Mel Todd's death, he was convinced of that. The fisherman who had lived in boats since he could first totter along the deck of his father's trawler. Who knew the lake shoreline as well as the lines in his own hand. Who died, leaving five thousand dollars stashed in his old boat.

He was sure that Todd had played a part in the smuggling. The trick was how to connect that up with the murder of Wes Sedore. Who else could have been near South Island that night? Oh to have a bird's eye view! Instead, he would have to soldier on with his limited human faculties.

So, dealing with the favoured scenario first.

Wes Sedore is on South Island.

Discovers Tice there, confronts him. Tice, in the grip of his uncontrollable temper, kills Sedore in a rage.

Did Keri Tice's find of the I-pod prove otherwise? Did the photos suggest instead, that Gerald Tice was busy searching for his precious airplane site, near the buoy. Maybe not, but say they did, who then killed Wes Sedore?

Extensive investigation had so far discovered no other likely suspect. Nothing the police had so far discovered, indicated that either Sedore's former wife, present girlfriend, workmates or bandmates had any motive to kill the man, let alone in a manner that would have involved a fair amount of planning and premeditation. If indeed any of those people had wanted to murder Sedore, it would seem quite a fantastic plan to kidnap the man and somehow spirit him away from South Island.

No, the plan to make it seem as if Sedore had simply disappeared was obviously an after-the-fact, poorly thought-out scheme cobbled together by a killer under stress. So the chief was probably right, Tice had killed Sedore. But could there be more to it, possibly some other motive, rather than mere simple rage?

He remembered what Detective Anderson in Cornwall had said about the hundreds of places on both sides of the lake where a man could hide a boat.

"All the coves and marshes the booze smugglers used during Prohibition are still there," he'd said. "Big messy overgrown marshes with lots of channels where boats can hide at night."

So, was there smuggling happening on the night of July second?

Was Gerald Tice a smuggler? The man had wealth enough from his salvage business. And he had his airplanes to look for, he didn't need another hobby. For some folks though, there was never enough money. And the Arrowhead search was a good cover for spending endless hours on the boat, all over the lake.

Had Gerald Tice, stopped that night at South Island to leave something, or to pick something up?

Had Wes Sedore surprised him at this activity?

He pictured the struggle on the shore in the night.

Or to think of it another way altogether. He and the chief might have been wrong to toss out so quickly the idea that Sedore was involved in the drug smuggling. Sedore might even have been a partner with Tice and the two men had an argument.

As for Sedore's possible involvement in smuggling, that was harder to figure. Maybe he'd reached that mid-life crisis the chief talked about. Or maybe he just wanted more for his kids. People could always find a need for money. And the smuggling rewards were so tempting to so many. Then Sedore's conscience might have begun to bother him, when he thought that his own kids might end up taking some of the very same drugs. He might have wanted to get out of the business and Tice argued with him. Said he knew too much to just leave, so Tice had killed him.

How connect Mel Todd to all this? He couldn't have witnessed the murder, they'd found his body two weeks before Sedore was killed. But he might have known about Tice and the smuggling. He was out on the water all the time in his battered old boat. Maybe he saw something interesting while he was out there and thought he'd found a way to buy his new boat motor. Maybe he'd approached Tice who had paid him for a while, then got tired of the expense and killed him.

Yes, the smuggling operation was the trail to follow. He just had to figure out the markers that led the way. He looked at his map where he had drawn several lines across the lake, from Bonville to the old smugglers' sites on the American side.

All the lines had to go past South Island.

Or in the words of the notorious Mr. Long John Silver, it seemed that X still marked the spot.

38

It was the morning of the Lighthouse Day picnic and breakfast at the Jakes' household was not going well.

"Just what are you saying here, Ali?" Pete said incredulously in mid toast bite, "That Tyler Cotes is a drug smuggler? What the hell gave you that idea?"

Ali was horrified. Why had she ever blurted it out? This was every bit as bad as she had feared. Worse.

But in for a penny, in for a pound. Might as well forge ahead.

"I didn't actually say that Tyler is a drug smuggler," she protested. "I just asked if you have ever considered that he *might* be."

"No, " Pete said rawly, "Actually I haven't." He pushed his unfinished food away. "And I'm not going to listen to this. You've never liked Tyler, right from the beginning. But this is just crazy."

She hated to have him looking at her like that. She reached across the table for his hand. "Pete, you know I wouldn't bring up something like this unless I had good reason. Won't you hear me out?"

He withdrew his hand, sat back with arms locked across his chest. "Go on," he said through rigid lips. "If you have to."

She repeated what she had told Chief Halstead.

"Go and see Tyler yourself," she said. "You'll see that he's walking and moving just fine."

"He explained that to you," Pete said tersely. "He was going to surprise me."

"Ask him to explain where he goes in the boat all the time, and what about the navigational maps."

"Like he says, he's been filling in time. He likes being out in the boat. He's hardly been concealing any of this."

She sighed. "How well can you know him?" she asked. "You haven't seen him in three years. Maybe he's changed."

"Somebody's changed, that's for sure. In future, I'd appreciate if you would stick to your teaching and leave the detective work to me."

He left, slamming the door. Nevra cried, never having seen her daddy like that. Ali felt like crying too.

* * *

Halfway to the village, Pete pulled off the road to cool down. Normally even- tempered, he didn't like the feelings that were boiling through his mind. Anger, hurt, raw disbelief. And something else, something even more disturbing.

Could it be unease, maybe even an unwelcome suspicion that Ali might be on to something?

Could it be possible that what she said was true?

His mind veered away from the thought.

Reluctantly, though, he felt the police part of his brain start to sort through the events of the last few weeks. Tinkering with various loose bits, trying to link them up in that way of his that sometimes drove the chief nuts.

The recent local drug smuggling did seem to have begun around the time that Tyler arrived on the Island. But that could just be a coincidence.

On the other hand, he didn't really know much about Tyler's movements during the past couple of months. Tyler could be going anywhere, at any time of the day. Or night.

And what was wrong with that? Tyler was a grown man. Pete was a buddy, not the guy's keeper.

O.K. calm down, work through it, the way he would with any other suspect – not that Tyler's a suspect. The process was just as useful to clear away suspicion. Think of it that way.

So, Opportunity. Yes Tyler would have had lots of opportunity.

Motive. Well sure, the same as for most people, he guessed. Money, pure and simple. Well, maybe not so pure.

But he'd never heard Tyler complain much about lack of money. Even when they were sitting in some crummy canteen, drinking crummy weak beer, sand and grit from the day's manoeuvers in their hair. Even when the other guys were dreaming about winning the lottery, buying a Lotus or an island in Hawaii. Tyler never entered into the game. He'd just sit there with a grin on his face, enjoying the crummy beer. Looking forward to the challenge of the next day's adventure.

That was the way he thought of army life, just like it said in those hokey television ads. *Today's army -- Join the adventure!* Tyler had wanted to be in the army since he was a kid. He wasn't always dreaming that he was somewhere else. He was where he wanted to be.

But that could play both ways.

Maybe adventure-loving Tyler had become too bored, waiting around to be rehabilitated. Dangerously bored. Look at what he'd said about fishing on the lake, how dull he'd found it. Maybe he thought he'd spice up his life a little. Or maybe he really was worried that the army might not take him back. And when he talked about getting into some kind of business he'd meant the drug business.

And then there was that request about the bank loan. Pete had thought Tyler need some money to tide him over and been more than willing to help. But actually, Tyler should have had a fairly healthy bank balance, put away over the years. He was single, had no mortgage anywhere. Why should he need money now? Maybe he had unknown debts.

Pete shook his head angrily to clear away the unwelcome thoughts. He might just be able to imagine Tyler enjoying a speed chase on the water, outwitting the coast guard and the police. But peddling tablets of ecstacy to teenagers? That was harder to picture. Much harder. On the other hand, for all Pete knew Tyler had been involved in the drug trade overseas, for the past few years. As Ali said, did he know the guy at all anymore?

So he and Pete had looked after each others backs in some pretty dangerous situations. Did that buy loyalty forever?

Maybe not. But it did buy Tyler the chance at an explanation.

The chance to speak up for himself.

Pete certainly owed an old buddy that much.

He'd arrived at at the village but was in no state to stop. As he passed the station, he radioed Jane that he would be late coming in. Then he headed for Cedar Grove, his thoughts swirling.

It's one hell of a dilemma.

If he confronts Tyler and he's wrong, he loses a friend.

If Ali's right, he loses a friend.

It's bad either way.

But waiting wouldn't make it any easier. If he was going to have it out with Tyler, it might as well be now.

* * *

Everyone was ecstatic about the weather. The day was warm but not humid, with a light breeze and no rain clouds in sight.

"A perfect day," Beth Harrison was beaming. "I knew that Bonville weather man was wrong. He always is."

Ali forbore from pointing out that Beth had been the biggest doomsayer of the group about the threatened rain.

"All's well that ends well," Miranda whispered, rolling her eyes.

Yes, the big day was here, every moment of the morning crammed with tasks to get ready for the opening of festivities at noon. That was fine with Ali, still shaken from the argument at breakfast. She was glad to be busy. Nevra was spending the day with Tracey and the kids, who would keep her for the night as well.

So, into the fray. First there was set-up of the tables and various booths. As Ali was one of the younger members of the group, she threw herself into the work. Beth cruised here and there with her master scheduling sheet, busily issuing commands and checking off items. Ali and the other volunteers each had their own photocopy of the sheet with their specific duties marked.

There was a full roster of activities. Throughout the afternoon, Joan and Steph would be conducting informational tours of the exterior of the lighthouse and the old lifeboat. Under Miranda's tent canopy, there was a table displaying the information pamphlet and offering Save Our Lighthouses pins and buttons for sale. Visitors could also buy a raffle ticket on a watercolour of the lighthouse. And for the children, there was Pirate Ali's fish pond and doubloon hunt. The food truck would be selling burgers, corn, cold drinks and ice cream throughout the afternoon. All this activity would culminate at dusk in the ceremony of lighting the lighthouse lamp. Actually two lamps but it was hoped that the effect would be of one strong beam.

By ten someone got the sound system set up and soon infectious mariner jigs rolled out from the speakers, making the work go easier. By eleven Benny and his catering truck had arrived. The teasing smell of frying onions soon filled the air.

The tables set up, Ali left to don her pirate costume and to get her own booth ready. She slipped into the baggy trousers and vest. Then tied up her hair in the red kerchief and struggled to paint on a mustache in her tiny purse make-up mirror. She hadn't thought of that difficulty.

"Smile!" Miranda popped up like a jack-in-the box from behind the booth.

She held a camera. "As I'm not much use anywhere else," she explained, "They've set me to taking pictures."

Ali posed and Miranda clicked.

"Is there anything wrong, dear?" she asked. "The outfit's jaunty but you look a bit under par."

Glumly, Ali told her of the breakfast argument.

"It was terrible, Miranda. We *never* argue."

Miranda went directly to the main point. "So you think that Tyler is a drug smuggler. I can see how that might upset Pete just a tiny bit," she added drily.

Ali squirmed miserably. "I don't know what I think anymore."

Miranda shook her head sympathetically "I assume you had some reason to do such a thing. I *hope* you did."

"He was acting suspiciously," Ali babbled, "He was always out in that boat of his —he lied to me…. Oh! I don't want to go into it all now, but yes, I had my reasons."

"Then maybe you did have to say something," Miranda said reasonably. "Stranger things have happened."

Ali sighed."But now all my so-called evidence doesn't seem like anything much at all. Please don't mention this to anyone else," she said miserably. "I feel terrible about what I've done. I've been wondering all morning what Pete is going to do. Will he go talk to Tyler? I've just wrecked everything and for nothing. I'm probably wrong anyway."

Miranda patted her hand. "I hope you're wrong, too. But you're a smart cookie, Ms. Jakes. And if you're right, you might have helped Pete solve a case."

"Now my Pirate Gal," she said briskly. "Let's get these fishing rods set up for the children."

Privately, Miranda too wondered where Tyler Cotes could be. But she said nothing. Life was full of mysteries, and often none so mysterious as the actions of her fellow human beings.

39

Cedar Grove Cabins. Weekly and Monthly Rates.
Housekeeping Services Available.

Pete stopped the cruiser before turning into the driveway. He hated himself for feeling this way. On the alert, wary. Now that he'd cooled down even more, he realized that he could hardly barge into the cabin and start telling Tyler about Ali's crazy theory. What did he expect – that Ty would just fess up?

More likely that would get good buddy Jakes a punch in the face, and he would deserve it. He might react in the same way if faced with a similar wacky, out of left field accusation. Anyway Tyler was likely already at the Lighthouse picnic, helping set up. According to Ali, he thought wryly, Tyler was fit enough to do the work. He wondered how she would cope for the day, working with her supposed criminal assistant.

"Aargh!" He groaned and gripped the wheel in frustration.

Once again, he went over Ali's reasoning – if you could call it that. Then contrasted that with his own gut feelings that she couldn't be more wrong. There was only one sensible way to go ahead. He had to follow the same procedure as he would in any other investigation, with any other suspect – he winced, there was that word again. He would go back to the station, do a records check on Tyler and talk the case over with the chief.

He turned the cruiser round, thought briefly about checking in on how things were going at the Lighthouse Point picnic. Amend that thought -- truthfully he wanted dearly to check in with Ali. To wipe out the memory of how he had left the house that morning in a blaze of anger, the hurt look on Ali's face, little Nevra near tears as well.

But no, the best way, the only way to make things better between them was to clear up the situation about Tyler. And the only way to do that was to do his job, to start acting like a policeman, even if meant investigating his friend. Ali had mentioned her visit to the Peterson's Marina, that was where she had picked up some of her so-called 'evidence'. He would stop there on his way into town.

* * *

Young Jimmy Peterson was alone at the Marina store counter, texting someone on his phone. But he looked up politely when Pete came in.

"Morning," Pete greeted him. Is your Grandpa up at the house?"

"Likely having a nap," the boy said. "Old folks sure nap a lot – after breakfast, after lunch, after anything."

Pete was reluctant to disturb them. "Maybe you can help me, then. I think you know my friend, Mr. Cotes."

"Sure," Jimmy said, "The army guy."

"Has he been by today for gas?"

Jimmy shook his head. "No, I haven't seen him. Mr. Storms is the only one who's come by this morning. He's still down there at the dock."

"Thanks Jimmy."

Pete headed across the lawn, thinking he'd say hello. He wondered how he could bring up the subject of Tyler and realized he wasn't being very professional. He still wasn't comfortable with the idea of asking questions about Ty but it had to be done. And Art knew a lot about the doings on the lake.

Once on the dock, he paused to watch a stilt-legged heron lift itself awkwardly from the shore, and launch itself into the air on slowly flapping wings. Then his gaze dropped idly to the boat that was tied up at the dock. Gradually realization grew. He was looking at a boat bow embraced with a distinctive wide blue stripe.

What the hell? He thought he'd got that damn boat out of his thoughts.

Was this Art's boat? *Sea Gal* it was called. He realized he had always associated Art's water travel with the police launch or the ungainly tub that was used to train the kids in search and rescue.

He had never seen Art in his *own* boat.

And so what, anyway. Big deal, a coincidence. As the chief had pointed out, the SpeedCrest was a popular boat. Out of curiosity though, he found himself looking for the serial number on the bow. He would have to get closer to see if there was a four in the registration number.

"Ahoy there," he hailed in the usual way, as he approached. He couldn't see Art, who must be down in the cabin. He moved closer to the bow, leaning down to check for the -set of numbers. And there it was.

ON89604.

For a moment the numbers actually seemed to sear his brain, as if they had been physically branded there. He stood like a stunned fool, finally realizing that Art had appeared at the rail. A bulky shape against the bright morning sun.

Pete put his hand up to shade his eyes. "Permission to come aboard," he managed to say.

Storms was wiping a screwdriver off on a rag. "Permission granted," he said as Pete stepped across the short gap between the boat and the dock.

"What are you doing down this way, Jakes?" he asked with his usual bluff interest.

"Ali asked me to pick up a couple more cases of bottled water at the store," Pete fabricated glibly. "They need it for the picnic at the Point."

Storms looked up at the sky. "They got a good day for it. The rain held off."

He tossed the screwdriver into a green metal toolbox and picked up another. "I was just about to take off on a little fishing venture. A day away from the kids on the crew, sometimes I need the break."

"Where are you headed?" Pete asked.

Art waved vaguely eastward, "I'll probably just poke around the south shore. Catch a few bass."

"Nice boat," Pete said, running his hand along the neatly painted rail.

Art shrugged. "It's an oldy. I bought her last year. She gets me around."

"It's the SpeedCrest 98?" Pete said. "Twenty-eight feet, 50 hp?"

Art looked surprised. "You've been boning up."

Pete shrugged. "I might get a boat myself some day. Figured I'd read up on the subject."

Storms grunted, "Well, it's nothing like that *Finders Keepers*. That boat's likely got a gold-plated toilet."

"Did you ever run into the *Finders Keepers* out there on the water?"

"Nah, we were working different parts of the lake. Tice was fishing for those plane models, I fish for bass. But why do you ask?"

"Just curious," Pete said, looking up towards the bow. "Tice's daughter brought some photos into the station showing a buoy marker. There's a date and a time on the shots, the I-pad does that. She thinks they show that her dad was telling the truth when he says he wasn't near South Island the night Sedore was killed."

"What do you and Bud think?"

Pete shook his head. "There was nothing conclusive. She didn't realize the time frame of the murder was wider than that."

Storms shrugged. "Can't blame the girl for trying to help her old man."

"Some of the photos were kind of interesting though, in another way."

"How's that?"

"In the background, you could see a couple of boats meeting up just off-shore. I doubt they were of any interest to Tice. I could only make them out after I'd enlarged the photos. One of the boats had a big blue stripe like this one."

Art held the screwdriver up to the light, seemed satisfied and tossed it into the tool box. "There's likely hundreds of these old SpeedCrests out there, maybe thousands. Particularly this 98 model. It was a good boat, still has a decent resale value." He added deliberately. "And they all had blue stripes on the bow."

"It was nearly dusk in the photos. The boats didn't have any lights on."

"You seem pretty interested in this boat."

"Could be helpful in our investigations. Could be helpful for Tice, if the driver of the boat could verify Tice's story. But nobody's come forward."

"A lot of people don't like to talk to the cops."

"But you *are* a cop."

"What's that supposed to mean?"

"I think you were out there that night in this boat. And the only reason I can think why you wouldn't volunteer the information is because you don't want want anyone to know that you were there."

"Is that so?"

Too late, Pete noticed that Storms was advancing on him with a heavy wrench he must have picked up from the tool box. He raised his arm in an affort to deflect the blow, but Storms had the advantage of momentum. He came down hard and caught Pete a cracking whack on the temple.

That was really dumb of me, Pete thought as he fell.

40

Halstead looked lazily past his raised up shoes, dreaming of the season's first big feed of sweet corn. Fresh from the field was the sweetest. He heard the phone ring and hoped it wasn't for him. He even scrunched a bit further down in his chair. Not that it ever did any good. Jane was relentless. It was no good turning the speaker off either, the station was too small for that to have any effect.

No phone calls, he'd told her when he came in. I've got paperwork – he did too, somewhere. But here she stood in the cubicle doorway.

"Vern's on the phone," she said. "He wants to talk about the waterfront festival."

Halstead grunted. "I'm not here."

"He'll have seen your truck out front," Jane pointed out the obvious.

"I'm still not here." Halstead waved a hand. "Make something up."

"I said you were at your zumba lesson," Jane said on her return. Halstead didn't hear or at least didn't acknowledge the joke.

Jane noted the file on his desk, his slumped posture, he wasn't even spinning his chair.

"What's up chief?"

Halstead sighed. "Ah, I'm not happy with checking up on Tyler Cotes behind Jakes' back. It doesn't feel right."

"It's the nature of our biz," Jane said sympathetically. "I'm sure you check out all the rumours about me."

He laughed. "Only the interesting ones."

"So, what have we learned about Tyler Cotes?" she asked.

Despite her wide gossip network of relatives and friends, Jane was the soul of discretion in matters regarding her work. She couldn't have kept her job otherwise.

"Nothing much," he said, flipping open the file. "He was born in Battleford, Saskatchewan. Went to high school there, was a star on the football team. He racked up one minor charge, drunk and disorderly at a local bar, with the rest of the team after a win."

Jane shrugged. "Pretty standard for a football team. That could describe my son."

Halstead nodded and turned a page. "He went to community college, then I guess decided he wanted more excitement out of life and joined the forces. His army record seems blameless enough. He signed up when he was twenty-two, so he's been in there twelve years. Served in Iraq - then Afghanistan, that's where he met Jakes."

"Sounds impressive," Jane said.

Halstead nodded. "Solid enough anyway. No record of drug use – although a lot of those army boys like to smoke some dope. No record of drug peddling at any rate."

"Any weddings?" Jane asked.

"One, back in Saskatchewan during that year in college. Divorced a year later."

"No kids?"

"No kids. No child support owing."

"Where did he get hurt?"

"In Afghanistan, shot on a patrol."

He sighed. "I guess I could call him in, discreetly ask a couple of questions."

Jane didn't have to say anything, her look said enough.

"I know, I know," Halstead said. There would be nothing discreet about a visit to the Middle Island police station. Not in broad daylight at any rate.

The phone rang and she left him to his thoughts. No longer the peaceful contemplation of his cornfield, but a review of what he knew about the smuggling operation.

It was true that the spike in local drug action seemed to have begun just about the same time that Tyler Cotes had arrived in the area. Could be just a coincidence, but as he'd often told Jakes, a good policeman was always wary of coincidence. And apart from his injury, Cotes was by all accounts a man capable of quick thinking and quick action, qualities as useful to a successful criminal as to a professional soldier. Throw in some cunning and a lack of fear and you had a powerful combination.

Still, that wasn't much to go on. He missed having Jakes' input into the problem. He'd come to appreciate the younger man's intuition and willingness to follow up even unwelcome lines of investigation.

"Jane," he called. "Can you get me Detective Anderson in Cornwall. They haven't got back to me yet." He had asked the detachment office to check whether Tyler Cotes had any connection with the recently arrested men.

Halstead knew Anderson slightly from a police services conference a couple of years back. Now he picked up the phone and exchanged the obligatory manly conversation about the Toronto Blue Jays baseball team and their standing in the League, before getting down to business.

"That connection down your way you were asking about," Anderson began. "I don't have a name but I did get a description from one of the men we arrested. He gave us a load of information in exchange for a sentencing deal."

"Shoot," Halstead said, pen at the ready.

"Thanks," he said when Anderson was done. "It doesn't sound like our man at all but I appreciate the call."

"Anytime," Anderson said. "I've sent the file to you on the computer as well."

"No go, eh?" Jane said when he put down the phone. "But that's good news, isn't it? Good news for Ali anyway."

"And for Cotes," Halstead said. "But it still leaves us with a big puzzle."

"What's it say?" Jane said, leaning in to look at the computer, where the message had already appeared. "Oh I see. For a start, Tyler Cotes is only about thirty-five, right? This guy is fifty or more, with greying hair."

Halstead laughed, "Sounds more like me."

Jane read on, "Heavily built. That's not you, you're a long drink of water. Always have been. " She chuckled, then said slowly,

"Here's an odd detail. The man they're describing chews those nicotine tablets and coughs a lot."

"What?" Halstead asked, pushing past her to the screen. "What did you say? Anderson didn't say anything about a cough."

They stared at the computer screen together, transfixed.

Then said simultaneously.

"Art!"

"What the hell?" Halstead said after a long moment. "Come on now, lots of people chew that stuff when they're trying to quit. Art's one of the good guys - the man is working with the coast guard auxiliary himself, for god's sake."

"Pretty well the perfect cover for moving around the lake," Jane said numbly. "And the rest of the description could fit. Policemen do go bad sometimes, Bud."

Halstead looked to the outer office, to the duty roster above Jane's desk.

"Where is Art now?" he asked urgently.

She shrugged helplessly. "He's been out on the boat today, like always."

"I'll call the Bonville Marina," Halstead snapped. "You try to get him to answer on the radio. Find him!"

He glanced at the roster chart. "Where's Jakes? I need him to get his butt in here fast."

But Jakes' IN marker wasn't on the chart.

Jane looked stricken. "I haven't heard from him for hours either, Chief. Just one call earlier this morning when he said he was running a bit late."

41

There was darkness and there was movement and there was noise, a steady rumbling noise.

And there was soreness, terrible soreness.

His head hurt, true, but the soreness seemed to be concentrated around his wrists and ankles.

Cautiously he tried some movement. First his head, but that was not a good thing to do. For a time he battled nauseating dizziness, unable to register anything else. Eventually, he realized that he was lying prone on a wooden surface. He couldn t move his arms or legs. Panicking, he thrashed like an insect on a pin.

More dizziness. This was getting him nowhere. Time to smarten up.

His wrists and ankles were obviously bound. How long had he been trussed up like this? Judging by the soreness and his raging thirst, it had been awhile. Hours anyway, surely not days!

Again he fought down panic, trying to recall a sequence of events that led to his current imprisonment. Memory trickled slowly back. Danger. Something hard hitting his head. Falling.

Something about a boat.

A boat.

He was on a boat now, the steady rumbling sound that he'd awakened to was the motor. This was a piece of knowledge to hang on to. A fact.

Maybe that was enough for now.

The dizziness was back. He slid into the darkness again.

* * *

"Hey Mrs. Pirate," said the excited little boy. "Look at me! I got the blue fish."

Ali smiled and reached for the blue metal fish that dangled from the pole. "Yes you did!" she said. "And now you get a prize."

She handed the boy a treat bag, one of fifty that she had packed the night before. Each bag held a balloon with a parrot on it, a strip of pirate ship stickers, and a telescoping kaleidoscope. Other, older children had been turning in the doubloons for their prizes. Attendance was brisk, she hoped she had made up enough bags to last through the day. When Tiffany Beck, a grade ten high school student volunteer, came to relieve her at the booth, she gratefully accepted. She needed a bathroom break.

She also took the opportunity to take a little tour around the site. The volunteers staffing the other booths excitedly shared news of attendance counts and rapidly filling cash boxes. Over a hundred people had already come through the site. Later there would be the supper time crowd, who would be staying on to see the lanterns lit in the lighthouse tower.

Other volunteers were taking donations and signing up memberships. It looked as if the take would be several thousand dollars overall, not a bad launch for their campaign. Beth Harrison was so excited that she was actually handing out praise to the other volunteers. She even complimented Ali on her outfit.

"Love the blouse, dear. Very dramatic!"

So the day was going well, everything the committee had hoped for. Too bad that personally, all Ali could think of was the disastrous morning argument with Pete. Despite the distractions at the picnic, she'd had an aching heart all afternoon. And now, checking her phone for the twentieth time, she saw again that he hadn't called.

What had she been thinking? How had she ever deluded herself that Pete would accept her suspicions calmly, that he would even thank her for revealing the truth about his friend. Instead they'd had the worst fight of their married life. And it was all her fault! Now, looking back over the past few weeks, she felt she'd been behaving like a madwoman. Tracking Tyler, spying on him. Then weaving a lunatic tale, all based on little more than her own dislike.

She checked the phone again, doubting now that Pete would even arrive to help with the evening lantern ceremony. Miserably, she trudged back to the fish pond booth, a crestfallen pirate.

* * *

Jimmy Peterson came into his grandparents' kitchen for lunch, hungry as only a hard-working teenage boy can be.

"Hey Gramps," he said, "Did you see that police cruiser is still parked up at the lane?"

Ralph looked up from his copy of *The Record*. "How's that?" he asked the boy.

"I said that police cruiser is still parked up the lane. Officer Jakes hasn't been back to pick it up."

"That's strange," Edna said and she left off stirring the soup, to look. "The boy's right," she told Ralph.

Ralph sighed and put down his paper, then followed suit. That made it official, the cruiser was still there.

"Jakes must have gone fishing with Mr. Storms," Ralph said, ending the discussion or at least his part in it. "He'll likely be back by and by."

"Come and eat your soup, you two," Edna said. She didn't like food to get cold.

Later, though, when his grandparents had settled in the lounge chairs for their after-lunch naps, Jimmy approached the cruiser, a blue sedan with a red glass siren on top. A wire net barrier separated the back seat from the front.

Neat! he thought.

The driver's window was down and he could hear a voice on the car radio.

Double neat!

He leaned into the window to hear. The sound was sort of crackling but he thought he recognized Mrs. Carell at the police station. She was probably looking for Officer Jakes. Maybe there was some emergency – like maybe a robbery going on right now at the village bank!

He'd better answer her and explain that Officer Jakes wasn't there.

He opened the driver's door and slid into the seat. He was a clever boy and like most kids of the age, he was handy with technology. It took him only a couple of seconds to figure out the right buttons to push.

"Hello," he said hesitantly. "This is Jimmy Peterson. Is that Mrs. Carell at the police station?"

Pete hadn't had the dream about the explosion in a while.

And in a way, he was almost used to it. The stifling heat, the slightly dazed look of his companions in the tank-like vehicle. The look that everyone wore in that country. Not exactly patience, more a dulled resignation, a submission to the relentless heat, the smell of sweat, the endless dust, the necessary languor of existence. All combined to make the noise of the exploding bomb that much more shocking.

So he braced himself in the dream for the terrible images that usually followed. The screaming, the blood, the chaotic tumble of bodies in the smoke-filled interior of the mangled vehicle. His own panic and the subsequent pain of his wounds.

Instead there came a magical vision of water, cool green-blue water. Shimmering like a mirage before his dry, desert-scoured gaze. Amazed, he stepped thankfully into the liquid embrace, let the water lave the fear of the dream away. He leaned his head back upon the soft, pillowing wave, delighted to watch a line of cormorants stitch a thread across the blue blanket of sky.

For long moments, he was soothed, then heard an approaching sound. Irritated at this invasion into his sanctuary, he turned his head to look. The sound grew louder, increasing to a roar. The birds scattered like feathered black missiles, that had been shot roughly into *the air. The broken pieces of sky tumbled into the water, so near that he felt the chill droplets on his face.*

…. The sound is now very close, it's a boat, the prow rearing out of the water. He can't get away, he feels himself being swamped, swept under. The cold water clogs his nose, chokes his throat. He's gasping for breath, but there is only the water. His last view of the surface is the blue band around the prow of the boat. Incongruously, someone on the boat is singing.

Yo ho ho. And a bottle of rum.

Consciousness was back. Not so dizzy this time. The boat motor was still rumbling, they were moving quickly over the water. It was all coming back to him now, in a rush, like a coloured picture in the dim cabin. For that s where he must be. In the cabin of the *Sea Gal*.

Art Storms' boat.

He could see it all over again, Storms lunging at him, face distorted with effort and anger. Wielding the heavy metal wrench. He winced all over again at the thought.

How long had he been tied up? It was only about ten in the morning when he arrived at the Petersons. He had a feeling now that it was much later. Evening at least. He wondered where they had been all day. He wondered where they were going.

His head reeled with the weight of the questions. Best to concentrate on the task at hand, trying to free his wrists. It wasn't going to be easy, the ropes were tied tightly, the knots stiff and immovable. Carefully, cautiously, he tried twisting his hands. Winced. The raw chafing was painful. Still, there was no choice but to forge ahead.

For long painful minutes he struggled but to no avail. He lay back, exhausted, fighting back panic. What help could he hope for? He doubted that the Petersons or Jimmy would sound an alarm. They would likely think that he had gone off on an impromptu fishing trip with Art.

The motor sound was changing. The boat was slowing down, coming in for a landing. Pete tensed, his every sense alert and braced for what was to come next.

* * *

Halstead held the phone so tightly it was a wonder he didn't crush the instrument in his hand. Since the conversation with Jimmy Peterson and his grandparents, he had figured out one, that Jakes was with Storms. And two, that Storms had disabled Jakes somehow. Because if Jakes had any way of contacting the station, by cell phone, beeper, or boat radio, he would have done so.

Jakes must have discovered something that threatened Storms. Halstead could only guess that it had to do with the smuggling operation. Storms had then reacted on the spot, attacking and disabling him. *Disabled* was the most optimistic term Halstead could think of at the moment.

"Where the hell is this guy?" he now barked into the phone. "Any sign of him?"

"We've got the word out to the border check-points," the coast guard dispatcher said. "But he's not likely to go there."

Halstead agreed. Why would Storms risk running into border guard interference when there were miles of unguarded lakeshore to make a crossing.

"I've got four boats out," said the dispatcher. "We're looking, but it's a big lake. Lots of places to hide."

"Yeah, well keep looking. This guy's got one of my officers."

Halstead switched the phone off, restraining an impulse to toss it across the room. Lots of places to hide, that was an understatement. The lake was inset with hundreds of bays, inlets and coves. And Art Storms knew most of them.

Christ, he wanted to tear his greying hair out A cop gone bad, a cop gone rotten. Such a terrible betrayal of the man's oath, his responsibilities, his duty. And most galling, it had all gone on right under Halstead's own nose! He had worked with Art Storms for years, talked with him daily and all the while suspected nothing.

Maybe Vern was right, maybe he should retire. He wasn't fit to hold the office.

But not today. Today he had to find and save young Jakes.

It was now going on five o'clock. From what Jimmy and the Petersons had said, it seemed that Storms had already had five or six hours to get to a hide-out.

Traipsing all over the lake wasn't going to help Jakes. He had to *think*. Think what might be in Art's mind, what he might be planning to do.

* * *

Pete stumbled ahead of Storms, along the deck of the *Laker Gal*. Storms held his police issue revolver at the ready, but at the moment hardly needed it. He had freed Pete's ankles, but the surge of returning blood circulation had made Pete weak. He limped painfully forward, absorbing what physical details he could. It seemed to be evening, as he had thought. He guessed about eight o'clock, the cormorants were heading back to their roost, and dusk was settling down on the water.

He knew more. Could it be? Yes, he knew where they were. Storms had brought the boat to the dock at South Island. That did not seem like a good thing.

His captor, who had said nothing so far, indicated that Pete should jump to the dock, not an easy challenge with his hands still tied. Storms had to grab his arm so he wouldn't fall into the water. So Storms didn't want him to drown. Not a great comfort, actually. There were lots of other ways to kill someone.

Pete moved along the dock, a part of his mind noting with grim humour, the registration number on the bow of the *Island Gal*. ON89604.

He recalled the hours he had spent on the computer searching for the damn thing. Well, now he'd found it. Be careful what you wish for, as the saying goes. Because you just might find it.

* * *

Ali removed her pirate headscarf and eyepatch and looked worriedly out over the lighthouse park. Dusk was falling, the crew of volunteers were packing up the booths and tables, getting ready for the evening ceremony.

She checked her cellphone for what seemed like the hundredth time that day but it was still frustratingly empty. Besides, she'd had the phone on all day and would have answered instantly if there'd been a ring. She'd also talked to the baby sitter at supper time on the off chance that Pete had called, but no message there either.

She groaned miserably. She had hoped desperately that he would somehow magically appear to help light the lamps. They had been looking forward to sharing such a special experience together, but now it seemed certain that was not going to happen. Still, she must rally and help with the ceremony. An audience was waiting, the show must go on.

Miranda appeared round the corner of the booth. "Still no sign of Pete, dear?"

Ali shook her head. She continued doffing her pirate gear and changed quickly into jeans and a hoodie for the cooler night air.

"Have you called the station?" Miranda asked.

Ali sighed. "No, I was hoping to apologize to Pete in person. It's not really the kind of conversation you want to have over the phone."

Now though, she even dreaded the thought of going home. Maybe she could just stay here in the park and become another Island legend. The crazy lady who lived in the lighthouse and never came out.

"Here comes Stephanie. I'd rather not explain why Pete isn't here, thanks."

Miranda nodded. Steph had come to report that there had been no word from Tyler Cotes either. He had never appeared to help Joan at the catering truck. Fortunately, Ali didn't have time to think about that, there was too much to do.

"Men!" Miranda said it for all of them.

"I guess it's just us then," Steph said. Luckily Joan's son and his highschool buddy had lugged the equipment up the day before.

She stopped Miranda's protest before it even began. "And no, we're not going to let you go up those rickety stairs. Just get yourself a good ringside seat for the show. You deserve it, you made all this happen."

Ali opened the narrow door of the lighthouse tower and looked up the stairs. She was glad of the flashlights that she and Steph carried. Wayne Jessup had mended the most obvious gaps and dangers, replacing the broken boards with new pieces of wood and shoring up the staircase itself with strong struts of two by four.

Moving gingerly, they climbed the steps up to the platform at the top. They'd only been up there in daylight before and now the small space seemed filled with dusk, as if the night had begun to flow in through the windows from the outside. On the grass below, people were gathered in little clumps, many holding up children to see the coming show. The children had coloured light sticks that made patterns in the air.

Ali looked out the windowed eyes of the tower at the darkening lake and thought of the keeper of old, diligently monitoring his solitary beacon in the night.

A lonely job.

She had never felt more lonely herself.

43

Dusk was settling quickly over the island. Sweat ran in Pete's eyes and his face smarted from scratches. He couldn't raise his hands to protect himself from the branches of the cedars along the path. The best he could do was to squint his eyes, which made progress along the stony path even more difficult.

His head had begun throbbing again, now with tension as well. Desperately, he tried to concentrate. Behind him, Art was eerily silent. Like a good, trained cop, he was quietly, methodically going about his task and ignoring distractions. Distractions such as feeling any guilt or remorse about what he was planning to do.

"Where are we going?" Pete asked. But Storms only jabbed the gun more roughly into his back and said a terse "Keep moving."

"You can't get away with this," Pete went on, risking another blow. "The Petersons will find the cruiser and wonder why it's still parked at the marina. They last saw me with you. They'll call the chief at the station."

"None of that's going to help you," Storms said. "So just keep moving."

They emerged from the clawing bushes to an open spot on the rocks. Pete recognized the area as one of the sections on Wes Sedore's grid map, though he couldn't remember whether it had been marked as cleared of danger. He gulped air and stared bleakly across the water. Ali was over there, only a few miles away as the cormorant flies. She'd be wondering where he was. She'd be thinking that he was still angry, so angry that he wouldn't come and help light the lighthouse lanterns.

To think that their last moments together should be an angry fight – he groaned in helpless frustration. But he had to put such thoughts out of his mind. If he was going to live to see his wife and daughter again, he had to think about now, right now.

"Stop," Art said. "This is far enough."

Ominous words. *Far enough for what?*

"Sit down," Art said, giving him a half shove.

Pete sank down to a slab of rock, his hands held awkwardly out in front of his chest.

"What now?" he asked warily.

Storms moved towards a canvas bag wedged in between a couple of big rocks. Pete realized he must have stowed it away at some earlier date. Still gripping the revolver in one hand, he hauled out the bag and carefully lifted out a small cardboard carton. He deposited it gently on the rock, then dropped to his knees, put the gun down and opened the flaps of the box.

"Art, what the hell are you doing?" Pete burst out. It was not a time for subtlety. The next few minutes were crucial. He had to try to inject some sanity into the situation.

Storms turned, his big face pocked with shadows in the dusk.

"This here is a grenade, fella. When they find what's left of you they'll think you accidentally set off one of those UXO's that Sedore was looking for."

Pete felt as if he'd been slam-dunked in the chest. For a moment, he couldn't catch his breath.

"Jeezus man, you're a fellow police officer. I've got a wife and kid!"

"I thought about that and I'm real sorry, Jakes, but I'm in too deep now to get out of this any other way."

"So you *were* the local smuggling contact." Pete said bitterly. There was little satisfaction to be proved right.

But, anything to keep Storms talking. To give himself some more time. He couldn't free his hands, but he still had his feet, his legs. Maybe when Storms came closer he could launch himself at the guy and knock him over.

Storms nodded, not looking up as he considered his deadly package. He spoke absently, absorbed in his task. He seemed preternaturally serene, relaxed, as if he was coming to the end of something.

"I spent way too much time in those damned casinos, and I owe way too much money to some way too scary guys. It was either help them or end up in the lake myself."

"You could explain that to the authorities. That you were coerced."

Storms shook his head. "They wouldn't let me explain away a couple of murders."

A couple of murders.

Pete let that sink in for a minute. "So you did kill Wes Sedore. And Mel Todd, too."

"Yep," Storms said in the same dispassionate tone. "I used him as a lookout for awhile and paid him well. But the fool was as gabby as a damn woman when he was in his cups, I couldn't trust him."

"So you drowned him."

Storms shrugged. "It didn't take much. Todd had already fallen into the water. I gave him a little shove but he likely would have drowned anyway."

Not according to Roger Huma. Pete thought. But it wasn't a good time to bring that up.

"And what happened with Wes Sedore? Why him?" Pete asked, as casually as if it was a couple of weeks ago and the two of them were just having a workaday conversation.

Storms looked around, frowning with concentration and chomping on his gum. Planning the details of his macabre show, Pete guessed.

"My employers used various places as drop offs, that damn buoy you were so interested in for instance. But I'd also left a small cache of drugs on the Island. It was a handy place but when I went back that night to pick the stuff up, Sedore spotted me. I thought he'd gone to bed but he was trying out some new infra red equipment so that he could scan the area at night. You might say he caught me red-handed."

Storms didn't laugh at his own joke, though. He shrugged, "I had no explanation for why I was sneaking around the shore at night, so it was bad luck for Sedore. Really bad luck. I wacked him with the wrench too."

That was not cheering news. Definitely not.

Storms' glance, containing nothing but abstract calculation, skimmed past Pete to the brush beyond. "Then I saw I could pin it on Tice. That part was almost fun. The jerk deserved it."

"I don't deserve this though," Pete said desperately. "For god's sake man, just leave me tied up here and take off. You'd have a good head start. Your employers could get you into the States."

Storms snorted. "Are you kidding? They'd give me the same treatment I gave Sedore and toss me in the lake. My cover's blown to hell, I'm no use to them anymore."

"So turn crown's evidence," Pete said. "Maybe you could make some kind of a trade for info on the bad guys you've been working for."

Storms didn't bother to answer that one.

What else could he say to convince the man?

"You must know that you can't get away with another murder. There are a lot of questions out there, the hunt is heating up. The chief is never going to believe that I blew myself up over here. You know he thinks the whole story about UXOs on the island is a crock."

But Storms was long past being swayed by any logic other than his own warped plans.

"I'll be long gone by then," he said with finality. "I've got a cabin on the other side where I've been stashing my money. No bank account to trace. I've got a car waiting for me there and then I'm off to New York, to take a plane down to the Bahamas."

He reached for his box. "Now shut up, I've got to concentrate."

Pete watched with mesmerized concentration himself, as Storms pulled out the grenade. It was an old piece, probably a souvenir from the Korean war. Or even older than that. Pete had read that thousands of returning WWII soldiers had smuggled home souvenir weaponry in their backpacks. They kept them in their sheds or basements or even in mounted displays in their homes. Many of the souvenirs were live and turned up at auction houses where a knowledgeable staff would immediately call bomb experts.

Art might have inherited this one from an uncle or other family member, or he might even have bought the thing over the internet. Unfortunately there was no bomb expert here to overcome Art and defuse it.

Frantically Pete cudgeled his memory for details. How long was the delay period on these old models, once the pin had been pulled? Not that it made much difference – Storms was bound to toss the grenade good and close to his victim. He'd likely throw it from a safe distance so that he could make his own getaway.

Numbly, Pete tried to think over his options.

Put simply though, he had none.

How crazy was that, to survive the fighting in Bosnia and a road bomb in Afghanistan, only to get blown up in his own country.

He could only hope it would be quick.

44

"Here we go!" Steph said excitedly. She'd wanted to wait till dark to get the the full effect.

Ali struck a match and began to light the lamp wicks.

Steph clapped her hands, "Oh, isn't it lovely!"

And it was. Inside the tower space, as the wick flames were multiplied in the shiny reflector panels, the effect was magical. Like being in a fairyland of mirrors, Ali thought. A chorus of oohs and aahs rose from the people watching on the ground, accompanied by enthusiastic clapping. Ali hoped that Miranda had a good view. She was sorry that Pete wasn't there but she was proud of being part of such a special moment.

Then the night was shaken by a far-off boom, dimly echoing in the air.

"What the heck was that?" Steph asked.

Ali stepped to a window. The people down on the lawn seemed okay, they hadn't been swallowed up in an earthquake or something similarly dire.

"Ali!" Steph called from another window, "Look, over there!" She pointed southeast, where a red glow rose like a bright line of fire in the darkening sky.

"Is it the fireworks in Bonville?" she asked in a shocked whisper.

Ali shook her head, "No, that would be in the other direction. And the waterfront party doesn't happen till next week."

"That's over at South Island," Steph gasped. "An explosion. There were UXOs there after all! Somehow one's gone off and started a fire!"

She turned to Ali whose face was a pale oval in the dark. " Are you all right?"

"I'm frightened," Ali said, the words tumbling out of her mouth. "I'm frightened for Pete. He hasn't answered my calls all day."

Steph looked puzzled. "But why should the explosion have anything to do with Pete?"

"I just know that it does, Steph. Today had such a bad beginning. We had a fight and Pete and I never fight." She wondered where Tyler Cotes was. He had never turned up to help with the picnic. Was he somehow involved in this?

Steph gave her a hug. "You're just in a bit of shock, dear. We both are. But whatever is going on at South Island, there's nothing we can do but wait till we hear more. The coast guard will be on the way there soon."

But Steph looked anxiously out over the water too. Fear was catching. She thought the police launch was likely to be headed to the island as well.

In the tower, the lamps still flickered in the reflector panels. Ali wondered if the light was visible from South Island. The light that had saved so many lives, that had led so many homewards. She sent out her hopes for her husband's safety, that he would be guided homeward too.

"Why don't you call the station?" Steph suggested. "Jane can just look at the roster and tell you where Pete is."

* * *

The station telephone line was busy. So was the back-up line and the message holder was fully loaded up too. It seemed the Island grapevine via landlines and cell phones, was working overtime. Everybody had heard of the fire on South Island and wanted to share the news with everybody else.

Halstead had already been on his phone with the coast guard. "Yes, I've heard about the fire," he said drily. "I'm going to get the launch now, I'll be headed over there right away."

"Call Greg Jackman," he said to a harried-looking Jane. "Though I imagine he's already on his way."

There was a crowd gathered outside the Island Grill, gabbling like a flock of excited geese. As Halstead drew up in the cruiser, they surged towards the car, Vern Byers at the forefront. The clerk barely gave Halstead time to get the door open.

"You've got to get some control, Bud! Some kid are talking about taking a boat over there. They want to see the spaceship leave."

Vern was right for once. The last thing they needed right now at South Island – whatever was happening there – was a bunch of wild, excited kids. He saw Gus near the Grill door and called him over to give Vern a hand.

"Nobody's going anywhere right now but me. That means no other boats are leaving this dock. Stand at the entrance and keep them away."

As he was heading down to the police launch, a car drove alongside and Tyler Cotes stuck his head out the window.

"Hey Chief," he said. "What's going on? I was in Toronto signing my army re-enlistment papers, and I come back across the causeway and see everybody all stirred up."

Halstead looked at Cotes and made a snap judgement. Cotes was strong, smart and trained in military action. Just the man he needed at the moment.

"Looks like some kind of explosive went off on South Island," Halstead said. "I think Pete's over there and if he is, he's in trouble. Want to help?"

Cotes was out of the car in a second. "What are we standing here for?" he said. "Let's get a move on."

What the hell had happened?
He was living the nightmare again. Only this time it was for real.
Red and orange light seared his retinas even through closed lids.
There was heat too, scorching his face.
Where was Storms? Was he still alive?
Sightless, he crawled along the seared rock. Heading toward where
Storms had been.
But the fire was too hot, his hands were scorched. He reeled away.
Anywhere would be better than this.
He would have to try to find some help.

The launch sped towards South Island. The two men aboard were grimly silent, straining to see across the dark water. Halstead had tersely described the situation to Cotes but the only real detail the man needed was that Pete was in trouble.

Halstead spun the wheel and veered the launch at the dock. Which was still there, he noted gratefully but the entire east side of the island seemed to be in flames. He saw snakes writhing into the water away from the sizzling rocks.

"The coast guard should be coming along soon," he hollered to Cotes.

Cotes leapt to the dock and hastily tied up the boat. "Which way?" he mouthed.

Halstead looked around desperately. The air was loud with the sound of crackling brush and he could taste the smoke. Christ what chance was there of finding Jakes alive in this?

"Towards the fire," he shouted. "They must be where it started. Take something to put over your head."

Cotes took off his shirt and threw it into the water, soaking it. He wrapped it around his head and set off at a run.

* * *

He knew that he was moaning because he could feel the sound in his throat. He just couldn't hear it.

He would have to think about that later. If there was a later.

He couldn't see either. But he felt some lessening of the scorching heat.

He wondered if he could stand up but the effort seemed beyond him. So he kept crawling.

Something moved beside him on the rocks, long and sinuous. It moved across his arm. A snake!

The snake would know how to get to the water. He must be going in the right direction. Doggedly, he crawled on.

* * *

Frightened bats darted through the hot air. Luckily the brush was so scanty that the flames were already dying down because of lack of fuel. On the other hand, it was getting darker and now there was little light to guide them. Halstead had brought a couple of powerful flashlight from the launch and followed Cotes over the hot rocks and crunching brush embers, the raw odor of lingering smoke stinging his eyes and throat.

The younger man was running much more quickly, Halstead could barely keep him in sight. He thought briefly and ironically of Ali's visit to his office, of her concern that Cotes had been concealing his recovery. Whatever the reason, he could only be thankful now to have a helper in such top condition, when every moment counted.

Suddenly, Cotes stopped, almost teetering over on the rock. "Jeezus!" he gasped.

Halstead slowed too, then moved forward in dread.

When he looked down, he could just make out the blasted-out circle on the ground. It was obvious that this charred spot was ground zero for whatever disaster had happened.

Christ, Halstead thought. No one here when the blast went off, could possibly have survived. Cotes looked about for his bearings. He shushed Halstead with a cautioning hand, then just stood silently, listening. For a long moment, nothing, then he straightened as if galvanized by an electric wire.

"Hear that, chief? It's coming from somewhere over to the right. Over by the water."

* * *

He fell into the water face first. The water was so cool, blessedly cool on his skin. For a long moment he just lay there, gulping it in. Rolling his body in the gentle lapping shore waves, like a hippo or an elephant after a trek in drought season. When he finally dared to surface and opened his eyes, he realized that the darkness he feared might be permanent, was only night.

He didn't know whether those were tears of gratitude on his face, or water from the lake.

Then amazingly, appearing magically from somewhere, there were Tyler and the chief and strong, supporting arms pulling him up.

He was saved. The realization flooded his being with warmth. Some time soon there would be salve for his burnt hands, medicines for his hurts, blankets, coffee. Safety, sleep, *home.*

He was saved.

But there was something he had to tell them first. Something important that was hard to remember right now. It was like trying to catch a slippery fish. Ah there it was it.

"Storms," he managed. "Where's Art? ....grenade ..... tried to help him..... Couldn't find him. He killed Sedore..... not Tice."

Task done, he passed out.

46

"So what the hell happened here?" Halstead asked.

Morning on South Island. The fire and ambulance boats had left earlier and now a light mist rose like steam from the scorched black circle on the rocks. Charred cedars stood like bony black skeletons in drifts of grey ash from the burnt grass. Halstead was thankful there were no sightseers at this hour. He could already hear the stories – it wasn't hard to imagine that a spaceship had blasted off from such a launching pad.

Chris Pelly shook his head. He looked as grey-faced and exhausted as Halstead felt. Even his cowlick looked dejected. It had been a long and gruelling night, after they'd packed Jakes off on the ambulance boat. Tyler Cotes had gone with him, he couldn't be torn from his friend's side.

They got little more from Jakes before the boat left and had to attempt to put together the pieces of the night's events. Literally put together the pieces, as Pelly had commented with morbid humour. Working with spotlights and four people scanning the still hot rock surface with flashlights, they'd found Art Storms pretty quickly. Or at least what was left of him. It wasn't pretty. Even Pelly and his assistants were pretty grim-faced over the discovery.

"It took more than a grenade to cause this damage," Pelly had concluded. "That blast must have set off another, older piece of ordnance. Some kind of pyrotechnic device." He looked at the ring of blackened cedars. "When the flame hit these trees, they went up like dry kindling."

After a hasty examination in the make-shift circumstances, they'd bagged Storms up and sent the body off by boat to the coroner's office at the hospital.

By that time it was nearly four in the morning and it was well nigh impossible to find anything else until first light. Halstead and Pelly had dozed fitfully on two small hard bunks on the police launch. Now they hunched chilly shoulders around thermoses of coffee – fetched thoughtfully from the mainland by Pelly's young assistant.

"That kid will go far," Halstead said gratefully.

Pelly's face brightened and lost its gray pallor as the combination of heat and caffeine did its magic.

"The right leg was pretty well gone," he said, with chipper interest. "And there wasn't much left of the hands either."

Halstead didn't need reminding. He wasn't likely to forget that macabre picture, spotlighted on the rocks. Still, he'd begun the discussion. He grimaced. "And to think that Storms brought that grenade here himself."

Pelly kicked at a bit of charred wood and sent it skidding along the rock. "It's amazing that the thing didn't go off long before this."

Halstead nodded. "We'll be looking into Storms' background. Most folks have someone in the family who fought in Europe. Either there or Korea."

It was sobering to think that the grenade and others like it could be sitting in attic trunks or in garages anywhere in the country. Waiting on a hair trigger for more than sixty years. Ready to blow itself and anything nearby to smithereens. It seemed that as well as searching old military testing sites, the Department of National Defense might be better occupied in warning people to search their own homes.

Halstead looked uncomfortably down at his own shoes. "Makes you wonder if there's any more of that old ordnance here."

Pelly grinned. "Hopefully that fire cleared out this half of the Island anyway."

Halstead shuddered. "Jeezus! You have to admit it's ironic though, or some kind of cosmic justice. Art Storms killed Sedore and then he gets killed by a piece of UXO, just the type of old weaponry that Sedore was looking for."

"Sedore?" Pelly asked. "I thought you arrested some other guy for that one."

"We did, but if what Jakes said is true, then that other guy is soon going to get some very good news."

And double that for his daughter, Halstead thought. One good thing out of all this, Keri Tice would be happy.

"So why did Storms kill Sedore?" Pelly asked.

Halstead tossed out the dregs of his cup. "I guess we'll have to get the rest of the story from Jakes. And thank god he's alive to tell it."

* * *

Somehow he knew that it was morning. Something about the light, even here. The hospital room was immediately recognizable. You could never mistake a hospital room or a hospital bed for anything else.

Then out of that sterile whiteness Ali appeared, smiling and holding back tears at the sight of his bandaged hands. She stayed for a time, hopping into the bed beside him and silently leaning into his shoulder. They didn't need words right now. Words could wait until later.

The next time he woke up it was another morning and there was another face. Not nearly so pretty but a friend for all that.

"'Lo Chief," he said, sounding like a rusty-voiced crow.

Halstead eased into the room, almost tiptoeing. "How are you lad?"

"I'm O.K." Pete said. He held up his hands. "Guess I won't be holding a fork for awhile though."

"How's your hearing?" Halstead asked. "I'm not talking too loud am I?"

Pete shook his head. "I've still got some ringing in my ears but there's no permanent damage. Doc said I was lucky."

That was the understatement of the year, Halstead thought.

"Steph sent cookies," he proffered a ribbon-topped tin. "Her special peanut butter recipe. James Bond couldn't wrangle that secret out of her."

He put the tin on the bedside table and drew up a chair. "Feel up to a little chat?"

"Sure thing. Just swing my water glass over this way first, thanks." Pete leaned awkwardly towards the plastic straw and took a drink.

Ali came in then from the hallway, advancing in high protective mode.

"Chief – you're not going to tire him out! He's barely woken up."

Halstead raised his hands. "I'll be careful, I promise."

A little mollified, she bent to kiss her husband on the cheek. "You send him away, Pete, whenever you feel like it. I'll go home for a bit and check on Nevra."

"Give her a kiss for me," Jakes said.

With a last warning glance at Halstead, Ali left the room.

Pete grinned, wincing as the slight movement pulled at the bandage on his forehead. "She's a tiger when she's roused."

Halstead chuckled, "I'm properly warned." He was a policeman though and there were things to be learned. He took a cookie from the tin and pulled the chair closer.

"So, what happened out there?" he asked, munching appreciatively. "I've put together a lot of it, but I'm still left with a pretty cock-eyed picture."

Jakes nodded and gingerly pulled himself up a little further against the pillows. Halstead leaned forward to give him a hand.

"It was pretty cock-eyed," he agreed.

"Art was trying to kill you," Halstead said drily. "I figured out that much at least."

Pete nodded. "Yeah, he was trying to kill me."

"You knew too much. You found him out."

"Not until I met up with him at the Petersons. Not until I was on the damn boat actually. The boat that I'd been trying to find for days."

Halstead shook his head. "Art must have kept the boat at some other marina. It was news to me."

"Anyway there it was," Pete said ruefully. "staring me in the face. The 98 SpeedCrest, with it's big blue stripe. Everything fit, even the number. It all fell into place."

"Must have been quite a shock."

"Yep, and Art was watching it happen. He was swinging that wrench at my head before I'd even finished figuring things out."

"And what exactly had you figured out at that point?" Halstead asked.

"Not that much actually. Not right then. Recognizing the boat was sort of like fitting something together that you haven't been able to fix. Like struggling with a piece of machinery and then there's suddenly that click and you know you've got it right. But all I really knew then, was that Art had something to do with the smuggling. Something to hide."

"He certainly did."

Halstead filled him in briefly on the information and description that Detective Anderson had sent. How he and Jane had come to the same incredible conclusion, that Art Storms was the smuggling connection they had been seeking.

"It was Art all right," Pete said. "It was him all along. He had gambling debts, he told me. He was in really deep and didn't see any other way out."

"Must have been pretty big gambling debts." Halstead said. "Even if he only began with small runs of weed, he had moved up to moving bigger shipments and stronger drugs."

His mouth tightened. "And then the guy starts *killing* people. Planning to kill a fellow officer! The man was breaking every code in the book."

Pete nodded soberly. "I guess he was desperate, too far gone. I couldn't talk him out of it."

Halstead shook his head, warding away the image of that charred rock and what he and Chris Pelly had found there. "So, tell me about Wes Sedore."

"Art had used South Island at times as a cache for the drugs. That's why he got off his boat at South Island, he'd left something behind. Sedore was out in the dark, testing some infra-red equipment and saw him there."

"Shoot!" Halstead said disgustedly. "Sedore was probably just curious. You'd wonder why Art didn't make up some story – say that he was just checking in on Sedore to see if he'd had any more trouble with Tice. Sedore had met Art before, he'd have no reason to be suspicious."

"Maybe he couldn't think that fast." Pete said. "Or he knew that Sedore would likely mention the visit to his department at the Ministry or to us the next time he saw us and he couldn't risk that."

Halstead frowned. "It must have been more than that. He must have actually caught Storms away from the shore, obviously going somewhere else, away from Sedore's campsite. Sedore would have heard about the smuggling arrests, the story was big news. He must have said something, confronted him."

Pete took another sip from his straw. "Like I did, poor guy. And Art decided not to risk it. He killed him."

They were silent for a minute, picturing the scene. Dusk on the island, Sedore grunting softly in bewildered shock, then falling to the ground.

Halstead sighed. "A case of being in the wrong place at the wrong time. And Art wasn't any better off for killing the guy. He'd jumped right out of the frying pan and into the fire. Now he had a whole other mess he had to figure out."

Pete nodded. "Like we talked about before, only we saw Tice as the bad guy who had to figure out what to do with Sedore's body."

"So what did he say," Halstead asked curiously. "Was it the way we figured out with the diving tanks? Only it was Art framing

Tice. That was pretty clever, had me fooled anyway," he said ruefully.

Pete shook his head, "He didn't talk much about that part."

Halstead chomped absently on a second cookie. "Dammit though, it would have been tricky. And a tight time-frame too."

"Not so tight, we didn't find Sedore for another week."

Halstead thought out loud. "It would have to be sometime when Tice was off his boat and that wasn't often."

"Art got gas at the Peterson's Marina regularly, he could have found out Tice's habits. Tice kept his SUV there for instance, he must have come into town some evenings to get food and booze."

"Nevertheless, Art would have had to move a couple of heavy diving tanks from one boat to the other, without Jimmy for instance seeing him. He was damn lucky."

But as a long-time cop, Halstead knew that often the difference between a successful criminal and the one who ended up being arrested was exactly that, a combination of daring and pure blind luck.

He snorted. "Plus he was helped by the fact that Tice is such a belligerent jerk. The man practically built a case against himself. His fight with Sedore, his battle with the diving shop over the tanks. Storms probably couldn't believe how Tice played into his hands, refusing to say where he was that night.."

He looked at Pete, "But what if Sedore's body hadn't turned up? How could Art count on the tank working loose, or that someone would find him."

Pete shrugged. "I don't think Art really cared either way. The circumstantial evidence against Tice worked for his purposes – he meant to be away out of the country long before Tice went to trial."

"So we arrest Tice and Storms thinks he's got away with it." He frowned. "With the murder maybe, but he's hardly solved his problems."

Pete nodded. "He knew by then that Anderson and his team weren't going to give up on the smuggling investigations and they were bound to close in on him eventually. He knew he'd have to bail out and soon."

"Only you got to him before he could leave, " Halstead said drily.

Pete looked chagrined. "Yeah, well we know how that turned out. He would have made his escape too, except for that grenade. And the ordnance it set off."

Halstead leaned forward and clapped him on the shoulder. "And we're all mighty glad that you didn't go up with it too, lad."

A nurse lurked in the doorway, a signal that Jakes had probably had enough for now. Plus he'd better leave some cookies for the patient or he'd never hear the end of it from Steph.

But there was one last thing. "And you were right about Mel Todd – Storms killed him too."

Pete nodded. "Art used him for awhile as a lookout and to cache some of the stuff on his boat. But he had a loose mouth when he was drinking and Art was worried that he would blab something to his cronies. And of course he did."

"He was so damn happy about getting that money. I hope it can go to that grandson of his, the way Mel wanted."

Jakes was looking wan. Halstead gave way to the nurse and her capable ministrations. When he looked back, he gave silent thanks to whatever powers might be that Jakes was there and not in a body bag like Art Storms.

47

DARING RESCUE ON SOUTH ISLAND
COPS SOLVE PUZZLING DRUG CASE

Bob Denys had restricted himself to the facts in the story, omitting the gory details. For which Halstead was thankful. The mood at the Middle Island police station was gloomy enough with just Jane and himself rattling around in the place. Even Jane's normally ebullient spirits were seriously dampened. She'd been positively short with Vern this morning. Then she'd banged the phone down, and looked again at the newspaper headline.

"How does something like this happen, chief?" she asked miserably. "He was going to kill *Pete*. It makes me sick. You think you know someone but something like this makes you wonder whether you really know anybody at all."

She sighed, "Do you think if he'd talked to us, we would have been able to help him see a different way out?"

Halstead shook his head. "Maybe earlier on, Jane."

She turned tiredly back to her computer. "I guess you're right, he was just in way too deep."

"He sure made a good job of closing all his exits," Halstead said. "The rotten, poor, sorry jack-ass."

Fortunately there was always work to do. Specifically, addressing the station's staffing needs. Jakes would be on leave for at least two weeks, though it had been hard enough to convince him of that. Bonville Mayor Stuckey had assured Vern that the Waterfront Committee had enough volunteers to supervise both sides of the Bay during their event and the clerk had grudgingly expressed his gratitude.

On Halstead's desk there were four resumes answering his advertisement for a constable. All four candidates were city raised. Three were for recruits fresh out of training college, one mentioned six month's experience in Edmonton. He wondered if any of them had ever been seen a cow or a tractor or even a country road.

* * *

"You don't have to go," Steph said, as she patted down his shirt collar.

He shrugged. "Funerals are half my social life these days."

She tutted and rapped him lightly on the shoulder. "It's not *that* bad."

He frowned. "I guess not. Two funerals do not a summer make." He tugged frustratedly at the neck of his jacket. "I'm already hot. Why don't churches have air-conditioning?"

She smiled. "I guess we're expected to suffer some to properly cleanse the soul. At least the ladies' auxiliary have brought in seat cushions for the pews."

He looked out at the lawn where Steph's weekend clients, a half dozen middle-aged women, were posed in various positions of *tai chi*. Realized he was procrastinating.

"Ah well," he said. "Must go."

"This is hard for you," Steph said. "Really hard."

"It's a bad one," he agreed. "But I can remember the other Art, before all this happened. I'll try to think of him." He checked again in the mirror, wished he hadn't.

Who was that guy? Had his face always been this tired, this drawn?

"It's not only that, Steph," he said. "Do you think that Vern might actually have a point? That maybe I *am* getting too old for this job, That maybe I should retire. I didn't see this one coming. I didn't see it at all."

"Nobody did," she said. "Jane knew him as well as you did. You'd both worked with him for years." She kissed him and he gathered up his wallet and car keys.

"Maybe it will mean something to his family, " he said, "to have Jane and I attend. Some of the kids from his search and rescue training crew are coming too. They liked him, at least the Art they knew."

It was as tough as he'd expected.

He stopped in at the Grill on his way back from Bonville.

"Get me a brew, will you, Gus. This has been a bad one."

"It's on the house," Gus said. "And I'll join you." He left a helper in charge at the counter and carried a couple of dewy-glassed brews to the corner table where Halstead sat.

"Cheers," Gus said. They raised their glasses.

Halstead couldn't help but reflect that only a month ago, he and Art Storms had bid adieu to Mel Todd in this very same spot. Sometimes time moved way too quickly. On the other hand, the time that he had spent working with the colleague he thought he knew seemed a thousand years ago.

He smiled wearily at Gus. "Was it always this hard to be a policeman, I wonder? I must have been made of tougher stuff back then."

Gus laughed ruefully, "We were all tougher back then." He tugged at one of the few tufts of grey hair that remained about his shiny pate. "We were all prettier too."

Halstead laughed, "You know it." He looked towards the motel parking lot out back. "I guess your pretty, young guest has gone now. Her and her fiance."

"Yep," Gus sighed. "That one sure brightened the place up. She was a nice kid. I'm glad that things worked out for her, even though it didn't seem to improve the old man's personality much."

"Not at all," Halstead said drily.

He hadn't seen Gerald Tice personally, but had received a blistering letter from the salvage dealer's lawyer. Accusation of wrongful arrest, claims for financial compensation for stress and damage to reputation.

Halstead had replied with a brief note referring them to the provincial office where they could lodge their complaint. Very few complaints ever went any further than that. The police had to pursue wrongdoers and sometimes they made a mistake. At times this made Halstead uncomfortable but it was the system he worked within and from what he'd read of history, far from the worst.

So the Arrowheads were gone, for this summer at least. Ralph Peterson had reported that the *Finders Keepers* crew had weighed anchor yesterday morning. With nary a nod to South Island, Halstead suspected. He doubted they would ever be back if young Keri had anything to do with it.

"So, what's going to happen with South Island?" Gus asked. "Is the government going to send somebody else over there to replace their man?"

"I don't think so," Halstead said. "Wes Sedore had checked out half the island on his grid and as far as the rest goes, what didn't burn has been pretty thoroughly tramped over in the last few weeks. Anything that was going to explode, probably would have by now. I never thought there was much to that map of theirs anyway."

Gus shrugged. "I kinda enjoyed the martian story, it was good for business. But back to normal, I suppose. I hear that Vern wants you to run for Mayor -- what do you think about that?"

Halstead raised his brows. "And have to deal with all those pothole and garbage complaints? Now *that's* a tough job. No thanks."

He guessed he'd stay on being a policeman for awhile yet. There was worth and dignity to the job. He still believed that.

48

The Bonville waterfront festival had proceeded without further incident, and Vern Byers was thankfully free of that trial for another year. The Jakes didn't attend. Pete was just newly home from the hospital, and said he'd had enough of explosions, big or small, to last him a lifetime.

Tyler was leaving. Ali had invited him for a farewell dinner, though having been raised in boarding schools, she was not a confident cook. However, she had researched recipes on the net and was attempting to make a pilaf, a dish of Turkish origin. Miranda and Emily Dickinson were invited as well and arrived bearing fresh sliced peaches and whipped cream for dessert.

"We're celebrating too," she said. "We cleared nearly three thousand dollars at the Lighthouse picnic. That will give us a nice down payment to give Wayne for the new staircase."

Pete's face sported a few nasty scratches but the bruising had gone down. One hand was still swathed in gauze wrapping but the other, though still tender, was open to the air. All week, Nevra had been enjoying watching mummy feed daddy. She was eager to help, which had made for some rather messy mealtimes. Lots of giggling though, before Ali took over.

Now she had set the men to watching the little girl in the backyard while she and Miranda put the finishing touches on dinner.

"So you're going to have to keep in touch," Pete said. "No more three year wait till we see you again."

Tyler nodded. He looked relaxed in civvie trousers and shirt. No cast on the foot. "Yep. I took the boat back to Bonville yesterday."

"It's been great seeing you bud, we even managed to stir up a little excitement for you." Pete waved his mittened hand. "I can't promise that for next visit."

"I don't need excitement here," Tyler said seriously. "Not that kind anyway. There's lots of other good reasons to come to Middle Island."

He looked towards the lawn where Nevra was tossing a ball for Emily Dickinson. She wasn't a very good thrower but the dog didn't seem to mind. Often they just fell into the grass, the little girl's pink dress and the the black and white of the dog's coat making a colourful tangle.

Tyler smiled, "While I've been laid up, I've been thinking a lot. Never really had time to think before. Never really wanted to, I guess."

He sighed. "Never been hurt before either. Oh a couple of scratches, but nothing really bad like this. I was beginning to think that I was special, to think that the bastards would never get me. That all those other guys just had really bad luck."

"But now I know different. Your number's going to come up some time. And when it does, you want to have something to show for the time you've been here. And that sure as hell better be something worthwhile."

From the kitchen window drifted the sound of the women laughing, like soft bells upon the breeze.

"So, I've been looking at my options," Tyler said. "I'm not quite back up to par for full service but the doc says I will be. I could stay at Halifax for a few more months, then I could go join the anti-terrorism forces in Mali."

He forestalled Pete's frown. "Or I could check out that disaster relief work you talked about, that DART helicopter that drops troops into affected areas. I'd need some training for that job."

Pete looked the question.

Tyler grinned. "Long story short, I guess I'll be be practising how to dangle at the end of a rope from a whirly-bird.."

Pete clapped him on the back. "That's good news bud, really good news."

"I won't be needing that loan either, thanks. Now that I'm not going into business."

"I'd have been happy to guarantee it, any time."

* * *

Ali had talked to Tyler one morning at the hospital, outside Pete's room.

"I'm sorry," she said helplessly. "What can I say – I feel like such an idiot. Imagining you were some kind of pirate smuggler when all along you were thinking about investing in a restaurant!"

Such a simple explanation for Tyler's trips to Bonville. He'd been meeting with realtors and visiting various downtown prospective Bonville locations.

"Too much *Treasure Island,*" she said, mortified anew.

"It's not your fault," he said. "I can see how it happened. There you were, hearing about the smuggling every day from Pete and there I was going out secretly every day in my boat."

He shook his head ruefully. "I was looking for that goddamned plane. Crazy I know, but I thought it would be fun to scoop all the others. I couldn't dive but I had some fun with the map."

The map. Ali blushed at the memory of how finding it had furthered her suspicions.

"No," she insisted, "I don't deserve to be let off the hook so easily. I'm the crazy one. Mind you, I did a lot of thinking over why you were concealing the fact that your foot was so much better."

"I was a dope," he said. "I haven't exactly been acting my best. I don't know why it seemed so important to keep my plans secret."

Ali laughed. "Well let's not stand here arguing who is the bigger dope. We'll share the honour."

The crickets were chirping, the fireflies darting about on the dark lawn. Time to say goodbye. Nevra had long gone to bed, cuddled with the stuffed bunny Tyler had brought her. He'd given her a big hug.

"Bye sweetie. You take good care of your parents."

They saw Tyler to the car.

Ali hugged him, "Take care of yourself," she urged. "We're already looking forward to your next visit."

"I'm off too," Miranda said. "Good night, Jakes family. Sleep tight." Emily followed her down the driveway.

Ali leaned back into Pete's shoulder. "Sure you don't wish you were going with Tyler?" she asked.

He kissed her cheek. "I'm sure."

"Not even in a teeny part of you? Not even in one molecule?"

"How could you think that I would want that life back? You saved me, we got out of that chaos and came here."

He wouldn't tell her that sometimes his new life was actually more frightening than the old. When he'd been tied up on the island, helplessly awaiting the grenade blast, he'd never in his entire life been so scared. Not even in the toughest of battle situations. This was different, because he had so much more to lose. His wife and daughter.

Love made you more vulnerable than ever.

To a chorus of crickets, they walked back to their house, hand in hand.

EPILOGUE

It's only early August but dusk is already coming on sooner. The birds and ducks who have summered on the lake are beginning to get restless. There's a stirring in the flocks of swallows, but the cormorants won't be leaving for a few weeks yet.

Tonight the ragged line of black silhouettes is flying as always, low across the water. On the shore, the lighthouse stands like a blind sentinel above the rocks.

The line of birds pass over the blackened cedar stumps on South Island.

Something happened there recently but it doesn't concern them.

For the cormorants, it's just been another summer in the unending stream of the millenia.

Fishing is done for the day and it's time to go to roost.